LUNCH WITH THE DEADLY DOZEN

PETER BERRY

BLOODHOUND
BOOKS

www.bloodhoundbooks.com

Print ISBN: 978-1-916978-68-3

For Cait and Ella with love

1

'And then, finally, there is Monica. I have deliberately left her until last because she is, as you'll hopefully discover, rather special.'

Thomas Quinn studied his dining companion with interest, having looked up from the half-eaten contents of his plate, originally filled with the lightest, most flavoursome sage and butter gnocchi he had ever tasted. He must have passed this small Italian restaurant with the slightly faded, hand-painted signage hundreds of times over the years and never ventured in.

He couldn't fathom exactly why that was, yet his suspicion was that his late wife of almost forty years had never been a particular fan of pasta. Not when going out anyway. Alice had always been fairly conservative in her choices and had tended to prefer her own home-cooked food. On the odd occasion during their mundanely happy marriage when they had decided to go out to eat, Thomas and Alice had often left home with the intention of finding somewhere new to experience and yet somehow always ended up at the same Thai place. The owners, two brothers, were always welcoming and knew what Alice liked to order. Alice enjoyed the familiarity.

The other reason Thomas had never stepped inside this Italian restaurant until now was that it had always seemed unnervingly full, both at lunchtime and in the evenings. If he was honest, it also looked a little loud with, he estimated, around fifty customers all chattering away excitedly to each other, competing for volume.

This particular afternoon, however, late on an overcast Tuesday in mid-October with the light already fading, it was virtually empty. In fact, the only people in the room were Simone the elderly owner and, for this afternoon at least, head waiter, sommelier and, for all Thomas knew, the one doing the washing up; a chef whom Thomas had never seen, although the quality of the food suggested that she or he was a remarkable talent; and the softly-spoken, erudite eighty-one-year-old man seated opposite. His name was Lexington Smith and he had already polished off some tomato and basil bruschetta as a starter and a generous plate of risotto Milanese despite having done most of the talking for the best part of an hour.

A week earlier, Thomas had returned home from Portobello Road, his local place for fresh vegetables and bread, to find the telephone ringing. The landline. This was most unusual because everyone he knew would ordinarily contact him via his mobile phone; even in his late sixties, Thomas did his best to keep up with technology, if only to be able to see what his eight-year-old granddaughters were up to on social media. He had considered disconnecting the landline many times since Alice's death, but it had remained a comforting fixture under the mirror in the hallway, rarely troubling anyone and steadfastly deterring cold callers with its friendly but definite answerphone message.

On this occasion, however, something made Thomas pick up the receiver. He had momentarily thought it may be a distant aunt, one of those Christmas card list mainstays, calling to announce the death of an equally distant uncle. It wasn't.

'Thomas Quinn,' the quiet, somewhat theatrical voice had

announced confidently. 'My name is Lexington Smith. I should very much like to buy you a late lunch or an early dinner, depending on which way you look at it. I appreciate that this may appear a little forward on my part, but I do hope you'll agree to my invitation. I have an important proposal for you, and before you start to worry, I'm not selling anything. Trust me.'

Lexington had gone on to explain, in the broadest and least specific terms, that he was part of a group of retired specialists who had an undercover role in the general day to day running of the city. 'I suppose I am the leader,' he explained humbly, 'as much as anyone is, although I try hard not to come across as some kind of authoritarian enigma. There are quite enough of those around as I'm sure you'll agree. I'm afraid I can't really go any further into detail until we meet. The conversation we require is categorically of the face-to-face variety. Does next Tuesday suit? Perhaps *brillig* – that's 4pm in the new money – at La Stella on Moscow Road. I'm sure you know it. It's barely a ten-minute walk from Colville Square.'

'How do you know where I live?' asked Thomas with a mild degree of concern, although there was something about Lexington's voice that he found entirely unthreatening. Calming, even.

'I simply looked you up in the increasingly slim phone book,' Lexington replied. 'Hence the landline call. Of course, I have known your address for some time as well as your mobile number, but as I am a child of the 1940s, I still cling on to some of the old ways. Often, they remain the better option, don't you agree?'

The following overcast Tuesday afternoon, Thomas made his way through the delicate lattice of streets around Westbourne Grove towards La Stella. His mood was buoyant yet with a constant hum of the low-level melancholy with which he had become familiar over recent years. It lingered like fog over him, thickening from time to time into something that alarmed him.

A conversation over the weekend with his daughter, the latest in a series of gently nudging talks, had put Thomas in an upbeat state of mind. Emily had pointed out that it was almost six years since Alice's death and, although her father hadn't exactly been moping around his house on his own for all that time, it was perhaps a good moment to branch out a little bit and explore new opportunities. 'Maybe join a book club or something,' had been her exact words, delivered kindly and with a forehead kiss.

He hadn't mentioned to Emily the strange phone call; Lexington had suggested he keep their chat secret. Nonetheless, his daughter's enthusiasm had given Thomas an unexpected impetus to at least hear what was being mysteriously proposed.

Peering through the window, he could see that Lexington had already arrived and was seated at a table in the farthest corner of the restaurant despite apparently being the only customer. Seeing Thomas, he gave a cheery wave and gestured for Simone to unlock the door. Thomas, knowing Lexington's age, had expected his host to be frail, but the man who greeted him with a warm handshake was nothing of the sort. Lexington was tall and slim with a kind face and a radiant smile. His thick, grey, shoulder-length hair was neatly combed and he wore a dark three-piece suit without a tie. Thomas thought that he resembled a distinguished former movie star and felt mildly underdressed in jeans and a V-neck.

'Allow me to introduce you to Simone.' Lexington beamed as the aroma of garlic and fresh herbs permeated the room from the direction of what Thomas guessed was the kitchen. 'He opened this place in 1971 when he was merely a child and I have been a sporadic yet generous visitor ever since. I believe I may even have been here on his first day.'

'I was twenty-four, Signor Lexington,' scowled Simone

jovially. He turned to Thomas, gripped him by the shoulders and kissed him on each cheek. 'So lovely to welcome you, Signor Quinn. I arrived from Amalfi with only a few lire in my pocket, but I worked hard and here we are. There were so few Italian restaurants in London at that time. Now, they are everywhere. But we hope that we can still provide the best pasta and risotto you can find north of Rome. We have had the pleasure of many wonderful guests over the years as you can see. You have dined with us before?'

Thomas, although slightly thrown by the kissing, pointed out that he'd always seen the place full otherwise he'd have surely visited. He decided against mentioning Alice's aversion to restaurant pasta in case it caused offence. He was keen to make a good first impression. At Simone's direction, he looked around the walls of La Stella, which were adorned with dozens of photographs of film and music stars who had clearly eaten there and loved the place enough to return and sign their images. A brief glance around the room revealed that previous patrons had included Frank Sinatra, Dustin Hoffman, Robert de Niro, Cher, Elton John, Oprah Winfrey and Tom Hanks. As they sat down to eat, Thomas noted that just above Lexington's head was a black and white photograph of Marlon Brando taken, Thomas estimated, at some point in the seventies between *The Godfather* and *Apocalypse Now*.

After they had ordered and after Simone had uncorked a bottle of vintage red wine, Lexington explained that, for the last five years, he had been the leader of a select group of twelve people, all retired and each with a specific talent from their former careers, which contributed to the success of their area of business. Whenever a vacancy arose, a new member of the group, which had been in existence for almost 200 years and currently comprised eight men and four women, was invited to join after being distantly monitored and vetted over a long period. So far, nobody invited had ever refused. Today was Thomas's turn.

'Timing is key,' Lexington explained. 'The group has been watching you for a while, but you have not been ready. It was entirely possible that you would never have been ready; the group watches a number of potential candidates at any one time because, at our age, one recognises the dangers of just the solitary, precarious basket of eggs, if you understand me.'

Thomas nodded, curious. 'You were spying on me?' he asked with the mildest sense of unease.

'I prefer to think of it as observing from a distance. Simply to ensure that by the time we come to this particular part of our journey, nobody's time is wasted. It's broadly the same as when you used to visit different athletics clubs during your career to check out the opposition.' Lexington reached for a grissino. 'When Alice died in 2015, you took a baby step closer to being ready, but if we had indulged in this delicious meal at any point over the last few years, then you would have surely turned my offer down. Of that I am certain. Like many others, you were channelling your grief elsewhere. Fortunately, there was no appropriate vacancy until recently so the situation did not arise. Now, I imagine you'd be keen to know what our little specialisation might be. Would I be right?'

Thomas glanced up at the photograph of the middle-aged Brando, glaring ominously. 'Yes please,' he replied. He felt certain it would be something to do with charity work, or possibly some sort of board game collective, but that would be fine. He was at a loose end much of the time anyway. And he was rather partial to Cluedo.

Lexington leaned forward with his elbows on the table, his hands clasped. A broad smile formed across his face.

'We assassinate criminals,' he said, calmly.

2

At that moment, Thomas was aware of a faint yet persistent knocking on the restaurant door. Lexington's change in eyeline confirmed it. Thomas turned and saw a couple of anxious-looking women peering through the door at them. One was waving plaintively. His first thought was that they might be part of Lexington's mysterious group, but he dismissed the idea as they were too young – Lexington had already listed the four women, including Monica, who were involved, and they were all in their sixties or older. These people at the door were clearly younger if not by more than a fortunate decade.

Simone unlocked the door and, as politely as he could, asked what they wanted. It quickly became clear that the women were American, were flying home the following day, and had been desperate to eat at La Stella before they departed, only to be thwarted by the restaurant's online booking system, which had shown no availability. Deciding on a whim to pay a flying visit just in case of a cancellation, they had seen two gentlemen doing what appeared to be dining when the restaurant was meant to be closed. They decided to chance their luck. Simone, however, was charmingly yet firmly dashing their hopes.

Lexington rose from his seat, leaving the word 'assassinate' hovering above it like an elephantine hummingbird. 'Would you please excuse me for a moment,' he said. 'I'll just sort this small matter out.' He strode purposefully but with a slight limp towards the trio, now engaged in some form of polite stand-off. 'Do I detect the harmonious vowels of a North Carolina accent?' he asked with a knowing grin.

The two women looked up, star-struck. 'Why, y-yes,' stuttered the taller of the two. 'Wilmington. Do you know it?'

Lexington held out a long-fingered hand, which the first American gently clasped. 'Intimately,' he gushed. 'Lexington Smith, at your service. And may I please ask your names?'

'I'm Brianna Andrews and this is Madison Kowalski,' said the shorter and more flamboyantly dressed of the two. Both of them giggled, all thoughts of food momentarily superseded by both events and charm.

Lexington straightened and offered his hand to the second American. 'Madison. After the Avenue. How delightful. Just like myself. We are nomenclature twins, merely two blocks between us!'

'Oh my gosh!' said Madison, suddenly entranced to the point of light-headedness.

'Oh yes. My parents conceived me in a New York apartment in 1938 and decided to name me after the location. I'm just eternally relieved they weren't staying on Fifth Avenue.' Madison and Brianna paused for a moment while they connected the geographic dots and then simultaneously burst into laughter. 'Now, I understand you wish to dine and yet there is no available table. I may be able to help. It's just past five and I shall be done with my private table within the hour. I know that it is free for the rest of the evening and so, with Simone's blessing, I bequeath it to you.'

Lexington looked to the Italian for approval and Simone

responded with an acquiescent wink. 'In addition, your meal will be my treat,' he continued. 'It's the least I can do for residents of the Old North State. Now all we need to do is to arrange what you can do for the next hour. Have you been to Primrose Hill?'

Madison and Brianna both shook their heads, seemingly unable to form coherent words.

'Then that is your next hour beautifully occupied.' Lexington leaned out of the restaurant doorway and waved ostentatiously to a London taxi that was parked opposite. 'Martin!' he called, musically, as if summoning a cat in for its dinner. The cabbie, an older man with a grey, neatly shaped beard and a shaved head, wound down his window. 'Martin, dear. These ladies are visitors from Wilmington, North Carolina. I'm sure you know it. They are dining here as my guests in one hour, but until then the city is their playground. Could you bear to please take them to Primrose Hill and then park up and show them the glorious view? They've never been and we must rectify this oversight. It's a mild evening so the view should be spectacular as it gets dark.'

The cabbie turned on the ignition, swung the taxi round so that it was just outside La Stella, then got out of his driver's seat to open the passenger door for the tourists. 'Your carriage awaits,' he growled with a lupine grin.

Lexington asked whether the cabbie had anything appropriate as a soundtrack to their journey. '*Oklahoma* 1969 Original Broadway Cast Soundtrack good enough?' Martin grumbled.

'Give my regards to the Bellamy Mansion Museum when you get back to Wilmington,' called Lexington. He cheerily waved the Americans on their way before returning to the table where Thomas was attempting to make sense of what had just happened, as well as process the earlier assassination information.

'That was… generous,' he said, as Lexington lowered himself gingerly back into his chair. 'And, if I may say so, charismatic.'

'I try to engage in a random act of kindness every day. The

others in our group do the same. Charity work, volunteering, bake sales. It helps to mitigate the more unpleasant aspects of our work.'

'And were you really named after Lexington Avenue?'

Lexington sipped his 2010 Barolo with an expression of deep satisfaction. 'Oh, absolutely. My parents were in New York before the war; my father was a diplomat like me and my mother was a writer. She decided on the name as she wanted something a bit more memorable and exotic to go with Smith. My father wanted Winston, which would have been a disaster thanks to Orwell. I met him once. George. In 1947. I was nine. He came to a party that my parents were hosting in their London house and he offered me a Liquorice Allsort before I was ushered off to bed. Anyway, where were we?'

'Assassination, I think,' said Thomas with no small degree of uncertainty.

'Oh yes, of course…'

———

When Thomas returned home just after 6.30pm that evening, his overwhelming feeling was one of exhilaration, if tinged with fear. On the plus side, the nagging melancholy appeared to have subsided a bit and that in itself was something of a relief. The emptiness of the house felt slightly less overwhelming, his familiar patchwork of emotions shifting perceptibly. Thomas poured himself a whisky as, somehow, the day seemed to require a toast even if there was, as usual, nobody with whom to share it.

Lexington had, over the course of an hour, explained how The Twelve, as they were informally known, were formed in 1831 as a covert organisation working alongside the newly initiated police force to quietly and efficiently eliminate certain criminals. Originally The Twelve were mostly former members of the military, however, the group quickly became so adept and inventive at both remaining undercover and, at the same time, exterminating their targets without suspicion or evidence, that soon The Twelve became open to men of all backgrounds who were getting on in years.

Around the 1890s, the then leader of The Twelve, one Maurice Arthurs, decided to extend the employment criteria not only to other skill sets, but also to women – The Twelve was always ahead of its time in terms of social change. The organisation remained secret, merrily dispatching the more unsavoury members of society throughout the twentieth century. By the time Lexington sat down with Thomas at La Stella, the group included a former surgeon, an eminent linguist, a retired plumber, an ex-pathologist and a cabbie, Martin – 'You've no idea how important it has been to have someone who knows their way around the city and whose vehicle has such a nimble turning circle'.

According to Lexington, the only types of people who never seemed appropriate were politicians – 'The relevant skill set simply isn't there with most of them, and those who might have a semi-chance seem to have a moral aversion to the whole "killing" element' – and writers, 'especially poets. First of all, they rarely actually retire, but secondly, they're far too easily distracted by fauna to be of any use in the field, as it were. Assassination requires focus, as you'll find out. One's gaze simply cannot be drawn by crows or pigeons when one is meant to be concentrating on humans.'

And, of course, there was Monica; one of four women currently within The Twelve. Born in Gujarat in the early 1950's, Monica Lodhia had been one of the most renowned chemists of her generation. Her unrivalled knowledge of poisons and corrosives was the envy of universities across the world. She had retired early in 2012 after serving out the final years of her career as Head of Chemistry at Middlesex University. Naturally, she had been on the radar of The Twelve for many years and yet there had been considerable opposition to her eventually being approached.

Some within the group had passionately argued that she was far too damaged on account of her past. Lexington had personally campaigned hard to invite her anyway on the basis that the tragedies in her life made Monica even more likely to thrive and become indispensable to The Twelve's operations. To him, Monica was uniquely placed to provide expert knowledge as well as possessing a steely determination, which other candidates at the time lacked.

Naturally, Thomas had many questions. Did The Twelve use guns? Absolutely not. Nor knives. Their methods were always far more subtle and generally always had been, except in emergencies. 'In the early days,' Lexington had explained, 'most of the victims ended up in the river or in burning disused buildings after first being knocked out with laudanum or opium. Unnecessary suffering on the part of the victims has been frowned upon, especially since the 1970s when The Twelve went through a bit of a brief "hippie" period. Over time, the methods of dispatch have become more refined. These days it's more likely to look like a suicide or alternatively we have ways to make people disappear completely.'

Had Lexington himself assassinated many people? Yes, he'd had involvement of some kind in twenty-three cases since joining the group just under twenty years before – 'We're not exactly prolific,' he had admitted matter-of-factly. 'It's very much quality over quantity. In recent years, my role has been more administrative than active, but in my younger days I personally bumped off fourteen or so.'

Over coffee, and just before the two Americans returned safely from their unscheduled trip to NW1, Thomas had agreed that he would fill The Twelve's vacancy, seduced in part by

Lexington's persuasion, but also simply by the opportunity to meet some new people. If nothing else, he felt it sounded like a far better use of his spare time than board games. Whether he actually had the capacity to assassinate was uncertain to him, but Lexington was unwaveringly confident, assuring Thomas that he wouldn't have been chosen otherwise. 'Our meeting is not an accident,' he had stated with calm clarity. 'I've done a few of these now and I've never yet been wrong. I've been anticipating our meeting for a very long time.'

'Why me?' had been the burning question. Lexington's answer was enticingly unclear.

'Have you read Solzhenitsyn?' he asked. Thomas confessed with embarrassment that although he was reasonably well read for someone whose background was primarily in the sporting arena, twentieth century Russian novels remained very much a grey area. 'Then I would recommend *The Gulag Archipelago* when you have a spare week or so. "The line dividing good and evil cuts through the heart of every human being." Never a truer sentence written.

'As for why you,' Lexington continued, 'your humility, first of all. As you'll find out, I have spent a long time crafting The Twelve into a group that is free of arrogance. Devoid of ego. I simply cannot have any sense of gung-ho when it comes to such serious matters. That's not to say it isn't fun, as you'll also find out. But…' at this point Lexington leant forward and looked deep into Thomas's eyes, 'as for the other main reason, I suspect you know.'

3

The following morning, the reality of Thomas's decision hit home with the arrival by courier of a new mobile phone at Colville Square. Eleven numbers had already been programmed into it and there was an accompanying handwritten note from Lexington asking Thomas to check his WhatsApp.

There were eleven new messages in the solitary chat group, the first of which was an introductory message from Lexington thanking Thomas for his company the previous day, congratulating him on his wise decision to join The Twelve and inviting the others to welcome him as warmly as they possibly could. Lexington's text also gave the briefest overview of Thomas's career in sports training, culminating in the success of three of his athletes at the 2012 London Olympics. Mention of it made Thomas feel both humbled and exhilarated in equal measure.

The subsequent ten messages were all variations on a welcoming theme from each of the other members. They ranged in length from a couple of words – 'Alright, mate?' from a Terry Wilson whom Thomas recalled being a former locksmith with a

14

passion for baking – to a small essay from a linguist named Belinda Olorenshaw who greeted him in eight languages before going on to express how excited she was to have a new person to work with. Monica's message, the last to be sent, was of particular interest. 'I simply cannot wait to meet you, Thomas,' it read. 'I've heard so much about you.'

Thomas took the new phone into his kitchen to make a cup of black coffee while deciding how to respond. As it would be his first message, he wanted it to be friendly, but not overly so. He stared at the messages as he slowly sipped his coffee, then he began typing before rejecting his first draft, deleting it and starting again. It was the fifth draft which he decided to send. It read simply, 'Thank you all for your kind words of welcome. I look forward to meeting you all in person, whenever that may be'.

Lexington had suggested that, as The Twelve had no ongoing project, Thomas might like to meet with various members in smaller groups or even with individuals. He had even intimated that his first acquaintance could be with a plumber named David Latham as he was 'probably the friendliest of the bunch. Not that the rest of us are unfriendly, you understand. It's simply that David is more... immediate. You cannot help but warm to him.'

After lunch, however, a new text from Lexington indicated that there would be a full meeting of The Twelve the following morning as a new case was pending. The meeting would take place at one of The Twelve's safe houses not far from Thomas's house in Notting Hill Gate. The commissioner of the Metropolitan Police would also be in attendance as she was the one who was bringing the case for their consideration. Lexington ended his message, 'No gentle easing into it for Thomas, I fear. Sorry about that.' There was also an emoji that looked, Thomas thought, as if it were grimacing. He tried not to dwell on it. Nonetheless, perhaps sensing that the newest member of The Twelve might be feeling mildly perturbed at the thought of action quite so soon, Lexington's subsequent telephone call was welcome.

'If you wish to take more of a back seat on this first one, Thomas, then that's entirely understandable. Or you can just dive straight in. See how you feel at the meeting tomorrow. Don't worry about the commissioner. She's ever so friendly and I've told her all about you. You can find your way to the venue, I trust?' Thomas confirmed that he would be in the right place at the right time.

Over an afternoon cup of tea, Thomas decided to familiarise himself with what the other members of the group looked like using their WhatsApp profile photos. All had photographs of themselves – conveniently for Thomas, mostly close-ups – apart from David the plumber, who had a map of Trinidad, and Terry the locksmith who had a picture of an impressive-looking cake. Terry had texted the group to say he would be baking for the meeting with the commissioner so this, in part, explained that image.

The rest of them were all standard, smiley photographs of people in their sixties and seventies, some obviously taken on holiday somewhere. None of the small, circular pictures showed a partner.

As he was due to meet her for the first time, Thomas devoted an hour or so that evening to diligently researching the commissioner of the Metropolitan Police, Suzanne Green. He wanted to leave a good impression, both with the commissioner and his new... *What was he to call them? Workmates? Colleagues?* He settled on "comrades" with the option to adapt if necessary.

Commissioner Green, he learned, had assumed the role in

2016 after almost thirty years in the force, and was, by all accounts, one of the most competent holders of that esteemed yet challenging post there had been for some time. She appeared to be highly popular both with her team and, unusually, with the media – owing to her willingness to communicate on friendly terms with pretty much all of them regardless of political persuasion, a rare balancing act to perfect for someone in such a delicate position. She also had something of a reputation for plain speaking, which didn't seem to play well in the corridors of Whitehall. Calls for her resignation were commonplace although she had, according to Thomas's reading, always managed to deflect them with consummate skill.

During the early evening, Thomas noted a considerable amount of chatter on the WhatsApp group, but he didn't feel it was right to get involved, as he wasn't entirely sure what they were chattering about. There appeared to be a lot of talk about the last case in which The Twelve had been involved, that of a paedophile named Raymond Hunt who had been lured to his death by lethal injection in an East End bar and then dissolved in an acid bath in Beckton before being flushed into the sewage system and, eventually, out to sea. Monica appeared to have played a decisive role owing to her knowledge of concentrated acids although Thomas noticed that whenever she messaged, it was often to deflect attention away from her own actions, while passing praise to other members of the group.

Quite naturally, all the talk of morphine syringes and sulphuric acid with enough concentration to dissolve bone did give Thomas pause for thought; he did wonder at various points during the evening whether he'd made the right decision in La Stella. A group message from Lexington appeared to recognise these concerns. 'I appreciate that you're all still a bit overexcited about the Hunt business, but I would politely remind you about our newest member. I am keen not to scare him off within hours of persuading him to join us. Perhaps those of you with direct involvement with the Hunt case could take it offline and preferably to a pub at some point.' A series of muted apologetic texts followed until the chat went quiet around 8pm because everyone wanted to watch *The Repair Shop* without interruption.

———

The location for the meeting with the commissioner was a stucco, Victorian terraced house set back from the main thoroughfare of Notting Hill just behind an old converted cinema that hadn't shown a current movie for years. Conveniently for Thomas, it was only a short walk from Colville Square and the home he'd bought with Alice in the early eighties.

He zigzagged through the geometry of terraces and crescents around Ladbroke Grove thinking about how the area had changed. He and Alice had watched the neighbourhood with great interest as it passed through its gentle metamorphoses over the years. There was its ragged bohemian cool stage in the late eighties, which slowly made way for upmarket grandeur in the nineties, particularly after the influx of tourists following the movie that made the neighbourhood famous. Thomas had rather preferred the former incarnation with its patchwork cast of colourful, expressive characters from all over the world, while his wife had favoured the apparent security of the latter.

Their medium-sized mortgage had been paid off by the close of the twentieth century, leaving the two of them sitting on a reasonable fortune in investments and pension pots before the diagnosis and rapid progress of Alice's illness. After this the whole nature and meaning of the terms 'fortune' and 'quality of life' had changed utterly and forever.

A weak autumn sun was battling a thickening of clouds and a

stiffening breeze as Thomas slipped onto the narrow street leading down the side of the cinema just as Monica was arriving from the opposite direction wearing a pair of jeans and what looked like a white T-shirt under a scarlet raincoat. A smile of recognition suggested that she too had checked out his WhatsApp photograph the evening before, although it crossed Thomas's mind that she may even have been monitoring him for months without him realising.

'Good morning, Thomas Quinn,' she beamed, brown eyes sparkling under a powder blue beret that completed her outfit. 'It's a great pleasure to meet you in person.' She extended a gloved hand.

'I'm in the right place then,' said Thomas, suppressing nervousness. 'Didn't want to be late on my first day at school. Is this someone's house?'

'Good Lord, no,' replied Monica. 'It's one of twenty properties that the group owns around the city. We'd never meet in someone's house. Imagine the clearing up! Especially after Terry's been in the kitchen.'

'I thought Terry was a locksmith?' said Thomas, feigning ignorance of Terry's hobby.

'Terry *was* a locksmith, but since retiring a few years ago after his wife Irene died of liver cancer, he's absolutely immersed himself in cooking and baking. He's got a library of cookbooks in his house; there'll be something delicious today for sure. Anyway, how are you feeling on your first day?'

Thomas thought for a moment. A small dog being walked by a muscular man in tight, fuchsia shorts on the opposite pavement started barking suspiciously. 'Slightly nauseous, if I'm honest.'

'Good. Welcome to The Twelve,' replied Monica with a matter-of-fact half smile. 'You'll get used to it. We'd better go in. Time to meet everyone else.'

Monica walked up a couple of stone steps to the large, navy-blue door and keyed a code into the pad to its right. 'Terry is so very fond of his three-digit code locks,' she said. The door clicked open to reveal a bright entrance hallway lined with what Thomas thought looked suspiciously like sketches by the American artist Jackson Pollock. Once inside, the two of them could hear animated conversation, which suggested that they were amongst the last to arrive. The hallway opened out into a spacious reception area with ample space for thirteen.

Thomas took a quick scan of the room. He recognised Martin the cabbie from the previous day and also Lexington, of course, who gave a wave and meandered over to greet the new arrivals. 'I see you've met Monica,' he said. 'And she hasn't killed you yet, which is something of a bonus.' Monica glowered and gave Lexington a pinch on the bottom before sidling away to join a group of three other women whom Thomas recognised as Belinda, the linguist; Anna Hopley, a former pathologist with slightly greying, red hair tied in a high ponytail; and Catherine Daniels, an ex-newspaper editor. Within seconds of Monica's arrival, all four women had turned to wave at Thomas who decided it was only polite to wave back.

'There are still one or two to arrive,' said Lexington. 'Owen and Graham, predictably, but they'll arrive together and they shouldn't be long. They'd text if they were stuck. Come and meet David and Chris. Oh, and the commissioner, of course.' He guided Thomas to a pair of two-seater leather sofas where the plumber was sitting. He was in conversation with Suzanne Green, who was wearing casual clothes which threw Thomas momentarily, and Christopher Tinker, whom he remembered was a renowned surgeon in his former life and had acquired the rather grim but apparently affectionate nickname of The Cutter within the medical community. 'May I formally introduce Thomas to you all. We've rather thrown him in at the deep end, but I'm sure he'll get the hang of it reasonably quickly.'

'You'll catch up in no time,' said David, placing a firm, friendly hand on Thomas's shoulder. 'And anytime you need a chat, or indeed a plumber, you have my number. In fact, let's have a coffee after this meeting if you're free. I'm sure you'll have questions.'

Suzanne shook Thomas's hand warmly and assured him that he'd soon feel part of the family.

Chris's welcome was more subdued – a nod of the head and a simple, distracted, 'a pleasure'.

Just then, a stocky, jovial, bespectacled figure emerged from what Thomas supposed was a corridor leading to the kitchen with two plates piled high with delicious-smelling biscuits. 'I warned you I was going to bake,' Terry announced proudly, and gently placed a plate on each of the small tables in the room. 'There is no sincerer love than the love of food, according to George Bernard Shaw,' he announced to nobody in particular before turning his attention to Thomas. 'Hello, mate. Nice to meet you. Try one of these.' He lowered his voice almost to a whisper. 'I just warmed them up next door. White chocolate chip. One of my favourites. There's also a very subtle hum of cardamom in there if you can taste it; not everyone can. I only use one pod for this many biscuits, so as not to detract from the white chocolate, which isn't a strong flavour.'

The biscuit was, as advertised, delicious. He was just accepting a second one when two more men arrived. Thomas recognised them as Owen Pook, who had spent forty years working in surveillance, and an ex-police chief named Graham Best. Both made a beeline for Thomas and gave him a hug. After the kisses from Simone a couple of days earlier, such shows of affection, Thomas thought, were becoming commonplace.

'Could everyone please find a perch?' asked Lexington, who then waited while those unseated found somewhere to settle. 'It's lovely to see you all again and of course this gives us all an early opportunity to properly meet Thomas who, I hope, will feel very welcome. Many thanks to everyone for making the time at reasonably short notice. There is no formal agenda, as usual, however I should like to begin, if I may, by commending you all once again on your fine work dispatching the paedophile rapist Hunt earlier in the month. This operation was carried out with the expertise and precision we have come to expect and all of you should be very proud of yourselves, especially those directly involved.' He glanced at Monica, who blushed. 'I know that all of us sometimes have doubts with regards to the moral issues of what we do – if we did not then we would not be human – but when those challenging thoughts enter our heads, I would implore you to bring to mind the many dozens of young boys who will now never have to encounter the depraved Hunt. I'm sure Suzanne would concur.'

The commissioner nodded in agreement. She admitted, as she had at previous meetings, that like many in the police force, once she had risen to the senior rank required to even be made aware of The Twelve, her initial reaction had been one of disbelief. How, she wondered, had such an organisation existed for almost two centuries almost in plain sight, and yet avoided detection? Once she had navigated that particular hurdle, the moral and ethical questions started cascading in.

Over many conversations with both Lexington and with Graham, who could approach the subject from a relevant point of view, and after seeing the overcrowding in prisons and the bureaucracy involved in the legal system, Suzanne Green, like many before her, had come to the only rational conclusion. Any group which had successfully and efficiently been thinning out London's criminal population undetected for decades couldn't truly be all bad. The additional fact that they were generally all grandparents wasn't altogether unhelpful.

'May I just add,' she concluded, 'that these cookies are

extraordinary. I suspect they are Terry's work. Am I right? And is that the faintest hint of cardamom?' The delighted locksmith raised a mock-guilty hand. 'Then my deductive instinct remains intact despite the rather mundane desk job.'

'Beats a Rich Tea,' muttered Martin, and blew a theatrical kiss in Terry's direction.

A playful look danced elegantly across Lexington's face. 'As you all know,' he began, 'it has been eighteen years since I joined The Twelve and rarely has a day gone by in all that time when I do not myself question what we do. These doubts amble around my mind constantly like sullen ruffians murmurating outside a fast-food outlet. It usually takes a brandy in my hand and Bach in my ears to clear my mind.

'The weight of responsibility hangs heavy upon us all. Yet when I balance all the arguments, I – as you have, Suzanne – always reach the same conclusion. May I remind you though, as I regularly do, that we are not here to judge, merely to carry out our duty, unobtrusively and without fanfare. We exist in the margins of the grand story of this wonderful old city. We are pencil scribbles only. Ours is a tidying role, as much as anything. A dusting down of society's cobwebs, if you like.' Many of the group nodded in agreement, Owen Pook even venturing a subdued, 'Bravo!'

'Now,' continued Lexington, reaching for a cookie, 'speaking of cobwebs, to the main business of the meeting. Suzanne will explain while I have a cheeky nibble to assess whether my tastebuds too can winkle out the elusive spice.'

The commissioner reached into her briefcase and emerged with a thin sheaf of photocopied pictures, which she handed round the group. The pages showed what looked like a young homeless man with shoulder length dark hair and a gaunt, world-weary countenance. 'Thank you, Lexington. This young man is Sean Bay,' she began, straightening her back as the images were studied. 'He was twenty-eight years of age and had been homeless since the age of nineteen after being thrown out of his home by his mum and stepfather, a petty criminal himself but that is of no particular relevance here. Apparently, Sean was only really close to his paternal grandmother and when she died he went off the rails a bit. Nonetheless, he was popular both with acquaintances from the streets and with a few friends outside them. Unusually within the homeless community, he also had a couple of regular places to stay. One was out west in Hounslow with a divorced woman in her forties named Linda Morris, and the other down in Colliers Wood with another woman, a single mother in her late thirties named Nicola Thwaite.'

'Your use of the past tense,' noted Catherine, 'rather suggests Sean is no longer with us.'

'I'm afraid not,' explained the commissioner. 'He was hit by a southbound Underground train after falling onto the tracks at Oakwood Station late on the evening of October 7th. Ordinarily this would be no cause for investigation and we would simply chalk it off as misadventure; however in this particular case it wasn't the impact that killed him. Pathology has revealed that Sean was dead before he hit the tracks, owing to a large quantity of potassium cyanide hidden inside a tin foil-wrapped chicken sub roll, part of which he had recently eaten. The remains of the sandwich were found in his left hand, which had been severed by the wheels.' Anna winced. 'Needless to say, the chances of a homeless person going to the trouble of making themselves a chicken roll which they then laced with poison are reasonably slim. Monica, would you care to use your knowledge to explain succinctly what that substance does to a person? You'll doubtless do it more justice than I could.'

Monica shifted in her seat and leaned forward. 'Thank you, Suzanne, and thank you also for your kind words earlier about our little organisation.' She took a deep breath, as if addressing a lecture theatre full of undergraduates. 'Okay, let's think. Where best to begin? Of all the ways to die, potassium cyanide poisoning should be fairly low on anyone's list as it's very unpleasant, although at least it's quick. Poor Sean would have experienced painful and horrific multiple organ failure within seconds. Depending on how much of the substance he consumed, he would have suffered severe tissue damage to his mouth and throat, heart failure and breathing problems before losing consciousness. To the untrained eye, potassium cyanide looks a bit like sugar so it could easily be hidden in food, but it tastes bitter to most people and if you eat it in any quantity, even with a mouthful of sandwich, you'll lose consciousness pretty quickly, suffer a severe headache and soon your brain will be starved of oxygen and that will be the end of that. Does that help? I've only given you the basics.'

'Thank you, Monica,' said the commissioner with a look of admiration. Monica blushed again. Thomas smiled in her direction, but she didn't notice as she had lowered her eyes.

The commissioner resumed. 'We did a post-mortem before we knew who he was. Then a week ago Nicola Thwaite reported him missing as she was worried and thought he might have been beaten up on the streets. Apparently she has another homeless male friend who told her he hadn't seen Sean for a while, which rang the alarm bell. Nicola had a photo of him, which she kept on her mantelpiece. We identified him from that along with a couple of tattoos that remained intact despite his collision with the train. Three days ago, Linda Morris also reported him missing apparently, after hearing a rumour from another mutual acquaintance. We've obviously had to give both women the bad news, but naturally we haven't revealed how he died. As far as Nicola and Linda are aware, he simply fell on the tracks after a few drinks. They both accepted that it was not implausible, knowing Sean.'

'If I may,' asked Terry, 'why not tell them the truth?' A concerned look crossed the commissioner's face.

'Because I'm afraid Sean isn't the first homeless person to die in this very unusual way over the last few months. He's the second. At least.'

4

The commissioner frowned, adjusted her papers and held up a second picture, this time of an older man, bearded and darker skinned but clearly ethnically white with missing front teeth, a look of doleful resignedness and wearing a slightly tattered grey jacket. The picture was a police identification photo suggesting that this individual had spent time in prison or, at least, been arrested at some point.

'Please welcome into your world Daniel Neal, imaginatively known to his friends on the streets as Danno. Daniel – I refuse to call him Danno; after all this isn't Hawaii…' Martin almost stifled a laugh. 'Oh, thank God for older people, no offence.' The commissioner grinned with quiet satisfaction. 'I hoped that reference would play well with a more mature audience. I tried it on my deputy and just got a blank look, but then he is a bloody millennial or a Gen X or whatever they're calling themselves these days. I digress. Daniel was fifty-one at the time of his death on June 13th this year. He had been homeless for most of his life, in and out of prison for minor begging offences and once for affray. He was unconnected with the main criminal underworld owing to him being an alcoholic and utterly untrustworthy with any confidential information. As a result he was also of minimal interest to us, either as an informer or anything else for that matter. Until June. His life ended at Totteridge & Whetstone Underground station very late that Saturday evening. He had partially eaten a homemade ham and cheese wrap with salad, also wrapped in tin foil and also containing a fatal quantity of potassium cyanide. He didn't fall on the tracks this time but, as it was late, he collapsed in an obscured corner of the platform and wasn't found until 5am the following morning when the day staff opened up. You will, I'm sure, note the alarming similarities.'

'Second station from the end of the line both times,' announced David, proudly. Everyone looked at the plumber with a mixture of curiosity and confusion.

'I find that slightly geeky yet also strangely attractive,' pronounced Anna with an affectionate smile. David's expression shifted from one of pride to one of coyness.

'There's nothing wrong with geekiness,' replied David, softly, reaching for a biscuit. 'We're all geeks in our own different ways. Would you like me to list the Underground stations with an "x" in their names?' Anna pretended to swoon.

'I think we'll take what the Americans might term "a rain check" if it's all the same to you, David,' said Lexington sympathetically, 'although I've already thought of three of them – but only because I live in Pimlico.' He turned back towards the commissioner and asked whether there were any other connections between the victims, which may be helpful.

The commissioner sighed. 'Not so far. There doesn't appear to be any common link between the victims, apart from homelessness of course. The two men didn't know each other as far as we can ascertain, nor is there an obvious motive. The Neal death occurred much later in the evening, but that's probably simply because it gets darker much later in June and the murderer prefers darkness to operate – as well as a fairly empty train carriage – in order to minimise the number of witnesses. There were none in either case. If this is someone who has a violent hatred of homeless people, we naturally don't want to alarm that community by letting them know that they could be targets. Before you know it, the broader population will find out, there could be a state of general panic amongst commuters and we'll have no chance of catching him. He may already have gone to ground, as it were. We simply don't know.'

'You're sure we're dealing with a "him"?' asked Belinda.

'It's always a "him",' exhaled the commissioner, forlornly. 'Can you countenance a woman using an in-depth knowledge of lethal poisons to murder innocent people in such a painful and hideous way?' She glanced over at Monica who was conspicuously attempting to sink into her seat. 'Present company being the exception, and, like Mary Poppins, I mean that in the most delightful way, Monica.'

The former chemist smiled weakly. 'We've scoured CCTV of the stations and there's nothing hugely helpful. On each occasion there's a tall, thin man who leaves the train either at the station where the handover of poisoned food has taken place, or at the next one, and then walks away. We lose him fairly quickly because the coverage isn't that great in the suburbs, probably another reason why those outlying stations are chosen. On both occasions he's wearing a cap and gloves and what looks like a rudimentary disguise so we can't get a decent image. Forensics haven't turned up anything, ostensibly because of the time difference between the act of murder and the victim being found, coupled with the sheer quantity of DNA on your average Underground train. It's like the whole of London moults skin and hair on a daily basis.'

'Can you trace his movements back to see where he gets on the trains?' suggested Thomas, bravely interjecting.

'An excellent idea,' agreed the commissioner, causing Thomas to redden this time, 'and one that we've already looked into. The problem is that our killer is clever. He uses the same line to embark as he does to escape, but nowhere central. He gets on where the CCTV isn't brilliant and then keeps his head down under his cap to avoid a clear image of himself. He pretends to be snoozing until he's ready to attack. We know he got on the train at Osterley for the Sean Bay murder, and we can trace him back to a point just outside that station, but from there the coverage doesn't allow us to follow. With the Neal murder, the CCTV isn't available as London Underground doesn't usually keep it beyond thirty days or so. We were lucky to get the Totteridge images. These murders are planned in advance and meticulously executed. We're not dealing with an opportunist here.'

'Fingerprints on the tinfoil?' asked Owen hopefully.

'Nothing full,' explained the commissioner. 'And nothing from the partial prints that corresponds to anything on our database. The killer wears gloves, as we know, plus the nature of foil being what it is, any fingerprint if it existed would become crinkled and diminished. So, there isn't a lot to go on, but I wondered whether you might be able to see what you can do. I could put some resources of my own behind it but, as you know, we're rather stretched at the moment and the government is threatening yet more police budget cuts to save money. How they expect the crime figures to come down when the number of good detectives dwindles, I really can't comprehend, but there you have it. I'm not a politician so that breed of individual's increasingly random thought processes are as much a mystery to me as to the rest of us. Naturally, I'll forward any useful information that comes our way.'

'Bacofoil or the cheap stuff?' asked Martin suddenly.

The commissioner gave him a look pitched midway between bafflement and pity. 'I'm not entirely sure that that matters evidentially, Martin, but I'll certainly look into it.'

'All right,' concluded Lexington, calmly. 'There doesn't appear to be too much to go on at the moment, but we should begin by travelling those two lines late at night, in pairs for company as well as safety, and see if anything comes up. We'll do it up until Christmas or until there's another development in the case. I shall require four groups of two, initially. Do I have any volunteers for pairings?'

Within seconds, two pairs had materialised – Anna with Graham as they both lived in the same area of London and could get to and from each of the lines easily; and Terry and Martin who could leave his cab anywhere along the route and retrieve it after their shift before giving Terry a lift home.

'I'll take turns,' said Catherine, 'if anyone fancies joining me.' Thomas was in two minds about volunteering, but was half in a daze from all the information about poisoned sandwiches and, before he could react, Owen had put his hand up to team with the ex-journalist.

'Anyone else?' pondered Lexington. 'Otherwise I'll have to choose.'

'I'd love to help,' piped Monica, 'and perhaps Thomas would be kind enough to keep me company. As long as you're okay with that, Thomas?'

Thomas's torpor suddenly lifted at the sound of his own name. He hadn't needed to volunteer. Monica had done it for him. He smiled at Monica and agreed that that would be perfectly fine. It would give him an opportunity to find out a bit more about the group from someone other than Lexington.

'Excellent. Thank you, everyone,' said The Twelve's leader. 'I shall draw up a rota starting as soon as possible and distribute it at our regular yoga class which has, as you know, moved to tomorrow to accommodate this meeting. Don't forget that it's at 11am in the usual location. There will be no text reminders on this occasion. You don't need them. I shall see you all then. Now, the commissioner and I have a couple of non-Twelve matters which we need to discuss, so if you'll excuse us. Terry, you may leave the cookies.'

'I hope you don't mind me volunteering you, especially as you've only just arrived. I simply thought it'll be rather fun working on this together, don't you think, Thomas? It will give us a chance to get to know one another better.' Monica was adjusting her beret against the autumn breeze as they stepped onto the street. Although the day was now bright, London was noticeably changing colour all around them as the oaks, sycamores and planes had registered the shift in the air and had begun their annual regression to hunker down for winter.

'I can think of nothing better,' agreed Thomas. His immediate thought was one of satisfaction that he could finally spend quality time one-to-one with another member of the group, and Monica would, he felt reasonably sure, be most interesting company. 'I'll see you tomorrow at yoga, 11am. I have the address.' Monica gave him a warm hug and Thomas noticed that she smelt extremely good. He hadn't truly focused on a woman's scent for many years, not since Alice died at any rate. Monica's was a good smell, floral like peonies but with a hint of something else, something spicy that he couldn't place. *Maybe all chemists smelt good,* he mused, but that thought swiftly reminded him of the poisoned sandwiches and rather dampened his mood.

He watched Monica's back in a somewhat dreamy state as she sashayed in the direction of the station. 'Time for that coffee?' asked David's recognisable voice behind him.

There was a newish Danish coffee shop just over the road, which looked promising, and the two of them quickly settled at a quiet table by the window. 'You didn't feel like volunteering for

Underground duty, David?' enquired Thomas by way of small talk.

The plumber sipped his latte thoughtfully. 'I had a fairly major role in the last case. The Hunt one. So I thought I probably could do with at least a fortnight to decompress before throwing myself into another. Lexington understands. We only usually take one case at a time so that we can fully focus on getting it absolutely right. That also generally allows us to spread the emotional load a bit. This business takes its toll, as you'll find out. Assassination isn't a laugh a minute.'

'You killed him, didn't you? Hunt.' Thomas kept his voice low despite the nearest customers being deep in conversation themselves. David confirmed that he had indeed been the assassin in the Hunt case. Because the predatory paedophile had a preference for young, pre-teen black boys, David had volunteered to first befriend him and then lure him to a quiet bar where he could administer a lethal injection of horse tranquilliser into the drunken Hunt's thigh. Terry, who was also in the bar, then helped David carry the dying man to Martin's taxi and the trio then drove to the house in Beckton where Monica and Anna were waiting with an acid bath.

'It's a fairly new acquisition,' said David. 'Monica's idea about four years ago. We got talking and she wanted to know how easy it would be to plumb a gold-lined bath directly into the main sewer; it needed to be gold so it wouldn't be corroded by concentrated acids. I said that we'd need to find a house that was more or less on top of the sewer and close to a wide section of the river, but that it shouldn't be that hard. Within a month, Lexington had bought the perfect detached house in Beckton and the plumbing work began.'

'He just bought a house and a gold bath?'

David nodded. 'The Twelve has considerable financial resources. Anyway, once Hunt was in the bath, it was just a waiting game. His remains are now spread all over the North Sea – you just have to be careful to pull the bath plug when the tide's on its way out.'

Thomas thought for a moment. 'Surely CCTV would have picked up Hunt going into the bar and then being carried into the taxi?' David chuckled. 'Remember, everything is meticulously planned to the last detail. Owen is able to jam CCTV remotely so there is no coverage of him after he left work before walking to the bar. He simply disappears. Most of them simply disappear and those that don't get chalked down to suicide. How old are you, my friend?' Thomas replied that he was sixty-eight. The plumber placed a strong, comforting hand on his shoulder. 'You still have a lot to learn,' he said, 'but we all have time to teach you.'

It was just after 1.30pm when Thomas finally climbed the four stone steps to his front door, his mind filled with a range of emotions. The conversation with David had definitely answered some questions but had posed many more. He turned the key in the lock with an overwhelming but unexpected sense of admiration for David and the rest of the group.

Three years ago, the silence of the house would have crushed him, but today he embraced it. He made himself a quick pasta lunch with prawns and then sat in his favourite armchair with his book. After a few minutes he began to feel his concentration wane, so he placed the book on the floor, sat back and closed his eyes. 'I was a sports trainer,' he thought to himself as his eyelids drooped. 'I used to work with athletes. Now what am I doing?' He didn't have an immediate answer to this question but somehow it felt good to be alive. Alice ventured into his mind as she usually did at times like these. She was pleased that he had something new to occupy his time. Thomas smiled as he drifted into a light sleep.

Outside in the square, the gossip amongst the birds had begun to intensify.

5

Weekly yoga sessions weren't compulsory, yet, as everyone enjoyed them so much, it was extremely rare for there not to be a full house unless one member of The Twelve was particularly under the weather, or if the actual weather prevented attendance for safety reasons. The previous winter, Martin had slipped on some ice on the way to class and landed on his bottom, bruising it badly. On medical examination, Christopher had pointed out that if he had twisted his body ever so slightly during the fall, he would almost certainly have fractured his hip and as such injuries were a constant worry, slippery surfaces were best avoided even if it meant forgoing their downward dog for a week or two.

The discipline had been introduced in the early 1930s by an inspirational woman named Hilda Graham who was eighty-one at the time and had been a member of The Twelve for sixteen years, during which she had managed various levels of involvement in a remarkable thirty-three disappearances, at that point a record. Hilda had spent time travelling in India during her twenties and had picked up many of the key moves and postures from friends she had made in the local communities. As a result, it was Hilda's belief, ahead of its time in Britain, that older people would benefit from gentle exercises to strengthen their cores and their legs in particular. She felt that this in turn would lead to more successful Twelve operations, fewer injuries and a greater sense of calm amongst some of the rather mercurial members of the group. The proof of Hilda's karmic pudding was plain for all to see; she finally retired from The Twelve at the age of eighty-five and lived well for another four years before finally dying peacefully in her sleep at home in Wanstead after spending the previous evening practising her tree pose as best she was able, and then partaking in a regular bedtime brandy as the air-raid sirens blared. A few weeks after her death, the Luftwaffe bombed her house (and those of most of her less flexible neighbours.)

As a former sports coach, Thomas had always enjoyed yoga for its obvious physical advantages and he was sure this new opportunity would also allow him to get to know more of the group socially. The classes were led by Anna, who had taken it up in her forties – her forensic pathology career persuading her to consider more and more carefully her own inner workings, especially after slicing into so many unfit and frankly disgusting specimens, their organs constricted by fistfuls of lardaceous blubber. She was a sympathetic teacher whose classes were filled with both gentle humour and polite encouragement, with regular interjections such as, 'Remember to keep your feet at right angles for Warrior Two, David,' and 'Could we have just a smidgen more bend in your Cobra please, Terry. You're virtually horizontal.'

The usual location for these sessions was a nondescript house in an unspectacular side street between Euston station and the British Library, which had been purchased by The Twelve in 1954 for the very purpose of providing a suitable space for yoga. It had a large downstairs area, which had been cleared of furniture apart from a small table and a couple of chairs in one corner, and its floor was sanded and varnished to avoid splinters in bare feet or hands. If the neighbours were curious about the strange group of elderly folk who congregated every Thursday morning more or less, they didn't mention anything. Everyone kept themselves very much to themselves in that part of the city.

Anna's classes weren't generally strenuous – Philip was eighty-one after all, and although not exactly frail, he nonetheless struggled with many of the more challenging poses and on occasion had to be helped to extract himself from an unruly tangle – yet everyone always benefited from them. At his first class, Thomas found the ten-minute wind-down at the end particularly rewarding. He was encouraged to clear his mind as much as possible, which definitely helped him not to dwell upon the past and to focus more on the years ahead.

After Alice's death, for the first time in his life, Thomas had experienced an unfamiliar feeling best described as being unmoored. It wasn't pleasant. Being welcomed into The Twelve was quickly altering everything. Even though it had only been a couple of days, the chat with David and the promise of time with Monica had brought a renewed spring to his step.

Namaste. Everyone bowed their heads to signify the end of the class. Lexington remained still for a moment to recalibrate some balance, and then moved gingerly towards the back wall of the room and rummaged in his bag for a few seconds before finally extracting a thin file of papers. He then shuffled tentatively towards the small table, sat on one of the chairs and briskly rubbed his left knee before placing the file down as the others gathered around.

'A dynamic class, as ever, Anna. Thank you. Now, to business. I've discussed this with Suzanne and we feel that it would be best to start the monitoring tonight. I feel a sense of urgency surrounding this case so we may as well begin work as early as we can.

'Therefore, we shall start this evening at 8pm unless anyone has any pressing engagements. Owen and Catherine, if you could please take the Northern Line.' Both nodded in agreement. 'And if you, Thomas and Monica, could take the Piccadilly Line that would be splendid.' Thomas glanced at Monica, who was standing with her hands on her hips and smiling with satisfaction, while simultaneously glowing in the aftermath of the yoga.

'Then Martin and Terry can take the Northern Line tomorrow while Anna and Graham take the Piccadilly. On Sunday we revert to today's pairings and on Monday we go back to the Saturday pairings, et cetera et cetera ad infinitum, or more likely and more hopefully until there is an advancement in the case. And by "advancement" I mean either another murder or, more optimistically speaking, a sighting. We're looking out for anything unusual, anyone tall travelling alone late at night, after dark, acting suspiciously, wearing a baseball cap and attempting to steer clear of cameras. In particular please be aware of any homeless people travelling alone late at night. Don't engage with them at this point, except to give them money if you so desire, but be aware that they may need your protection, particularly if they are given a foil package by a lone stranger. We shall get an update next week here in this room and we shall see where we are. I have little expectation that much will have been achieved in six nights of surveillance, but you never know. All that remains is for me to thank Anna once again for another invigorating session and to wish you all a delightful weekend.'

'So where would you like to meet later?' asked Monica as they wandered back toward the Euston Road, both pulling their coats up tightly around their necks as one of the first autumn storms began to blow in from the west.

Thomas thought for a moment before deciding. 'How about the bar at the St Pancras Hotel just round the corner from here. I'll treat you to a cheeky cocktail before we set off.'

Monica gave him a friendly hug, enveloping him in her scent again, mixed faintly with sweat from the session. 'You're a man after my own heart. I'll see you there at seven.' Suddenly, she stopped, still holding on to his arm, stared up and tilted her head. 'You've got the most extraordinary eyes, you know. Grey on the outside but brown further in. The colour of wet pebbles.' She paused before stepping back, considering an unspoken thought. 'Anyway, I've got to pop into the West End for a few bits and bobs before I head home for a shower, so I'll see you later. Au revoir!'

For the second time in two days, Thomas watched Monica as she strode purposefully down the main road before hailing a taxi and disappearing into the traffic. Invigorated by their encounter, he pondered whether to walk home via the park but decided on balance that it was too windy, and besides there were buses aplenty.

Thomas spent much of the afternoon trying to establish what to wear for the evening's activities. It was a particular challenge; his wardrobe wasn't exactly blessed with garments for which the adjective "stylish" could accurately be used. He wanted to look nice for Monica but at the same time, they were both working on surveillance, and so needed to blend in. After several changes of outfit, he settled on comfortable blue jeans, a white T-shirt and a warm grey cardigan with a light, casual jacket in dark grey which could be removed if he got too toasty. The storm had rattled through, the worst of it much further north, but there was light drizzle forecast. Although he and Monica wouldn't be outside for any length of time, apart from crossing over to opposite platforms a few times for their return journeys, the autumn nights were becoming colder as November approached and Thomas felt it best to be prepared for whatever the elements might throw at them.

He dabbed himself with Blenheim Bouquet, a gift from his daughter Emily at Christmas because he'd read somewhere, and dropped into a timely conversation, that it was Churchill's favoured scent and had figured that it therefore couldn't smell too awful. It was either that or socks again, and Thomas had suspected that even Emily's twin girls Flora and Lucy were beginning to see through his faux excitement on opening yet another patterned pair.

At 5.30pm he glanced at the figure in his bedroom mirror, straightened himself up, puffed out his chest and sniffed. 'Not too shabby for an old fella,' he announced to no one in particular and then, seeing the photo of a smiling Alice in the wooden frame by their bed, added, 'I've really no idea what you'd make of all this, love. You'd probably think I've put my head on skew-whiff. But it'll keep me active, keep my mind sharp and, if I'm honest, it's an honour to be asked. I know you'd want me to stay busy and not mope around the place. Wouldn't you?' He paused, anticipating a reply. Imagining one. 'I thought so.'

Thomas kissed the photograph tenderly, his lips momentarily leaving a mark on the cold glass, which faded within seconds. Then he paced downstairs, opened his front door, strode down the stone steps and walked purposefully in the direction of Notting Hill station to get the Circle Line round to King's Cross. As the clocks were over a week away from changing, it was still early dusk as he joined the familiar bustle around the west London junction, although there was an ominous gloom in the air that seemed to herald the darker days ahead and the low, weakening sun was just disappearing beneath a thick quilt of cloud far to the west as Thomas gazed down Holland Park Avenue. He could have taken a taxi but had decided that the Tube would be quicker, and despite the fact it was rush hour, Thomas often felt more comfortable on public transport, generally being offered a seat by younger men whom he could tell were far less physically fit than he was.

He arrived at the bar of the St Pancras hotel at 6.40pm having squeezed off the Underground, negotiated the scurry of tourists and lovers heading to and from the Eurostar for weekends away, and climbed the stairs to the back of the hotel bar – stopping briefly to admire a statue of an entwined couple signifying the romance of travel. Thomas had always prided himself on his punctuality and settled himself into one of the high wooden chairs at a matching table for two. It was just inside the door of the bar leading out into the hotel lobby, where a group of recently arrived tourists was in the process of noisily checking in with a collection of over-filled suitcases in a variety of garish colours.

A waiter materialised at his shoulder and Thomas explained that he was waiting for someone and would order when they arrived, although this didn't deter the employee from hovering hopefully every few minutes in case he had changed his mind. Monica arrived at ten past seven, 'fashionably late', as she explained it, and greeted him with a warm hug and two kisses. She was wearing tight jeans and a fitted black wool jacket under a light grey coat and a bright blue patterned scarf, which was complemented with a dark blue beret. Thomas noted the same very pleasing smell as before and hoped his own fragrance wasn't too overpowering. Monica's breathy purr of 'Oooooh, you smell delicious,' implied that he'd managed to get the concentration more or less right.

The delighted waiter was dispatched with polite instructions to fetch a negroni and an Old Fashioned but, as Monica explained with a wink, 'Just the one because we are working.'

'Did you get everything you needed from the shops?' asked Thomas, by way of introductory small talk.

Monica's bright eyes sparkled. 'I did! There were only a few bits and I could have easily got them from nearer home but, you know when you have your very favourite places and just going into them makes you feel better. I go to a fabulous bakery in Marylebone and it's not far from a wonderful cheese shop, so I just popped into both to pick up some treats for tomorrow and Sunday. I live alone, as you probably know, and I haven't any visitors this weekend for a change so I can indulge myself a bit. Ah, the drinks are here.'

The waiter placed their glasses on small circular place mats, along with a bowl of apparently complementary crispy snacks, before retreating. Thomas could somehow sense that Monica was keen to dispense with small talk.

'Tell me, Thomas,' she began, after taking a sip of her negroni and licking her lips while looking deep into Thomas's eyes, 'Oooh, that's so lovely! How are you coping with this strange new existence?'

'The first three days have been a bit of a whirlwind,' admitted Thomas. His Old Fashioned would make him feel more relaxed, he felt sure, although he still felt inexplicably tense in Monica's company. 'So far, though, I'm very much enjoying it, thank you. I mean, I feel I should qualify that statement somewhat otherwise I'll come across as some sort of psychopath. Let's say I'm looking forward to getting involved and learning how it all works. Enjoy is perhaps the wrong verb.'

'It would rather worry me if you were the kind of man who enjoyed the idea of killing people, regardless of who they might be,' smiled Monica, mischievously, 'but you'll get used to it. And Lexington holds you in very high regard so don't worry about that. He was most excited when an appropriate vacancy came up.' She ran a fingertip around the top of her glass. 'How was your coffee with David? Enlightening I hope?'

It transpired that Monica and David were close friends, having joined within a year of each other and both coming from immigrant families. Monica was enormously fond of the plumber as he was someone who could 'make any room better just by being in it,' and also the sort of person who would always do a good turn with no expectation of any reward. 'The more you learn about him,' she explained, 'the more you realise that he may be some form of angel.' Thomas suggested that this might be why he struggled after each assassination, but Monica was quick to set the record straight. 'He doesn't usually. It's possible that with the Hunt business he had to get into character a bit and he saw some images of young boys that really upset him. In some ways I think that made the final act easier for David to commit, but it's understandable that he wants to take a few days before taking a major role in this next one. I have a sense that we could be working on it for a while so there's plenty of time for everyone to play their part. Do you know, on reflection, I think I might just manage another negroni before duty calls.'

Twenty minutes later, and with a second drink in front of each of them, the conversation became more gossipy. Thomas learned that Graham and Owen were lovers, but that occasionally they invited Catherine into their bed, a revelation that caused Thomas to have a coughing fit while Monica giggled innocently. 'They don't tend to broadcast it widely, although I've no idea why in this day and age, but you might as well be aware. Graham and Owen got together about a year ago, I suppose, maybe longer, and they both like to dabble in the straight world, having been married to women for many years. Catherine sleeps with them from time to time because, frankly, she's fiercely single and she enjoys the attention. I joined them myself once, back at the beginning of the year,' Thomas was again relieved that he didn't have a mouthful of whisky and bitters, 'but it wasn't for me. What's that they say, try anything once? Well I did, and I don't regret it… but equally I saw no reason to repeat it, despite their subsequent kind exhortations. Don't get me wrong; I wasn't exactly sitting watching the whole time, but let's just say the three of them seemed to enjoy it far more than I did. Too many wrinkly bums and things wobbling about for my liking. I put it down to merely part of the marginalia of my life rather than a juicy paragraph. I suppose at heart I'm quite traditional. One partner at a time is generally sufficient. Cheers!'

She raised her glass in anticipation, but Thomas just stared into space. He was unsure whether it had been Monica's intention to shock him, perhaps as a test of some kind, but his most pressing concern at that moment was that he had an image seared into his head that he really hadn't anticipated at the start of the evening. He rather wished it wasn't there.

'Oh dear, I see I've surprised you. I do apologise.' Monica's face looked anything but contrite. If anything it had an air of elfin mischief.

Thomas, grasping at some self-assurance like driftwood, somehow managed to gather himself quickly. 'Not at all,' he stammered. 'I just had no idea. I suppose it just hadn't occurred to me. Cheers, by the way.' They touched glasses. 'What are we cheersing?'

'To a new challenge!' Monica declared. 'And also to inspiring new partnerships. Mmmmmm, delicious. They do make a good negroni here. Tell me about your dear wife, Thomas. Alice, isn't it? Do you still miss her terribly?'

Thomas's head drooped momentarily. He hadn't really spoken about Alice to anyone new for a while. 'I think about her every day,' he said, quietly. 'I can't help it, but the pain eases with the passing months. It'll be six years in January. She was ill for a long time, that's one of the reasons I took early retirement. To be her carer. When the end came I was a bit all at sea, if you know what I mean. It's desperately hard to lose someone you love, but in some ways it's even harder to watch them suffer.' He raised his head and saw that Monica's brown eyes were shining, whether through tears or the reflection of the lights in the bar, he couldn't easily determine. Thomas decided it might be a good time to start being the listener rather than the talker.

'You've been married, haven't you, Monica?' He remembered some of the details Lexington had rattled through three days earlier, although it seemed a lifetime ago.

'Twice.' It was Monica's turn to lower her eyes. 'The first time was a complete disaster. It was the early seventies. He was an artist; Canadian with shoulder-length blond hair, cheekbones to die for and lovely green eyes. He was in London to take part in an exhibition of international young talent and we met in the National Gallery. It was lust at first sight. We were married three weeks after meeting. Needless to say, my father was utterly outraged. It simply wasn't the thing for a nice Gujarati girl to do, especially in the seventies. Dad didn't speak to me for two years. But sometimes lust fades quickly and after six months we realised we had nothing in common apart from the carnal desires which had drawn us together. I lay in bed with him one morning and thought, "I have nothing to say to you". He went back to Canada and I slunk off home to endure my father's furious silence and my mother's unbearable disappointment and wait for a nice, suitable Hindu boy to sweep me off my feet.'

'And did they?'

'No. Despite my father's intense efforts at matchmaking for many years. I never wanted to be the dutiful little housewife churning out babies and *dhokra* for the rest of my life. My career was taking off and the smart people in the chemistry world were starting to talk about me. Important people. It felt good to be noticed professionally and I could envisage an exciting life path ahead that simply didn't have a big Indian wedding in it. I was approaching thirty and my father finally washed his hands of me completely. He said I was left on the shelf; I was soiled goods that nobody could ever love. There's paternal encouragement for you.

Mind you, it was 1980 and there weren't many young Indian women role models around, to be honest.

'Then, two weeks after my thirtieth birthday and at the point when I had almost resigned myself to delightful singledom, I met Patrick in a bar. He was English but with Irish ancestry, dark hair, blue eyes and a smile that made me melt every time I saw it. He worked in finance and told the most fantastic tales of travelling the world. Well, that was that. We dated for two years – I guess I didn't want to make the same rash mistake twice – and we travelled together whenever my work allowed, declaring our love in cities from Paris to Melbourne and all points in between. Finally even my parents decided that we were soulmates who were meant to be together. We married at a small church in the Cotswolds, where his family lived, and then settled down in St John's Wood in one of those Georgian terraces. He took me around the world whenever he had meetings and I truly believed we would be together forever. True lovers. Never to be parted. Protecting each other always.'

'So what happened?' Thomas had nearly drained his glass without thinking as he was so enraptured by Monica's story.

Monica looked up, her brown eyes now empty of sparkle, but full of defiance. 'World Trade Center. North Tower, 98th floor. Wrong place, wrong date. Shit. I'm afraid that's what happened. Shit happened. The one trip I couldn't go on with him because I had a ridiculous conference here. I couldn't protect him. Not on that terrible day. All I could do was watch in disbelief on a television screen 3,000 miles away and wait desperately for a telephone call that never came.' Monica finished her negroni and smiled feebly before taking a deep breath that perked her up considerably. 'We should go. I've depressed you enough. We can continue our delightful conversation on the Piccadilly Line.

6

'Speaking of New York, as we were earlier, Lexington probably hasn't told you yet but there's a Twelve there too.'

They were just leaving Caledonian Road on the fourth trip of the evening and Thomas was beginning to wonder how many more surprises Monica had up her elegant sleeve. The intriguing revelation about Owen, Graham and Catherine had taken a little while to settle completely in his mind, but he nonetheless suspected that in terms of what might be loosely termed gossip, they hadn't yet truly scratched the surface. After all, Monica had been a part of the group for many years longer than he had, more than enough time to gather invaluable inside knowledge about everyone and everything.

'They fly over from time to time, the Americans. They claim it's either to share intelligence when it's relevant to a particular case, or to get advice from Lexington, but I rather suspect it's because our restaurants are better.' Monica smiled, smugly, and put a finger to her lips in thought. 'Their last visit was, let me think, about four years ago. Two men and two women. I slept with one of the women but only because it was the anniversary of Patrick's birthday and I was feeling vulnerable and, if I'm honest, slightly needy, although not so vulnerable that I wanted to have to bother with a penis and all the bizarre insecurities that often accompany them. Clare, her name was. Without an "i". Beautiful black woman from Queens. Former lawyer. Sometimes you just fancy a bit of fun and a warm body to hold onto without any complications. You understand that, don't you?'

Thomas lied that he did, although in reality he felt becalmed by the conversation, far from anything resembling a safe shore and with minimal means to propel himself back. Monica, meanwhile, was paddling forth into uncharted waters, undeterred. 'There was also one in Berlin for a while – a Twelve, that is – in the 1920s, but it was short-lived. They had to disband during the thirties because it was becoming too dangerous owing to the fact that most of their potential targets were in or around the government at the time. The majority of them had to go to America or Canada to escape being sent to the camps. One couple ended up here, inevitably living in Dorking where they ran a Post Office for a while. Friedmann, I think their names were. There's been talk of restarting the Berlin group every year since 1990, but it doesn't ever amount to much.' Monica glanced over to Thomas whose mouth was slightly open. 'Sorry, am I boring you?' she asked with an impish grin. 'You seem to have rather glazed over.'

Thomas wanted to explain that she was doing entirely the opposite and, in fact, he was beginning to believe that Monica was probably the most interesting person that he had ever met, yet he couldn't quite form the sequence of words that would adequately express this, and so he fell back on simply: 'Not at all. It's all most fascinating. Thank you.'

They had been travelling up and down the Piccadilly Line for over three hours, changing carriages regularly and observing the standard comings and goings of a regular Friday evening, but had seen no obvious sign of anything unusual. Generic drunk people of all ages, yes. The nascent makings of a fight which quickly dissipated when one of the potential combatants threw up, luckily into a paper bag of fast food being carried by his female companion, which had caused her to scream, 'Oi, Kevin! That's my fucking nuggets you've puked on!' There was nothing sinister to suggest a murderer at work.

'I appreciate it's early days, but is there anyone in the group you think you'd like to get to know better? Apart from me, of course.' Monica accompanied this question with a broad grin and a cheeky wink.

'I'm going to tentatively suggest that our first evening together on the city transport system has been a resounding success, Monica,' he grinned, feeling slightly clumsy in his choice of words but also amazed that he'd managed to construct any sort of coherence under the circumstances. He thought for a moment. 'I think I'd like to get to know everyone in time, although Martin seems a bit grumpy and Chris is a bit standoffish.'

Monica sighed. 'I know what you mean but I don't think you need to worry. Martin's all bark and no bite. He's an absolute softy when you get to know him. And has Lexington told you about those psychology tests that we all do every six months to check that we're not somehow turning into homicidal maniacs? Martin absolutely aces them every time. He's a very caring man, you know. The sometimes gruff exterior is merely a front. He does an enormous amount for charity on the quiet as we all do, plus he's very cultured and he's known about The Twelve longer than any of us. As for Chris, you should invite him out. He's a hoot!'

'His nickname is The Cutter,' whispered Thomas, remembering Chris's subdued handshake. 'I researched him. He was one of the greatest surgeons ever produced by this country. Even I had heard of him before I met him, so you can understand me being more than slightly in awe of the man.'

'Oh there's really no need,' said Monica, sympathetically.

'He's absolutely lovely, very humble and he has the best stories from his time in emergency medicine. Take him out sometime, give him a couple of whiskies and then just sit back and listen to the funniest tales you ever heard. He'll adore you and you'll adore him. Trust me. And let's not forget, they don't just invite anyone into The Twelve. Lexington researches and watches and discards dozens of possibilities every year, people who will never know what they missed. If either Martin or Chris weren't a perfect fit, they simply wouldn't be a part of our lives, just as you would never have met me and vice versa.' She gazed into Thomas's eyes and beamed. 'Anyway, it's past eleven so I think it's time to come off our watch. We're nearly back at King's Cross so I'll black cab it from there. Do you want to jump in and I'll drop you somewhere? Where do you live again?'

Thomas considered the offer but decided he had monopolised enough of Monica's time already. 'You're kind, but I'm Notting Hill so it would be rather a long way round to get to St John's Wood.' Thomas paused for a moment. 'I have to say that I've very much enjoyed this evening and I look forward to more on Sunday. Same time and place?'

Monica reached into a pocket and pulled out her beret, ready for the outside world. 'Bloody lovely. Can't wait!' she clapped.

Thomas escorted Monica to the taxi rank at King's Cross, using his jacket to chivalrously shelter her from the light drizzle as best he could, and ensuring that he was always on the side of the pavement closest to the road to protect her from any gutter spray. He made sure that she was safely settled into her black cab from where she blew him a kiss and gave a little wave before driving off into the night.

Thomas wandered in the same direction towards the Euston Road and the bus to Paddington from where he could walk home. He could have got a taxi himself – he knew there was always plenty of money from The Twelve for expenses – but there was something about the bus that appealed. No offence to Martin, but there had been too many times since Alice had died that Thomas had wanted a journey of reflection and contemplation and instead ended up with an earful about political correctness gone mad or the Mayor of London ruining the driver's life via some seemingly sensible regulation which, the loquacious cabbie maintained, had been drawn up purely to piss him off. Tonight in particular was a time for thought; about the case, about Alice – it would be her birthday the following Thursday, the 29th, so he would be visiting her grave with flowers on the Sunday – about Monica, about the World Trade Center and so much more. Their conversation had been wide-ranging and eye-opening, but it had left many questions waiting to be both asked and answered. He decided to shuffle them around his head and figure out suitable ways to pose them, perhaps on their next evening together, but perhaps not. There was, with any luck, time to spare.

The bus was fairly quiet, with only three other passengers that he could see, and Thomas settled into the back seat of the lower deck and stretched his legs to the side. He let his mind wander as his eyes half registered the lights outside refracted through the raindrops on the window. The WhatsApp group chat pinged into life. Catherine Daniels' message told The Twelve that nothing unusual had been observed on the Northern Line. Within seconds, Monica had replied that the Piccadilly Line was also free of incident, Lexington had thanked everyone for their evening's work and wished everyone goodnight. *Monica would probably be getting home around now,* Thomas thought.

7

The following day, Thomas busied himself with a visit to non-Twelve friends in West London as well as an impromptu lunch at a pub on the river with his daughter Emily and her girls. He had wondered, during an idle moment gazing out over the water, whether microscopic bits of Raymond Hunt might somehow be floating past. He decided that the paedophile was far out to sea by now, diluted and dispersed by wind and tide.

There had also been sporadic text chatter within The Twelve's WhatsApp group, but nothing out of the ordinary. The main conversation seemed to be one between Martin and David regarding the point of the clocks going back annually before Lexington politely asked them to take their discussion offline and actually talk to each other.

In advance of her birthday, Thomas's thoughts turned toward Alice. She would have been sixty-six. He tried to picture her at that age, still beautiful with warm eyes and freshly coloured light brunette hair, but the Alice his mind created wasn't that much different to Alice at fifty-five, before she had become ill. He preferred that image to Alice at sixty, a few months away from death, skeletal, weak and in pain, imploring him to somehow help her to end her life yet knowing in her heart that he didn't have that power. Thomas pushed this image away, his subconscious struggling urgently to replace it with something, anything happier. Eventually, it settled upon Monica, which made him feel both comforted and uneasy at the same time.

On the Sunday, Thomas checked the weather using an app on his new smartphone and decided on a light, waterproof coat for a brisk stroll. It wasn't a particularly cold day, but it was breezy and there was the threat of rain in the air. He left the house and the square and walked towards Ladbroke Grove, picking up some flowers from a stall on the corner of Lancaster Road.

There were no peonies, Alice's favourite; it wasn't the season. So, he settled for some pink roses, which the young assistant wrapped carefully in brown paper for him. Just over twenty minutes later, he was in Kensal Green cemetery at the graveside.

Thomas had always felt mildly uncomfortable talking out loud to Alice's headstone. He'd seen it done in the movies and tried it once, but if it was designed to comfort the living, then for him it had felt daft, frankly. So instead, he bent down, laid the flowers and had a few quiet moments with his thoughts. He missed Alice, of course, but he missed her the way she was before the illness tightened its terrible, unrelenting grip on her body despite courses of draining, difficult treatment. He certainly didn't miss the last few months of Alice's life and the feeling of helplessness and indignity on both sides. The tears and the pain.

His concentration drifted to The Twelve and Thomas wondered what the remainder of his life would have been like without this new opportunity. Doubtless he would have settled into some kind of gradual, steady decline, maybe become one of those ageing men who plays golf for their weekly exercise despite never particularly enjoying that sport. Otherwise, sedentary. Stationary. Inert. A tired, old man shuffling toward winter.

'I thought it was you.' The sudden voice behind him was familiar, sophisticated. It took Thomas a moment to register that it belonged to Christopher Tinker, the surgeon. The Cutter. 'Don't worry, I'm not stalking you. My wife is over there.' The doctor gestured toward a collection of newer gravestones by the Dissenters' Chapel and then offered his hand. 'Been there five years, poor old thing. I come on the last Sunday of every month, rain or shine. You?'

'Birthday next week,' said Thomas, shaking hands. The surgeon's grip was firmer and friendlier than the week before. 'She would have been sixty-six on Thursday. I try to visit when I can, but I suppose it's not as often as monthly.' Thomas knew it wasn't. He tried to think back to his last visit and realised, shamefully, that it had probably been June, or even May. 'I'm a sorry excuse for a husband, even beyond death.'

'I'm sorry,' bowed Chris, 'and I have little doubt that you were an excellent husband. I'm sure…' he leaned over to read the inscription on the stone, 'I'm sure Alice would agree completely. Perhaps you'd like to celebrate her impending birthday with a nice cup of tea? If you're available, of course. It would be good to get to know you a bit. I'm in no hurry myself. Nobody to slice open anymore!'

The breeze had picked up and was scattering coloured leaves across the plots as the two men made their way to a nearby cafe, a parliament of rooks taking flight from the distant trees behind them which shielded the cemetery from the canal. Chris knew a cafe on Harrow Road. It was owned by a friendly, young Greek couple and sold a dizzying array of teas with homemade cakes displayed under clear glass domes. Thomas decided on Earl Grey, while Chris plumped for Assam. 'Cake?' he proffered, smiling warmly. 'It is a birthday week after all. Can't have a birthday without cake. I'll choose for you, if I may. No allergies, I trust?'

They settled into a corner table. The café was largely empty except for a couple of young mothers sharing stories in hushed voices as their babies slept peacefully in pushchairs, and a teenage girl seated by the window, wearing headphones and nodding rhythmically while simultaneously engrossed in a book.

Thomas looked at the babies and smiled. 'Do you have children, Christopher?'

'Please, call me Chris. Yes, we have three.' Thomas made a mental note of the first-person plural. 'All of them girls. All of them foolishly followed their father into medicine despite my best efforts as a human deterrent. One's a GP in Surrey – busy with all those rich, old people with their brittle bones, fatty livers and disgusting arteries; one went into paediatrics and works at Great Ormond Street, and the other is about to graduate in cardiology.'

'You must be very proud,' said Thomas as the Greek husband arrived with a tray of tea and cake into which Chris dived straight away.

'Yes. I am. The last five years have been hard, of course, after Alison died, getting everyone through it and out the other side… but we're all stronger and we look to the future. It's all you can do. How about you and Alice? Kids?'

'A daughter and a son. Both grown up. Emily's a hotshot lawyer, divorced with twin girls. Simon does something in media. I've tried to understand it, but I don't really. I'm much closer to Emily than I am to Simon, which is a shame but that's families for you. They both have busy lives.'

Thomas looked down at his cake, which seemed to be lemon drizzle. He wasn't feeling especially hungry but forced himself to shear off a corner mouthful with a small fork.

'Then you'll know all about getting through a bereavement and easing everyone through it too. Everyone deals with it in different ways. I suppose it helps that you'll be busy now, Thomas. With all… this.' The surgeon waved his hands around to signify their common connection. Thomas nodded in agreement.

'What do you think of the current case? He's one grizzly bugger, eh? Picking on hungry, desperate people and poisoning them. It takes a pretty diseased mind, don't you think?' Thomas noticed that Chris had almost finished his cake and wondered whether the good doctor had missed breakfast.

'It's all still a bit new to me, to be honest. I suppose I really just hope we can catch him before we have too many bodies piling up. Until there's some clue with regards to a pattern, though, I'm not sure how we're going to go about it. We're flying blind a bit at the moment. Although, I have to say I'm enjoying the surveillance so far.'

'That's because you're with the adorable Monica.' The surgeon smiled as he lifted the cup of Assam to his lips. Thomas felt mild unease at Chris's choice of adjective, but he pushed that to the back of his mind too, aware that it was getting increasingly crowded back there. 'She's a sweetheart. Very, very smart. Very, very funny. And a genuinely good person. What happened to her second husband obviously hit her desperately hard. You know about the husband, I assume?' Thomas nodded. 'But she's survived, damaged and battered for a while but eventually improved, like a Formula One car that's been in a scrape and had a superpower makeover. We're all broken in our own way, Thomas. I suppose that's why this works.' He placed the cup back in its saucer and waved his hands around theatrically once more for effect, drawing the attention of the teenager with the headphones, who looked up momentarily from her book.

Chris used his fork to squash and then scoop up the last remaining remnants of spongey cake, which he devoured ravenously like a tiger who has just lucked upon a bunch of deer trapped in a ravine. 'Look, Thomas, I'm sorry we haven't had the opportunity to talk before today. That's my fault for not being more welcoming on Friday and I apologise. I was going to call you yesterday but we've all got our own matters to deal with and sometimes you just get caught up in everything. So I suppose running into you in the cemetery was fortuitous. I also thought, foolishly, that you might be annoyed about the bins.'

Thomas stared at the doctor in confusion. 'Sorry, the bins?'

Chris licked his lips and searched vainly for any remaining sweet morsels on his plate. 'Lexington didn't tell you? Sorry. I was one of the people who has been checking on you over the last few months. One of the things I had to do was rummage around in your recycling on bin day, just to check you weren't drinking too much or only eating junk food. I thought you must have realised, but clearly I covered my tracks quite well.' Thomas suspected that this information should probably have shocked him but he'd experienced so much upheaval in the last few days that nothing was a surprise anymore. Least of all an eminent former surgeon rifling through his refuse.

'Anyway, forgive me if I'm telling you things that you already know from Lexington or Monica, but apart from Anna and Belinda, everyone in The Twelve has lost their partners in a more or less devastating way. And as for those two wonderful ladies, their loss is in some ways even more tragic because although their husbands are alive, dementia has robbed them of any recognition. Anna visits her husband Alan every week, but to him she is a complete stranger. It's utterly heartbreaking. More often than not he calls her "Mummy," which upsets her greatly as she could never have children. As for poor Belinda, she used to visit Malcolm and was completely devoted to him, but it just became too difficult for her so she stopped. He started to get aggressive towards her so it was the hardest thing she ever had to do. It completely tore her apart, but it made her who she is. Belinda is incredibly strong. We all are. But it's a gentle strength as opposed to anything macho.'

Thomas stared at his half-eaten cake. Monica hadn't really gone into detail about the other women in the group, apart from the revelation about Catherine and her sexual preferences. 'I had no idea,' he said.

'If you look at the history of The Twelve, though,' continued Chris, quietly, 'the type of person invited to join has been refined over the decades to the criteria we know today. Obviously you have to have certain talents and obviously you have to have a particular mindset, and naturally you'd have to be reasonably fit. It wouldn't work if we were just a bunch of thugs and hooligans. Yet the crucial thing, one of the very key things at any rate, is that we have loved.' Chris emphasised the final word with a gentle thump on the table that tinkled the crockery and made one of the two young mothers glance over. 'We have compassion for our fellow men and women. God knows I've saved enough of them over the years. I've watched them come round after the anaesthetic wears off and it's like they're back from the dead. Often, they are, pretty much. As for The Twelve, we have also experienced grief and we recognise, whether we realise it or not, that that grief is the necessary counterbalance to the great love we were so lucky to find in the first place. We want to somehow mitigate the grief of others, protect people from harm, and doing what we do is perhaps an extreme response in some people's eyes, but it's a perfectly rational one in others. Are you finishing that cake?'

'No. Um, sorry. I had a large breakfast. Do you want it?'

'Smashing.' The surgeon reached over and swapped plates. 'Put it this way: what do you think you'll feel when you finish a case? When someone gets bumped off? When someone disappears. Gets bunged in the acid bath, or however they go. Your immediate thought before anything else.'

Thomas thought for a moment, imagining capturing the poisoner and being involved in ending his life. 'It's really hard to say,' he whispered. 'Sadness, I'd imagine.'

'Precisely. That's exactly what I feel. None of us feels

delighted or triumphant. There's no strut or swagger. None of that fist-pumping nonsense or what have you. All of us feel sadness. Sadness at the loss of a life but then also relief at the saving of so many others. And, importantly… a sense of quiet achievement. Listen, I'm a surgeon. Sorry, I *was* a surgeon. I saved hundreds of people. Some I couldn't save, including my own wife.' Chris gave a deep sigh. 'But with those I couldn't save, more often than not they were carrying donor cards, so others could live. They could give the gift of life, Thomas. The greatest gift there is. Sadness. Grief. Relief. Joy. Love. All part of the same crazy human puzzle, you see? We are in The Twelve, because in our unique and different ways, and whether we're conscious of it or not, we accept our place in that puzzle. Our particular position in the delicate ecosystem, as it were. The death of a loved one shoves you through the mangle at breakneck speed, but we somehow come out of it.'

'Weathered but robust,' whispered Thomas.

'Exactly!' exclaimed Chris as he polished off the last mouthful of lemon drizzle cake and leaned back against the cafe wall. 'Delicious!' he announced victoriously.

8

With another evening accompanying Monica in prospect, Thomas was glad to get back to Colville Square at a decent hour so that he could lie down and rest. Initially it was difficult to sleep, but he closed his eyes and was soon dozing contently, drifting in and out of consciousness and semi-aware of the gradually fading light. His conversation with Chris was still resonating, along with some of Monica's revelations from the beginning of the weekend.

Thomas must have fallen into a deep sleep as he woke with a start, troubled by a series of scattered fragments of dreams rather than one coherent narrative. Catherine was in them as well as Chris. And Alice too. He was glad when five o'clock came and he could focus again on meeting up with Monica for their second surveillance journey. Thomas changed into a clean T-shirt over which he pulled a checked shirt and then a short-sleeved cashmere jumper for an extra layer of protection against the cold. He dabbed himself lightly with the Blenheim Bouquet which Monica seemed to like and ran a damp comb quickly through his hair as it had become slightly unruly during his doze, with tufts of grey sticking up around his ears.

Once more they met in the hotel bar as it seemed easiest, as well as giving them an opportunity for a proper chat before the noise of the Underground made conversation more difficult. The same waiter was on duty again and appeared delighted to welcome them back. 'Happy Diwali,' said Thomas as Monica arrived, proud and a little amazed that he had remembered from one of their Friday conversations that the Festival of Lights was imminent.

'Oh, thank you, you sweetest man,' said Monica, kissing him gently on the cheek. She had chosen a purple fitted jacket with a navy blue coat, a matching beret and a colourful scarf which, to Thomas's untrained eyes at least, looked expensive. 'It's not for a couple of weeks, but I appreciate the greeting. Do you ever see any of the fireworks from your house?' Thomas admitted that he had never seen any from Colville Square but he had distantly heard them, usually to the north of where he lived, beyond the tree-filled square and in the direction of the cemetery. 'That'll be the communities towards Wembley and Harrow. They always push the Diwali boat out. I don't get to see much from St John's Wood. Occasionally there are a few over towards Camden, but if I want to see them properly, I'll walk up Parliament Hill and look out over to the east of the city and you get a few over in the west too, Ealing Road way. If it's not raining, it's a wonderful thing to do. I did it a couple of times with Patrick before 2001 and then took a break from it but went back a few years ago. On my own.' Monica took a deep breath and composed herself. 'Anyway, drinks.' Their waiter had been patiently awaiting his moment and was overjoyed when it finally arrived. 'I'm buying this evening. Old Fashioned again?'

Once their drinks had arrived, Monica again raised a toast, this time to a successful evening. 'What have you been up to today, Thomas?' she asked. 'Anything jolly?'

Thomas thought back to his conversation with Chris and

began telling Monica about it, confirming her belief that the two of them would get along famously, but when he began to explain that they had met by the grave, he became suddenly aware of an intense feeling of nausea building up from a place deep inside him. Except that it wasn't nausea, it was something else; something he hadn't felt for many years. 'I'm so sorry, Monica,' he managed to mutter and just about moved his glass out of the way before bursting into floods of tears, his body crumpling forwards with his head in his hands, all of his muscles convulsing as waves of unendurable sorrow overcame him. The tide had been drawn out in the cemetery leaving barren, ash-like sand; now, the tsunami was rushing in.

He was fully expecting to look up to see Monica with a confused or even shocked expression on her face, but instead he felt her soft arms around him, her wonderful scent enveloping him in a delicate yet secure chrysalis.

Distantly, as if he were in a tunnel, Thomas heard a waiter's voice asking if everything was all right, followed by Monica's gentle confirmation that yes, her friend had simply had some bad news and would be fine momentarily. He could also feel Monica stroking his salt and pepper hair, kissing his cheek gently, kissing the tears, rescuing him from his sorrow. After what seemed like hours but was really only about a minute, Thomas looked up into Monica's huge, brown, glistening eyes. There was no confusion, no shock, only compassion. 'I'm sorry,' he repeated. 'I'm so embarrassed. I don't know what just happened. I really don't.'

'I do,' whispered Monica, holding his face, stroking his hair. 'I know exactly what happened. I recognise that feeling far too well. Sometimes it just builds up and all it needs is a tiny trigger and then, boom! You've lost your soulmate and it doesn't matter how long ago that might have been, even something as silly as forgetting to buy milk or accidentally putting a dishwasher tablet in the washing machine with the laundry can set off the grief –

I've done that, believe me, with the dishwater tablet.' Monica smiled at the memory. 'The pressures build up and then suddenly everything gushes out uncontrollably. There's not a bloody thing you can do about it.'

'Has it happened to you often?' Thomas was dabbing his eyes with a clean white handkerchief, Monica now holding and delicately caressing his left hand.

'Oh, heavens! Many times,' she replied. 'Many, many times. Far too many to remember. I've been alone for almost twenty years, don't forget, give or take the odd short-lived, often ill-advised dalliance. I was fifty when the planes hit the towers. I'm sixty-nine now. There are countless occasions where I've completely and utterly crumbled, particularly in the early days. We wouldn't be human without it.' She entwined her fingers in his and squeezed. 'When was the last time you cried, Thomas? I mean properly.' Thomas admitted that he couldn't remember. It was probably when Alice died although he couldn't in truth recall any tears falling at her funeral; he was too busy keeping a stiff upper lip for Emily and Simon. 'Well then,' continued Monica, smiling kindly, 'I think this welcome outpouring was extremely overdue. And don't worry, you're not the first man who has cried on my shoulder and I daresay you won't be the last. Now, do you think you can carry on with this evening's business or shall I let Lexington know that we have to bow out for tonight? I'll tell him I've got a migraine; he won't mind. He'll find someone else to cover.'

Thomas took a big swig of his drink followed by a deep breath. 'It's fine,' he said. 'I'm fine. Thank you, Monica.' He smiled weakly and thought back to his chat with Chris in the cafe earlier that day. 'Chris said you were adorable. Now I know why.' Immediately he felt embarrassed and wished he could swallow the words back, but Monica appeared completely unfazed.

'I *am* adorable!' she exclaimed, 'as far as I know.' She kissed his hand softly before picking up her negroni for another toast. 'To tears. Both happy and sad. May we always shed more of the former!'

9

Nabil Shahin was unusually anxious. According to his diary, which he'd kept since leaving home, it was only his sixth week in the great city of London, yet it felt much longer.

This was a place he had dreamed about for years and one that his parents had spoken of with hope and a sense of opportunity, yet already an unfamiliar chill was beginning to concern him. He wasn't merely troubled by the physical and bitter cold that reminded him of harsh winter nights at home in Masyaf, drinking with friends under heaters at the bustling cafes in the shadow of the castle, but also the unexpected frostiness of the welcome he had been afforded since his arrival.

Nabil's father had promised him that the people of London would take him to their hearts. *How could they not?* Nabil was young, educated, a hardworking Syrian IT specialist with both talent and ability; and yet the opposite had so far been true. Everywhere he went, Nabil's attempts to begin conversations in his limited English had been met with hurried looks of disdain, angry words, occasional threats of violence, sometimes spit. This was not what his father had led him to expect. It was far from the dream for which he had paid many thousands of dollars, saved

65

over countless months, to cross Europe on his epic and dangerous journey.

There was no way to turn back now. Nabil would simply have to make the best of a challenging situation, pray five times every day and every night, and work harder to fit in. He would surely find some kindness soon, if Allah was willing, and someone to take a chance on him and offer him work – not necessarily in IT, but anything to get him through the bleak winter ahead.

He could clean; Nabil's mother was always praising him for how tidy his room was when he was growing up. He could work as a delivery man so long as someone gave him a map; he was used to maps by now. *Maybe today would be the day. Yes, today there would be a change in fortune. God is great. His prayers would be answered.* Something important was about to happen. Nabil could sense it.

The complex and multicoloured diagram of the city's transport system had become familiar to him at least. In addition, one of the Iraqis he had met on his second day had explained how you could get into the Underground train network with relative ease, either by sliding under the automated barriers during quiet times or by quickly dashing through them behind a passenger during rush hour, before they closed. You'd have to pick your moment and not do anything foolish like trying such a move in front of the station staff or, worse, the police, but after studying a couple of the Iraqis demonstrating their technique, Nabil had taken the plunge. He'd even become quite good at choosing which commuters to scurry behind; the younger ones were best as they moved faster and didn't seem to care about who followed them.

He'd learned that the worst you might get for your trouble was a harsh look or a terse word, nothing more. Once you were inside, cocooned beyond the barriers, you could stay there as long as you wanted, within the transport sanctuary, provided you kept watch for ticket police. You could ask for money and sometimes food, and it would be given freely if you waited long enough and smiled a bit. London people often responded positively to a smile, he'd realised.

This current method of earning a living wasn't ideal, of course, but it could sustain a man until something more acceptable turned up, that yearned-for cleaning job perhaps. There were places you could go to get work, no questions asked and no documents needed. He'd heard this from the many voices with different accents along his journey. He just hadn't found those places yet, but when he did, Nabil knew that he could start to build a new life and finally make his father proud, maybe even begin to send money home in the new year.

He liked to choose a different line on the Underground each day, although he had been warned against the purple one as it was the domain of East Europeans who, he had been told many times, would do worse than spit at him if they felt he was infiltrating their lucrative business. Sunday, today, meant the light blue line, the one named after Queen Victoria. This had been a propitious option on two previous Sundays – less so while it was going through the centre of the city, where it was often too busy and frantic for him to be able to communicate properly with people amidst the jostle and din – but at either end, after the carriages had emptied out at the big termini at Victoria and King's Cross, luck would often change.

These more sparsely populated extremities of the network were where he had managed to eke out just enough pennies and some silver coins to get through each challenging and perilous day. On one Sunday, he had even managed to obtain a few of the gold coins, the valuable ones, plus some chocolate from a smartly-dressed young Black woman who had given his heart a temporary glow, especially when she smiled at him kindly as she got off the train at somewhere called Stockwell. Nabil liked the idea of Stockwell; the sound of the word itself seemed somehow magical. Stock-well. Maybe he would get off there himself one day to see the sights. Maybe he would live there, in a big house or a mansion, when his fortunes changed.

This particular day had not been quite as fertile as the chocolate gift day. There were no gold coins in his ragged pockets. A few silver ones but mostly the reddish brown ones, which weighed him down. He was grateful for them, of course, but nonetheless he couldn't help but feel the pang of embarrassment when paying for a bag of crisps or a cheese roll with around fifty of them, counting methodically while the softly-spoken old Asian shopkeeper in his favourite platform kiosk waited patiently. Nabil had quickly learned not to visit during rush hour as that risked fury and abuse from the busy commuters queuing behind him for coffee in paper cups and anaemic croissants sealed in flimsy plastic. *People were not amused on Queen Victoria's line,* he had chuckled to himself on many such occasions.

As it was getting late, Nabil decided that he would need to bed down for the night, but where? Perhaps tonight one of the quieter outlying stations would suit him best. He could hide in a toilet or, better still, a waiting room and hope that the night staff wouldn't bother him until morning. That strategy had worked before. Sleeping in a toilet wasn't ideal, of course. You had to hope there wasn't too much urine on the floors or, if there was, that there were enough paper towels left in the holders to build a serviceable barrier; but at least it was shelter and if you could wait for the last train to offload its cargo of drunks and druggies, you could get four, maybe five, hours of uninterrupted rest to gather strength for the following day and whatever opportunities it might bring. He stood and looked with puzzlement at the map, struggling to make sense of some of the words.

'Excuse me, please,' he mumbled to a young woman whose

skin colour matched his own. The woman was rising from her seat to leave the train, but smiled and stopped, seeing that Nabil needed help. He reached over the seats and pointed to a station near the end of the line.

'Blackhorse Road,' said the woman. 'Is that where you're going? Stay on this train.' She pointed at the floor to signify that Nabil should remain on board. 'Good luck,' she added cheerfully as the doors opened and she vanished into the night.

Black horse road, he mouthed to himself. *It sounded promising.* Originally, he supposed, long ago, in the time of Queen Victoria, there would have been black horses living there. Maybe. His uncle had kept black horses at home in Syria so Nabil took this to be an auspicious omen. He could pray quietly, completing his *isha* a little later than required, get some much-needed rest and be ready for his journeys along the red line on Monday, filled with early Christmas shoppers visiting the big stores in Shepherd's Bush and Stratford where he'd seen people laden with colourful bags.

As the train scuttled away from Tottenham Hale station on its northward journey, Nabil realised he was being watched. The carriage was now virtually empty apart from a couple of giggling young girls at one end, engrossed in their conversation about something he couldn't understand because they were talking too fast and in an accent he couldn't follow. There was also a youngish man at the other end, regarding him with lowered eyes, who suddenly stood up and came towards him. Nabil assumed the man was young, although it wasn't easy to tell as part of his face was covered with a scarf and he wore a baseball cap pulled down over his eyes.

'You look like a man who needs help.' *Was this an unlikely angel to answer his prayers?* He was oddly dressed but sometimes angels came in unlikely guises.

'Help. Yes, please.' Nabil had known around twenty words of

English when he left Syria, but this had expanded considerably since arriving in London. For now, though, only the fundamentals would be required. 'Thank you.'

'I have something for you, my friend. For later.' The stranger reached with a gloved hand into his brown leather bag and offered Nabil a package wrapped snugly in tin foil. 'For later. You understand? Not now. Later.'

Nabil nodded that he did, although he was more focused on the fact that he had been called "friend," which made him happy. He had learned "later" in one of the camps in northern France while awaiting the final, terrifying transport across the summer sea. He carefully placed the foil package in his pocket. *A wonderful gift to be treasured.* It felt like bread of some sort, squishy but with a crust. *For later.*

'Good man,' smiled the stranger. 'Be lucky.' He pulled a beanie hat out of the bag and pulled it down over his cap. This had the effect of pushing the peak of the cap even lower so that it covered his eyes as he waited in the doorway of the carriage for the next station, Blackhorse Road.

'My station too,' nodded Nabil as the train started to decelerate, but the man ignored him. That coldness again, descending like a low, evening cloud after a brief burst of autumn sunshine. The doors opened and the stranger, head down and stooping slightly, walked briskly towards the exit. 'Thank you!' shouted Nabil, who then searched frantically for what other words might be appropriate. 'Your father, um, is proud,' he blurted out, but there was no response.

The Syrian stepped out of the train and pondered what to do next. His choices, as he weighed them up, were either to find a covered place to sleep within the station – it didn't appear overwhelmed with opportunity; there weren't even any obvious toilets – or leave the station to explore this part of London and try to find shelter where the black horses used to run. The third option, often the safest if there was uncertainty, would be to travel back into the centre and try his luck in one of the usual places. That would make his *salah* even later, but Nabil felt sure that Allah would be understanding, bearing in mind the challenging situation.

He would do the latter. King's Cross would be best. He knew a place near the station where people like him gathered. It had a roof and it was warm. Despite the late hour, he would surely be welcomed there. He was bringing food after all. He could share.

———

Lexington and Belinda were, unusually, late for yoga the following Friday, their usual day shifted again to allow Thomas to spend his wife's birthday in quiet contemplation. The week's monitoring of Underground lines had continued fruitlessly and a couple of members of the group had even fallen asleep during the later stages of their surveillance journeys.

The yoga session began as normal, but when the missing two still hadn't appeared halfway through, mild concerns began to be voiced more loudly. *Perhaps Lexington had had a fall and called Belinda to assist as she lived closest to him, just across the river near Wandsworth Bridge. But then someone would surely have sent a text, and there hadn't been one, which made the whole situation something of a mystery.* Finally, during the understandably distracted wind-down at the end of the session, the door opened. Lexington and Belinda made their way quietly to the table at the back of the class, where they sat in silence for the last few minutes in order not to disturb the *savasana* for the others.

After *namaste,* everyone gathered around the table, relieved that Lexington appeared to be in good health despite the slight limp.

'I'm sorry we were unable to attend today – you all know how I enjoy a good cat stretch as much as the next man – but I'm afraid I have some rather sad news.' The older man cleared his throat. 'Belinda and I have just had to watch a brave, young man die a somewhat unpleasant death. Our poisoner has been at work once more.'

Owen let out a long sigh. Catherine slumped into a nearby chair. 'I'm guessing this wasn't on either of the Tube lines we've been monitoring?' she asked. Thomas felt a sense of unease that something hideous might have happened under their very noses, rather like the experience of being reprimanded by a schoolmaster for something he could be certain that he hadn't done, although the very fact of the admonishment brought even certainty into question.

'Correct, Catherine. This was on the Victoria Line last Sunday night. The young man in question was a Syrian national named Nabil and was a recent addition to our delightfully diverse London community, one of those many desperate souls who have ventured from a distant war zone to seek safety and the promise of something better in the United Kingdom. He doubtless has a devoted family somewhere waiting eagerly for news. Sadly that news, when it eventually reaches them, will be the worst possible.'

'So what happened?' enquired Monica. 'Clearly not potassium cyanide again. Something slower and more insidious?'

Lexington smiled at her subtle recall of knowledge. Rarely did a day go by when he wasn't proud that he'd fought to get Monica on board seven years earlier. He had been more certain than ever that she was exactly what The Twelve needed, but there had been a small yet noisy faction which had lobbied hard for another, male, chemistry expert. Lexington had stood his ground, argued persuasively and finally got his way, although the repercussions had rattled on for a good few months.

'The type of location has remained consistent. The method has altered. Slightly. Yes, there was some food wrapped in foil, but this time it contained mercuric chloride which those of you familiar with such matters will know,' he glanced at Monica again, 'can, in certain cases, be rather more ponderous and stealthy when it comes to its action and its direction of travel... although it generally achieves its aim in the end. The commissioner called me this morning when the evidence suggested that he might be another victim. He had been in University College Hospital since the beginning of the week, but only yesterday did someone realise he was homeless and put the pieces together. Nabil's English wasn't the strongest, so I took Belinda as she is reasonably fluent in Arabic. The poor fellow didn't have much strength left, but we did manage to glean that he had been given the foil-wrapped food at Blackhorse Road, at the northern end of the Victoria Line. From there he had taken it to King's Cross where he shared it with another homeless man named Gary Bishop. Gary, as you might imagine, is also dead, owing to the fact that he rather scoffed most of the poisoned sandwich himself.' Lexington raised his eyes to the ceiling in weary disappointment. 'Nabil, being younger and stronger, managed to survive somewhat longer, but early this morning his body finally gave up. Belinda and I felt it best if we stayed with him so that at least his family would know he wasn't alone in his last moments. Hopefully this will be some small comfort to them. The Foreign Office is attempting to trace them as I speak and, when they are found, The Twelve will naturally make a significant donation to ensure they can at least live in comfort through their years of sorrow.'

Graham shook his head both in sadness and in disbelief. 'Belinda, did he say anything else of interest? About the person who gave him the foil package.'

'My Arabic isn't entirely up to scratch,' the linguist admitted, 'not having had to use it for a good ten years or so, but he did say "tall man", "hat" and also "smiling". That hardly narrows it down, I appreciate, but it didn't seem the time to properly interrogate, as I'm sure you'll understand.'

'If this happened on Sunday night,' posed Thomas, 'then the murderer was in action on the Victoria Line at the same time as we were on the Piccadilly. And Owen and Catherine were on the Northern. Is there some sort of pattern emerging, do we think? Or simply that he's switching lines to avoid being caught?'

Terry, who had been engrossed in a copy of the London Underground map on his phone, looked up. 'I would tentatively suggest that he's travelling around the outskirts of the city methodically, in a clockwise direction,' the locksmith announced. 'The furthest ends of the lines each time, presumably so there are fewer witnesses and the surveillance is shakier. He started with the Northern – midnight if you think of the map as a clock face – then the Piccadilly and now the Victoria. If this is indeed a pattern, the next on his list should be the Central. We just don't know when. Assuming there's a pattern at all. Which there might not be. Sorry not to be more precise.'

Lexington's phone rang, a harsh, metallic version of Al Dubin and Harry Warren's 'Keep Young and Beautiful'. 'I'm so sorry,' he stuttered, somewhat embarrassed, rising from his chair slightly stiffly. 'One of my great nieces who visits me every few days has put this song on my phone and I can't stop the blessed thing! It's the commissioner. I'll take this next door. Good morning, commissioner…'

'I'm no chemist,' David broke the brief silence, 'as you know, but is it reasonable to suspect that the chloride family isn't made up of the kind of folk you'd ideally want to encounter down a dark alley? And I'm also guessing that this new poison may indicate something significant.'

Monica was thinking fast, weighing up what the change to

mercuric chloride might mean. 'It's a very nasty substance David, but it's slower to take effect. It means a few hours or days of intense pain before, usually, kidney failure. There'll be a bit of vomiting blood and a few other equally unpleasant symptoms. It's best avoided if you can. I suspect this Gary character consumed more of the poison and so died faster. Nabil may also have been fitter so his body would have fought it better but ultimately the result is the same. It will have tasted slightly metallic, but that would probably have been masked by something else in the sandwich. The potassium cyanide in the previous two murders is more or less instant. Grisly but swift. Anna, have you encountered anything like this?'

The ex-pathologist was also deep in thought. 'Never mercuric chloride, thankfully. Various other poisons, yes. The potassium cyanide wasn't new to me. I've had a couple of those over the years. They leave rather a mess of a person's upper digestive tract, as you can imagine; quite a lot of corroded oesophagus and the surrounding area. My main concern at this point is where our murderer is getting all this stuff. It can't be easy to find. Well, it shouldn't be, at any rate. If we can somehow find out where he's buying it, then maybe we can use that to trace back and find him.'

'You'd be surprised,' chimed Owen. 'You can get pretty much anything in the shadowy corners of the internet if you know where to look. In addition, there's always the possibility that someone else is buying the poison and passing it on. Wouldn't you agree, Chris? You've dug around in there a bit.'

The former surgeon raised a quizzical eyebrow. 'With the internet? Oh yes, absolutely. I could get you whatever you want, pretty much. What's *your* poison, Anna?' He winked at the pathologist, who went bright pink and tried to hide behind her yoga towel.

'At least we have an idea where he's likely to strike next,' said David, as the sound of footsteps heralded Lexington's return, a weary look on his aquiline face. 'Assuming there's this pattern. The Central Line. Somewhere towards the end of it, out Essex way. Debden or Epping, or somewhere leafy like that. My guess is that we'll all become fairly familiar with the picturesque stations of suburban Essex before the year is out.'

Lexington pulled up a chair and collapsed disconsolately onto it. 'You're right up to a point, David, but not quite where you might imagine. It'll probably be somewhere further south and east, I'm afraid, if indeed our suspicions of a pattern are correct. According to Suzanne, our friend has had something of a burst of late October energy with regards to his list and has, it seems, already chalked off the Central Line.'

10

'BASTARD! I can't believe he poisoned a dog! Who does that? Who poisons a beautiful fucking dog that never did anyone any harm?' Martin Francis was so incandescent with fury that tears started pouring down his cheeks. The commissioner's call concerned the fifth and sixth victims of the year, a fifty-seven-year old homeless ex-serviceman named Lenny Davies and his faithful Staffordshire bull terrier Pongo, both found dead at Theydon Bois station on the southbound platform as they apparently tried to make their way back into Central London. The murders had occurred the previous day. *Alice's birthday.*

The remains of a tinfoil wrapped meal were found next to them and it appeared as though Lenny had shared his unexpected late-night treat of a chicken sandwich with his faithful, long-time companion. Unfortunately for both of them, the sandwich was laced with an especially unwelcome substance called botulinum, causing rapid paralysis and death. Just as before, CCTV had turned up very little of use; a tall man, his face hidden under a cap pulled low over his brow, leaving the northbound train at the same time as Lenny and Pongo and disappearing outside the station using a cash-bought day travelcard. 'I fucking hate people who hurt animals,' Martin had calmed down slightly and was wiping his eyes with a corner of his yoga towel.

Thomas decided that it wasn't quite the time to remark that this latest poisoning had happened on his departed wife's birthday, but a sympathetic look from Chris told him that one other person in the room at least was thinking of more than the untimely demise of a terrier.

'Settle down please, Martin,' urged Lexington calmly. 'I know it's upsetting but we have work to do, particularly as the frequency of these killings has accelerated alarmingly.' Martin apologised and explained that he'd been listening to the Blood Brothers London Cast recording from 1995, which always made him emotional. 'Tell Me It's Not True' destroys me every time, he whimpered, dabbing his eyes with a handerchief.

'Suzanne would like to arrange another meeting,' continued Lexington, 'and this time include the Chief Constable of the British Transport Police. He's had to be brought up to speed with our activities rather quickly and has obviously signed all the necessary paperwork as he wasn't previously a party to our, um, existence and specialisation. Suzanne is confident that we can trust him although I suspect there may be certain occasions going forward when we need to keep matters to ourselves, if you catch my drift. Two poisonings in the space of a week could mean that there is now a far greater urgency in finding and dealing with our subject.

'However, I should remind you that we still haven't established a pattern for the dates of these attacks so we're very much dealing with an open book as far as that is concerned. There could be another one tomorrow or it could be next month or even next year. It may be that our suspect is only a sporadic visitor to our city and the attacks rely on some other undefined timetable. Either way, it seems likely that the District Line will be next to be targeted.' Lexington's tone was perceptibly more serious than many of the group had ever witnessed before. 'Until we have had this meeting, I suggest we take a break from surveillance to conserve energy, although I wonder whether I might ask Owen to please have a very subtle hunt around the dark web to see whether we can trace any transactions involving these poisons. I strongly suspect that whoever is responsible is covering their tracks with great care, but it is nonetheless worth investigation. If everyone is agreed then I wish you a good day and I will be in touch in the fullness of time. Oh,' he raised his hands to face level and bent his fingers to assume the appearance of claws, 'and Happy All Hallow's Eve for tomorrow!'

As everyone gathered their belongings to leave, Thomas felt an arm around his shoulder. It was Chris. 'Are you okay, Thomas? Shitty old day for another attack.'

'What's happening here?' asked Monica, joining them.

'It was Thomas's wife's birthday. Yesterday. When Lenny and the dog died.'

'Yes, I know. God, I'm sorry, Thomas.' Monica gave him a big hug and a kiss on the cheek and then embraced Chris by way of a thank you for his sensitivity. 'I think we could all do with a coffee if nobody has any other plans.'

'It's a personal opinion, I'll admit, but I do find that Danish pastries are by far the best post-yoga fuel.' Chris placed a tray of sticky sweet treats and coffees on the corner table and immediately tucked in, ignoring the supplied wooden fork and diving straight in with both hands.

'Just out of professional interest, why aren't you the size of a house?' quizzed Monica. She was wearing a post-yoga ensemble of tight jeans, a grey sweater and an orange beret this time and, in addition, had given herself a quick dab of her fragrance after class, which was somewhat distracting Thomas from the pastries and indeed everything else in the vicinity.

'Darling girl, when you're fortunate enough to have a metabolism like mine, you burn the calories almost before you've ingested them.' Chris wiped some sticky pastry crumbs from his mouth with his index finger. 'Imagine this, if you will. I've cut into so many flabby rolls of blubber in my time as a surgeon that I know how not to get into that dreadful state. So when I'm not doing yoga or in meetings, I'm either running or playing squash or lifting weights or I'm on the exercise bike. I'm rarely just vegetating on a sofa, you know. Even when I'm reading, I'm usually walking around every twenty minutes or so. There was this one chap, I remember,' Chris's face creased wickedly at the thought, 'where we had to perform a colectomy, which is to say, remove a chunk of his large intestine, but the poor fellow was so obese that I simply didn't know where to start. Luckily, I had an intern working in theatre on that day, so I asked him to make the first incision. Honestly, the poor chap was chopping and carving away like a lumberjack with a fish knife for about ten minutes before we found anything resembling a diseased organ. It was like trying to find a small apple in a barrel full of brie, if you'll excuse the image.'

'What happened to him? The patient, that is,' asked Thomas, mildly horrified and also fairly certain that his own cake would end up inside Chris for the second time in a week.

'Oh, he died,' replied Chris matter of factly, between mouthfuls. 'Not on the operating table, I should add, because the team that day did an amazing job, but a few weeks afterwards. We managed to remove the offending piece of bowel eventually and sew everything back together but his heart wasn't in the finest fettle and it basically ended up drowning in fat during his recovery at home. I mean, that's not the technical, medical term but to all intents and purposes, that's what happened. Keep doing the yoga and fitness, my friends. The alternative doesn't bear thinking about. Particularly in our line of business.'

Undaunted by the conversation, Monica daintily forked a small piece of pastry into her freshly lipsticked mouth. 'Talking of fitness, it's my medical next week. Are you doing it or is Anna?'

Thomas shot her a surprised look. He was aware that their annual medicals were conducted by either Anna Hopley or the former medical practitioner in front of them, but he had always assumed that the women were examined by the ex-pathologist. 'I don't mind, Monica; whichever option everyone is comfortable with. See what Anna wants to do. We're both doctors so we're used to bodies, albeit cold and stiff ones in her case. Ha!'

Thomas was conscious that his pastry was in danger of being annexed if he didn't begin to focus on it soon, so decided to attempt to change the subject, asking whether either of them had any ideas regarding the increased regularity of the poisonings. Monica took a sip of her latte, leaving pink lipstick stains on the rim of her mug. She turned towards the window and focused on the shops opposite, suitably decorated for Halloween. 'I've been looking at the dates for the last couple of weeks and I haven't noticed anything obvious. One in June on a Saturday. Maybe that was a one-off or possibly a practice, or it was intended to be, but he got a taste for it and by October the urge to do it again was too powerful. So, we have the June one and then a Wednesday in early October, last Sunday and then yesterday.'

'There's the possibility that he's a visitor to London, but infrequently.' Chris was finishing his pastry and eyeing Thomas's with ravenous interest. 'Maybe a business traveller coming over every few months, taking his chances when he can and then flying out again. What do we think of that? Should we be looking at flight passenger lists?'

'I would suggest that these are far more planned than that,' countered Monica, who had clearly been thinking about the case far more than it appeared. 'I don't think it would be hugely easy to arrive in the city with poison, randomly make a sandwich, fill it with said poison and then wander out into the transportation system in the vague hope of meeting someone homeless and hungry. Personally, I think these murders are meticulously worked out. I think he lives here and he travels the lines for days or weeks, possibly in disguise, researching and observing everything and establishing the best time and place to strike, figuring out which are the best stations to escape from and how to disappear from there quickly. My priority questions would be these: What's he doing after he leaves the stations? Is he staying somewhere local each time? If so, we should be checking out hotels in the vicinity of the murders to see if anything correlates. Has he driven and parked nearby, knowing where he'll be getting off each time? Maybe there's some CCTV of that. A matching car registration number in each of the locations. Owen could explore that avenue easily. Right now, we don't know any of these things. Maybe he's just very fit and walks for miles using side streets to avoid cameras until he can get a night bus. Maybe there's a network of associates with whom he can stay, or who can collect him from a pre-planned location. There are a variety of possibilities at this stage.'

Thomas had listened with great interest. One aspect of the case had troubled him from the beginning and he decided that now would be the time to mention it. 'Personally,' he began, 'I'm a bit surprised that the Met Police haven't put more energy into this themselves. We are dealing with a dangerous serial killer after all.'

Monica drained her latte and lowered her voice to avoid being overheard. 'I talk to Lexington a lot, as you both know. The fact is – and this must go no further – Suzanne would love to put more of her people onto it, but the Home Office won't sign that off. Apparently they don't want to divert resources away from what they see as more important areas of policing.' An ambulance siren could be heard in the distance and Thomas immediately wondered whether another victim had been found, statistically unlikely though he knew that was.

'Essentially, homeless people don't matter because they don't vote,' surmised Chris. 'Deeply wrong and morally indefensible though that pronouncement may be.'

'That's pretty much it, I'm afraid. And I think the poisoner probably knows that too. If he were to suddenly attack a banker or a doctor or something, it would be all over the news in no time and the clamour for an arrest would be deafening. But homeless people don't pay taxes and that, with the current administration, is what it boils down to. As it stands, currently their best hope of putting a stop to the carnage,' Monica looked first to Chris and then to Thomas, 'is us.'

'Maybe this Chief Constable of the Transport Police fellow has some answers,' posed Thomas.

'I've met him so I doubt very much that he has. Regrettably,' frowned Chris. 'His name is Dennis Burrows and he's an odd sort of man. I won't say any more, because you should come to your own conclusion when you meet him, but I'd be interested to hear both of your impressions of him after you've had the pleasure. Meanwhile, Thomas,' the doctor licked his lips and raised an inquisitive eyebrow, 'I'm just casually wondering, do you intend to finish that pastry?'

11

The anticipated text arrived on Sunday evening, darker than usual with the clocks having gone back, requesting everyone to meet at 10am the following morning at the Hogarth Court location off Fenchurch Street in the City, an unassuming door in an even less assuming alley which could be accessed only by a keypad using the code: star one two star. Once inside, visitors would find themselves immediately confronted by a somewhat forbidding corridor with what resembled black leather walls and rather austere low-level lighting more commonly used in certain specialist nightclubs. This was ostensibly to deter anyone who happened across the unassuming door by accident and somehow guessed the passcode. At the far end of this corridor was a rather ominous, heavy black door behind which was an extremely welcoming library with books dating back to the nineteenth century – 'some first editions of classic novels which are quite valuable' according to Lexington, 'bought and stored by some of the early members of The Twelve. There are a couple of Dickens, some Wilkie Collins, even an Anne Brontë' – as well as a selection of large, comfortable vintage leather sofas and a well-stocked drinks cabinet.' From the outside, with its facade of grey office block mundanity, nobody but those with the most vivid imagination could ever conceive what lay within.

Lexington's Sunday text had been received by Thomas as he was sitting in his armchair in Colville Square watching *Countryfile* with a cold beer. It was followed a few moments later by another from Monica, separate from the group chat, asking whether he wanted to meet at Liverpool Street station and walk down together. The text ended with two kisses, which naturally threw Thomas into a state of emotional confusion and uncertainty as he wasn't sure whether he should also respond with two kisses. *What if he responded with one or none at all? Would that send some sort of wrong message? What if he responded with three? Would that somehow be even worse?* Text etiquette was so awkward to navigate in one's sixties. Emily would know what to do, but of course he couldn't ask her without a barrage of difficult questions and so Thomas decided he was on his own and would have to figure out the solution himself, and quickly. In the end, after several minutes, he decided to echo Monica's two and hoped that was the correct form with which to negotiate this particular social minefield. Monica's simple two kisses back implied, to his relief, that it was.

The arrival of November had coincided with windier days, which meant that Thomas had dug out a favourite black and white patterned scarf for the first time since March and it was this which Monica playfully stroked as the two of them met outside a leather stationery shop on the station concourse just after 9.30 on Monday morning, the area still thronging with commuters on their way from the home counties and day-trippers on their way to the coast or airport. 'That's good quality cashmere,' she stated, kissing him on the cheek. 'I'd love to borrow it, and perhaps you'd let me if I ask nicely!'

They walked in the direction of the river and detoured through the cover of Leadenhall Market to shelter from the wind. 'Are you feeling all right today, Thomas?' asked Monica as they passed a strange and incongruous sculpture on a corner.

'I'm feeling good,' he smiled, blushing slightly at the memory of his tears the previous week. 'Better than last Sunday evening. Thank you again for looking after me.' Monica squeezed his arm gently and Thomas felt a perceptible increase in his own heartbeat so decided to change the subject. 'Obviously I'm keen to delve more into this new investigation, but we'll have to see what the commissioner and this other chap have to say. Have you ever met him? The Transport Police fellow, Burrows? I've done a bit of background research and he doesn't seem the most inspiring type, I must admit.'

They were zigzagging their way through a flock of Spanish tourists who were taking photographs of themselves by another piece of modern art, Monica in a lime green beret and black puffer coat. 'Dennis Burrows? I've not met him, no. A few of the others have. Catherine for example through her work, and Martin, somewhat bizarrely. Nobody has a particularly good word to say about him. He's not a team player, apparently, which partly explains why crime rates on the Underground have gone up over the last couple of years. Catherine also knows someone who has interviewed him, and she says he's one of those people who loves to see himself in the papers and on TV, and likes the sound of his own voice. A limelight hog. I can't think of anything worse, personally. As far as I'm concerned, that's another advantage of our little group being below the radar. Can you imagine if I ever had to do an interview with anyone? I think I'd rather die.'

They weaved between office blocks under the shadow of the building known affectionately as The Gherkin after its curious pod shape, and arrived at Hogarth Court where they scanned around for anyone suspicious before entering the code. There was an almost inaudible click, which allowed Thomas to pull open the heavy door for Monica. He followed her into almost pitch darkness, pulling the door securely closed behind them, at which point the corridor lighting automatically increased so they could easily see their way to the library.

Lexington greeted them both with friendly handshakes and ushered them towards a figure they both recognised from their research. 'Dennis, may I introduce you to Monica Lodhia and Thomas Quinn. Monica is our resident chemistry genius and Thomas is our most recent acquisition from the world of sports and education. It's his first case so we're trying to be gentle.'

Dennis Burrows held out a pudgy, slightly sweaty hand, first to Monica and then to Thomas. He was average height, in his late forties, with receding brown hair that was slicked back with some sort of wax or gel. He was also carrying rather more weight than you'd expect for a senior police officer, and dressed in uniform, which struck Thomas as unusual as the commissioner almost always attended Twelve meetings in civilian clothes in order not to draw attention to either herself or to them. The uniform was also rather tight-fitting, which suggested that either Dennis had outgrown it, or that vanity had meant he had deliberately chosen a smaller size than the one most suitable.

'Very pleased to meet you both,' he said, his voice friendly but with an undertone which hinted that he felt the meeting was a waste of his time. 'Suzanne has brought me up to speed with your area of expertise, if that's the best way to describe it. I must say it's hugely impressive what you do, although I'm personally not sure how you can help in this particular case.'

'And what gives you that impression, Mr Burrows?' bristled Monica. There was a subtle yet detectable note of displeasure in her voice that Thomas hadn't heard before. He also noted that Burrows didn't suggest that he should be referred to as "Dennis".

'Well, for one thing, you don't know the identity of the person doing these poisonings and as a result you can't know how easy it will be to make him disappear. That's what you do, isn't it? You lot. Make people disappear?'

'This is partially true,' agreed Monica, calmly, 'but it's not all about disappearances you know, Chief Constable. You'll remember that corrupt oil tycoon a few years back who killed himself by jumping off the twentieth-floor sky garden round the corner from here?' Burrows nodded. 'That was us lot, as you so delicately describe us. And the former government minister Griffiths who was accused of sex with underage girls and found dead in a hotel room from a suspected heart attack? Us lot again. In fact, I could give you around forty notable examples of suicides, accidental deaths and untimely fatal aneurysms and they will all be related to the people you see around you in this room and those who came before them. If someone is designated for elimination, then that, Mr Burrows, is what will happen.' Thomas could see a fiery defiance in Monica's eyes as she stared directly at Burrows, particularly when she said the word "elimination". 'It would certainly be a mistake to get on the wrong side of *us lot*, Chief Constable. A smart man like yourself would never find himself in such a position, I'm sure.' She smiled demurely and arched an eyebrow, awaiting Burrows' response. Thomas moved next to Monica so that the two of them were confronting the policeman, now visibly shrinking, the various memories of those cases forming gruesome mental pictures in his mind.

'I see,' he spluttered sheepishly. 'Well then, let's hope we can all work harmoniously together to find a speedy solution. The homeless are a persistent plague within the transport system as I'm sure you can imagine, but nobody wants to see this… unpleasantness continue. Now, if you'll excuse me.' Burrows nodded and slunk off in the direction of the commissioner, who was sitting on a two-person sofa, deep in conversation with Anna.

'You're terrifying,' said Thomas in quiet admiration as they watched Burrows waddle away.

Monica straightened. 'I'm a pussycat with claws,' she whispered. 'I'm not prone to bad moods, but that man has managed, with remarkable efficiency, to rub me up the wrong way.'

'May I bring this meeting to order?' said Lexington. Those who weren't already seated shuffled purposefully around the room locating spare chairs or sofas. 'Once again thank you all for making the time at short notice. I believe you've now all met Dennis and he is, needless to say, most welcome here amongst friends.' Monica frowned dismissively, an expression which went unnoticed by all except Thomas. She had simultaneously squeezed his arm, causing him to look in her direction as well as tickling his heartbeat once more. 'If I may, I'm going to start by handing over to Suzanne for an update of where we are with these poisonings.' He settled into one of the dark brown leather armchairs nearest to a plate of sticky pastries and gazed longingly at the drinks cabinet before deciding that ten in the morning was perhaps too early for such indulgences, if only by an hour or so.

The commissioner stood up. 'Thank you. As you all know, we currently have five dead bodies…'

'Six!' shouted Martin gloomily. 'Don't forget Pongo.'

The commissioner looked towards Lexington, who shrugged his shoulders and closed his eyes in mild despair. 'We have *six* dead bodies and not much in the way of clues. Our attacker uses some rather exotic but effective poisons, which he procures almost certainly from the dark web using either crypto currency to avoid detection or, more probably, through a third party. He travels using cash-bought tickets to prevent tracking via the Oyster or credit card system; the tickets are purchased daily or weekly, again to make the trail difficult to follow. We have a very basic description thanks to Nabil before he died. We have snippets of CCTV footage too, which give us little more than Nabil's description. One thing we do know is that he changes location after each poisoning, travelling to the outer reaches of various tube lines starting north and so far slowly moving east in a clockwise direction–'

'The next one will be the District Line. Somewhere like Upminster or Hornchurch.' David Latham cracked his knuckles in a statement of pride.

'Yes, David, we believe so too,' the commissioner continued. 'The challenge we have, or one of the challenges at any rate, is that we have no idea when. There isn't any obvious pattern to the dates. There was one incident in June and now three in October. This could mean the poisoner is accelerating his attacks because he wants more people to die before he gets caught, which is very concerning. Or, he only visits London occasionally, or he only has access to the poisons at certain times, or none of the above. There could be another entirely different reason for the randomness of the dates of which we're currently unaware.'

'What's your view on the nature of the victims commissioner, and is it relevant?' Catherine's journalistic background gave the question an air of gentle interrogation but the police chief was unfazed. She had been interviewed by the media frequently and weathered so many storms that such matters held no fear for her. Besides, Catherine had become a good and trusted friend over the previous couple of years.

'Well, they're all men so far,' she stole a quick glance at Martin whose arms were folded in stern defiance, 'apart from Pongo who was of course a male dog, but that's probably because more men are homeless and they're also more likely to be begging on the transport system late at night. Homeless women will generally try to get themselves into hostels or amongst friends on the street before nightfall. That's just second nature for women, as we know.' She glanced at Belinda who returned a knowing look. 'Four are white British and one is Middle Eastern so there isn't really any likelihood that these are race crimes. The vehicle for the poison is something that only a homeless person would readily accept from a stranger, so the evidence suggests that these are indeed random attacks on some of society's most vulnerable people. The other key thing worth noting is that the suspect doesn't stick around to witness the poisoning taking place, which is in itself quite odd. Generally with serial killers, which is what this is now, they take pleasure from watching their victims suffer and die. This one simply doesn't care. It's almost like he's the ultimate psychopath, killing for no other reason than that he can.'

The commissioner was looking increasingly concerned. 'We've spoken to a number of criminologists and psychologists and most of them agree that this is perhaps the most worrying aspect. We have someone who has an obsessive mind and clearly plans these crimes with forensic care so that there is little or no evidence to give him away. There's a pattern to the locations, yes, but no discernible pattern to the timings and he knows that myself and Dennis can't spare the resources to patrol certain parts of the transport system indefinitely, particularly with the lack of evidence available at the present time.' Burrows nodded in agreement, his jowls shaking noticeably. 'Plus, even if we could spare the manpower, we can't exactly wander through the network asking to search people's lunch boxes. There would be panic within days. Furthermore, it's possible, even likely, that he would be watching us from a distance and waiting until we back off before striking again. It's not like we can simply arrest everyone wearing baseball caps, and he may not wear one when he's doing the background reconnaissance.'

'You say he knows you don't have the resources,' said David. 'Is there a possibility that the killer has some connection with the police force? A former detective or someone who holds a grudge against homeless people from having to deal with them on the beat?'

The commissioner looked at Burrows, who appeared deep in thought. 'It crossed my mind,' she had lowered her voice even though there was no one outside the room to hear them, 'but this is a young man, by all accounts, and I would like to think that none of my younger officers or even ex-officers would be capable of such a thing. It's a line of enquiry which we're exploring, of course, but nothing has come up yet. We're checking lists of former officers just in case.'

There was a brief silence while everyone in the room considered this possibility. It was finally broken by the soft, considered voice of Graham Best. 'How are you keeping this out of the media, Suzanne?'

'It's a good question with a rather depressing answer, I'm afraid, Graham. In each case, the victim hasn't really had close family or friends, not in the UK at any rate, and so there's been nobody to seriously question the cause of death or ask for a post-mortem report or to connect the killings. Even with Sean Bay, the two women in his life simply accepted his death without question, almost as if they'd been anticipating it or were certainly unsurprised by it. The teams working on the case both at my office and at Dennis's are all aware that a media blackout is best. Plus,' she took a side glance at Catherine Daniels, 'I guess we've been lucky. There aren't any journalists sniffing around the homeless network to put two and two together, and I don't think that community has strong enough internal communication to connect the dots either, at this point. Even the usual charities or the *Big Issue* team don't seem to be aware. Obviously the more deaths we have, the greater the likelihood of someone making a connection, which makes reaching a satisfactory conclusion even more imperative.'

Catherine smiled. 'Suzanne, you do know that if any journalist does come to you with a story, I can have it dealt with? You just have to ask.'

The commissioner knew that Catherine's connections with all the newspaper editors and owners of the more popular internet news feeds were second to none. Some of them knew a little of the existence of The Twelve, but chose to add its clandestine existence to their own personal treasure troves of secrets, along with all the celebrity indiscretions and political indignities which were destined never to come to wider public attention. 'I'm grateful to you, as ever, Catherine. Let's hope we don't need input of that kind, but you know I have your number on speed dial just in case.'

'Commissioner,' Thomas was sifting the information and calculating the possibilities, 'you said that the murderer could be watching the police and waiting until they get deployed elsewhere before acting again. He won't be watching us, though. A bunch of random old folk on the tube system. We're pretty invisible at the best of times and he won't know we exist.'

'Yes, you're quite right, Thomas. And this is one of the many occasions where the very nature of The Twelve positions you perfectly to make a significant impact. He won't be expecting that ladies and gentlemen…' the commissioner's mind struggled temporarily with the polite terminology, '…ladies and gentlemen of advanced years would have any role in his capture. And certainly not with a view to making the problem go away entirely.'

'To be clear,' added Thomas, aware that all eyes were on him, and quite enjoying the momentary spotlight, 'you don't really want the target apprehended. You'd rather the whole thing was just dealt with quietly and cleanly.'

The commissioner bowed her head in thought for a second or two before replying. 'If possible, yes please. Although that may change as we learn more so we need to keep open minds. Now, obviously this is an unusual case for you, and I understand that. We haven't got an identity yet for one thing. I suppose that as soon as we do, there will need to be another discussion and the plan may need to adapt and evolve, but the criminologists generally agree that we're almost certainly looking at a loner, someone with no obvious connections to any known group, otherwise we would have found something on social media, although he may be supported from a distance. This is someone who simply goes about his business and then just disappears into the suburbs, maybe staying in local B&Bs or walking for miles before taking night buses. We simply don't know.'

'Is it possible that he could be driving to each location and parking somewhere so he can drive home?' asked Monica, remembering the conversation in the coffee bar. The commissioner agreed that it was a good theory, but that Scotland Yard had done thorough checks on the registration numbers of all cars in the vicinity of each incident on the relevant dates and nothing had matched. They had also traced all hire cars acquired using cash; none of those were suspicious either. The only advantage to this particular line of enquiry was that Scotland Yard had managed to tip off the local traffic wardens with regard to some atrocious parking in the Cockfosters area.

Suddenly Burrows spoke up, mildly annoyed at being left out of the conversation up to this point. 'I'll be asking my officers to patrol the District Line for the whole of the rest of November,' he said proudly. 'If they see anything suspicious, they'll act.'

Lexington looked horrified but quickly managed to disguise it with a note of calm deliberation. 'Is that the right approach, do you think, Chief Constable? I don't wish to question your rationale or indeed poop on your party, but surely as soon as the suspect sees any police, he'll simply vanish. And you can't exactly arrest everyone tall carrying a tinfoil-wrapped sandwich. You'd have thousands in the cells within days. In addition to which, increased police activity on that line may well alert the media that something is going on. I imagine there are plenty of journalists using that line to get into work from Essex and it wouldn't take a mastermind to start asking some challenging questions.'

'Plus,' added Monica, bemused that Burrows appeared not to have listened to much of the morning's analysis, 'it's most likely he won't be travelling with a sandwich until the day of any murder. He'll be researching methodically, but without anything on him to arouse suspicion. If he sees increased police activity, he may just lay low for a while. Or try a different location.'

Burrows resembled a balloon whose air had been slowly and noisily let out. He glared at Monica, tightening his eyes into a porcine squint. 'Do you have any better suggestions, Miss Lodhia?' he spat.

'With respect both to you and your excellent officers,' Monica glanced at Thomas who was smiling admiringly, 'I think *we* are probably best placed to marshal the District Line, at least for the next few weeks. As Christmas approaches and there are more drunk people on the system, your officers will have their hands impossibly full anyway, particularly on that line. We can also work on the problem of the timings to see if we can save everyone's resources. If the psychologists say that our man is obsessive, then there will certainly be a pattern to the dates. We just haven't uncovered it yet, but we will. We have the time to spare. You don't.'

Burrows' crestfallen face resembled a cheap tin can crumpled under a heel. He looked plaintively towards the commissioner for some guidance, or even a morsel of support, but none was forthcoming. 'All right then,' he huffed, dolefully. 'But I want to know as soon as you've got anything useful!'

'Of course, Dennis,' agreed the commissioner. 'It's agreed. Now, if you'll be kind enough, I have some additional business with The Twelve which is unrelated to this case. Your car will be waiting where it dropped you. So…' She made a polite but dismissive hand gesture to Burrows to signal that he should leave.

'Well, um, yes of course,' Burrows blustered uncomfortably as he struggled to his feet. 'Thank you all for your time and your valuable input. And don't forget to let me know as soon as you have anything. Anything at all. That's most important.' He glowered at Thomas, then turned and headed for the door, making sure to pick up a couple of mini pastries on the way, one of which he wrapped in a serviette and placed in his pocket before opening the door and disappearing down the darkened corridor. Within seconds he returned. 'Can someone please help me to escape this sodding weird dungeon of yours,' he pleaded angrily through a mouthful of sticky sweet treat.

'I'm so sorry, chief constable,' said Terry, rising from his seat and moving towards the trapped police officer. 'Triple exit locks with fingerprint identification. My own new speciality. I'll help you out.' Burrows glared at him as the two of them paced back down the leather corridor towards the mid-morning bustle of the city.

'Additional business, Suzanne?' mused Lexington with a raised eyebrow after Terry had returned alone.

'A simple ruse to get him out of the bloody way.' The commissioner sighed, her eyes gesturing toward the exit. 'I honestly cannot bear that man. How he ever got the job, I will never know. There was an excellent alternative candidate. I suspect she didn't perform as well at the interview, or maybe it's something to do with the old boys' network. I've no idea.'

'I find that in any organisation of significant size,' suggested Lexington, 'there are usually one or two turds which stubbornly refuse to be flushed.' David pointed out that maybe the Met required a stronger cistern. Martin expressed his admiration for the use of a gerundive.

'Nonetheless,' the commissioner continued, 'as these murders are happening on what is essentially his "patch", regrettably he needs to be part of these complex discussions. That said, I probably don't need to point out that if you *do* happen to make any progress over the next few weeks, you really don't need to make Dennis your first call, if you get my meaning. Not yet at any rate. I can pass on anything relevant.'

Lexington nodded sagely. 'I think that's a given. As for a plan going forward, we shall monitor the outer reaches of the District Line daily until we have something new. If you acquire any useful intelligence in the meantime, do please scream. We will also try to figure out the pattern, if there is one, with regards to the dates. We shall travel in pairs, as we have been doing, until we have some results or hear otherwise.' He turned to the assembled group. 'Any questions from anyone? Are you happy to stay in your pairs or are you so dreadfully bored of each other by now that you wish to swap for fear of initiating your own crime spree on the Underground?'

Thomas looked at Monica and noticed with relief that she was grinning back. 'We certainly are,' she agreed, before adding, 'Happy, Lexington. Not bored in the slightest.'

'As it may be a long job,' Belinda Olorenshaw interjected, 'I'm happy to be paired up so that there are five groups rather than four. David, do you fancy joining me?' She looked over at the plumber who bowed approvingly.

'Thank you, all,' concluded Lexington. 'We'll resume tonight and report anything relevant via the usual channels. Suzanne, I shall be in touch as soon as we have news. Do please thank Dennis for his attendance today and,' he smiled cheekily, 'apologise from us for his difficulty exiting. Now, Thomas, I wonder whether I might have the tiniest of words with you alone.'

The two men settled in a quiet corner while the remaining members of The Twelve – along with the commissioner – made their way quietly out into the city morning. 'I'm conscious,' began Lexington, tenderly, 'that I haven't yet organised your initial psychologist meeting, Thomas. That is both a reflection of my own senile inadequacies and also because Mrs Mendoza herself has had a brief period of ill-health, physical not mental, I should clarify. Nonetheless, she is back to full fighting fitness now, so I wonder whether you might be available to meet with her sometime next week. I shall forward her number and address for you to arrange a time acceptable to both of you. She will be waiting for your call and your visit with great excitement, I'm sure.'

Thomas thanked Lexington and offered to help tidy up, an offer which was politely declined. 'It won't take long,' Lexington had said. 'And I have no other pressing engagements today. Plus, I may treat myself to a morning brandy and a moment of quiet contemplation before I leave here. As a reward for surviving the bleak company of Dennis Burrows.'

Monica was waiting outside in Hogarth Court as Thomas emerged into the breeze; a few dry leaves were skittering playfully across the pavement near her feet. 'Everything all right?' she asked. 'I hope you don't mind me waiting but I selfishly presumed that you might like company on the walk back to Liverpool Street.'

Thomas was touched and not a little overjoyed at Monica's thoughtfulness. 'Everything is just splendid,' he gushed, as his phone pinged with Lexington's text. 'I'm overdue my first visit to Mrs Mendoza. That's all. I'll call her when I get home. It's probably good timing actually, after last week's events.'

'You'll have much to discuss with her, I'm sure.' Monica smiled as she linked her arm with Thomas's, an intimate gesture which initially alarmed him but quickly felt somehow appropriate. 'We'll amble back to the station together and chat along the way.'

12

The psychologist Mrs Mendoza was the only person outside of The Twelve who knew broadly everything interesting that there was to know about its members, both present and future, although naturally her professionalism prevented revelation of all but the most rudimentary details unless she felt it was absolutely necessary. She had been instrumental in helping to choose new members for over ten years and was, the group collectively knew, one of the most important cogs in their particular mechanism, keeping everyone's mental health in good order and always available for advice or simply a friendly ear. Although meetings with members were, in theory, strictly confidential, Monica had already admitted that she found her own appointments so profoundly useful and invigorating that she'd often booked in an extra session, usually after the completion of a case, simply to rebalance her post-assassination mind. During their arm-in-arm conversation on the way back to Liverpool Street, Monica had been both envious and excited to the point of exploding when Thomas told her that he was due a first Mendoza visit. 'That woman is a saint and a magician and a superhero all rolled into one. What we'll do when she finally stops, I honestly have no idea, and she will stop one day. She's older than Lexington, for heaven's sake! They broke the mould with Mrs Mendoza.'

The Mendoza consultation room was on the second floor of a ramshackle old terraced house just off Brick Lane in one of the trendier, scruffier parts of the city, and next door to a Bengali restaurant from which the most delicious smells emanated from lunchtime to midnight. It was clear that Mrs Mendoza owned the entire building and lived on the other floors although whenever visitors ventured up the two flights of stairs, they would find every door closed and locked apart from two: the spacious toilet on the second level with its marble floor, blue and white tiled walls and neat stacks of tissues for every eventuality, and the consultation room itself, which was opposite. There was something reassuringly Dickensian about both the building and the street, as well as about Mrs Mendoza herself. The walls of her room were almost completely taken up with overflowing shelves of books and pamphlets, although even this maximum storage couldn't contain the sheer number of titles in her possession. As a result, a sizeable quantity had found either temporary or permanent homes on Mrs Mendoza's varnished wooden floor. In the small spaces between bookshelves were squeezed various drawings and paintings of squirrels, a creature for which Mrs Mendoza clearly had a healthy respect and admiration.

Mrs Mendoza was a slight-framed olive-skinned woman in her mid-eighties, with curly, white, cumulus hair tied back away from her face and a fondness for flowing tie-dye outfits in bright colours, which seemed hell-bent on engulfing her at any given moment. Nobody in The Twelve seemed to know her Christian name and, despite being the most welcoming and jovial of people, she never volunteered it, preferring "Mrs Mendoza" at all times. Even the solitary entry buzzer to her building read simply *'Mendoza'* in faded red biro.

'I understand you've been unwell, Mrs Mendoza?' enquired Thomas as he eased himself into a battered green leather chair, managing to avoid kicking over a pile of books precariously poised within leg's reach. 'I do hope it was nothing serious.' He had arranged the meeting for mid-afternoon on a mild, wet Wednesday when he had no other appointments and no evening travel with Monica to look forward to.

'My dear Thomas,' Mrs Mendoza grinned, pouring them both a cup of Earl Grey, 'it was an old war wound playing up and nothing more. And when I say "war", I don't actually mean "the war", you understand, merely,' she hesitated momentarily as if balancing her options, 'the bumps and scrapes of previous activities. A figure of speech. I am still here and that is the main thing. I should be here for a few more years yet, so long as an errant bus doesn't get me. One can never tell quite what is around the corner, but one can always take precautions. Now, as this is our first meeting, perhaps you could start by giving me an overview of how you're feeling about the events of the last few days. Take as much time as you require. We're not on the clock, as you know.'

Thomas had spent the previous evening making a mental list of the things he wanted to discuss, and began by explaining how he had, in general, been enjoying his time in The Twelve and been made to feel welcome by so many of its members, despite the unusual circumstance of being somewhat rushed into a first case. As a result, he felt confident about the current investigation. 'Those nasty poisonings,' announced Mrs Mendoza to Thomas's obvious surprise. 'Oh, don't worry, Lexington tells me all about the cases, especially if he thinks I could help.'

'And can you?' Thomas was hoping for any nugget or insight

that might bring them closer to the murderer. 'In this particular case?'

Mrs Mendoza leaned forward for a sip of tea. A large pigeon settled briefly on her windowsill to shelter from the rain before deciding there were better options elsewhere. 'I shall tell you what I told Lexington only this morning. I firmly believe there will be some connection between the perpetrator and the victims. I don't think he was homeless himself because I suspect that he would have more empathy if that were the case. It will be something else. A flimsier link but one which, in the poisoner's mind at least, makes absolute sense. If I think of anything else, I'll let you know. Meanwhile, back to you, Thomas. If I may. Tell me more about how you have bonded with the group? They're an eclectic bunch, but welcoming, I would hope. Are you integrating slowly?'

Thomas paused. He had realised that over the course of his life there had been many occasions where he had found it difficult to mix with people, his natural introversion overriding the desire to form close friendships. With The Twelve, whether because he was older and wiser or because their welcome had been so uncomplicated and warm, he felt different. There was an almost immediate sense of belonging. And his evenings with Monica had certainly contributed to this feeling.

Mrs Mendoza took a long intake of breath. 'Sometimes one is instantly drawn to another person,' she proposed, 'a friend or a lover, like a bee to the most abundant flower. At other times a friendship can take much longer, particularly when we are more set in our ways. Opening up to new people at our age can be daunting. Yet I don't believe it's something which should overly concern you, especially as your friendship with Monica sounds like it is developing promisingly. I would also add that from what I know of dear Christopher, which is a lot, I suspect you two will also become firm friends in time. It's important to be aware, though, that one cannot connect immediately with everyone, Thomas. Someone like Martin, for example, is naturally more challenging to befriend, delightful though he is once you get to know him. He is a slower burn but rewarding in the long term. The trick is to be liked by more people than disliked, particularly if one wishes not to spend one's final years alone and regretful, as so many sadly do.'

Thomas promised that he would make a concerted effort with Martin. He was interested that Mrs Mendoza had specifically mentioned Chris. He spoke about their meeting at the cemetery on the Sunday before Alice's birthday and their conversation over tea, although he held back from talking about his tearful outburst later that day. Mrs Mendoza listened intently, unsurprised. 'I suspect your father was distant, wasn't he, Thomas?' Thomas nodded, wide-eyed. 'And you are an only child, of course, as we know, which brings its own peculiarities. There is a part of you which is still, even at this late stage of your life, attracted to father figures. Lexington is the main one, of course, and a more excellent candidate for that role you couldn't wish to meet. Yet I would tentatively but confidently suggest there is another part of you which has always craved an older brother, another strong, male role model in your life. Perhaps Chris will gradually begin to fulfil that role. It's worth pondering.'

Fat raindrops continued to thump furiously on Mrs Mendoza's window while the faint aroma of spicy food from next door was making Thomas feel hungry despite an open rye bread sandwich which he had made himself for lunch before leaving Colville Square. Mrs Mendoza, somehow sensing Thomas's predicament, lit a floral candle and then reached under her chair to retrieve a medium-sized tin box in the shape of a squirrel. She opened the box and offered it to Thomas who saw that it contained what looked like homemade biscuits.

'Terry pops by every couple of weeks with emergency

rations,' she explained. 'He only lives up the road so I suppose he likes to make sure I'm looked after. These are lemon and ginger. Do try one. He baked them at the weekend so they're still good, if not quite as chewy as they were on Monday morning.'

Thomas leant forward and picked out a cookie. 'I suppose the other main thing I wanted to talk about, and I'm not really sure how to put this, but does everyone who joins The Twelve feel that they belong there? That they deserve it?' He shifted back in his chair and crossed his feet. 'I still wonder quite often, why me? Lexington talked about humility but beyond that, I'm uncertain.'

The Mendoza brow furrowed. She helped herself to a biscuit before gently closing the tin and returning it carefully to the space under her chair, then nibbled for at least half a minute before answering. 'You may recall back in the spring that you returned home to find some rowdy men verbally abusing a young lady on your square.' Thomas remembered clearly. Four men, perhaps late teens or early twenties, shouting obscenities at the daughter of a neighbour. He had paused, unsure whether or not to get involved and fearing for his own personal safety. Then he had heard Alice's voice in his head urging him to confront the men, which he did.

The young men, shocked that anyone would stand up to them, quickly dispersed. 'What did you feel when that happened?'

Thomas tried to recollect. 'Relief mostly', he suggested. 'As well as a brief sense of satisfaction that I could still stand up to a challenging situation.' But there was something else. 'I wished that those boys could suffer instead of my Alice,' he said quietly. 'And then I immediately regretted it because you don't wish cancer on anyone, especially the young.'

Mrs Mendoza inhaled. 'As I thought.' She smiled. 'You had been nursing a sense of injustice. I was watching you that day from a seat in the square. I had told Lexington only a week earlier that you were not quite ready. After that episode, I knew the situation had changed. Lexington was delighted. We knew you would spend longer than most preparing to believe you were right for The Twelve, but that day was a turning point. I felt it. Even from across the square.'

Thomas was still registering the information that Mrs Mendoza had been watching him and he hadn't even realised. *How could he have done?* On that day, he had no knowledge of The Twelve or their activities. Mrs Mendoza chose to ignore his look of bewilderment.

'Imposter Syndrome, as they call it these days, is not uncommon within The Twelve – as within society as a whole. As you'll know Thomas, I can't possibly divulge detailed information about your colleagues, but suffice to say that every one of you has been chosen very carefully and there is no reason to imagine that you, of all people, were not deemed fully able or worthy. I vetted you myself and I knew full well that you would have self-doubt, but not to such an extent that it would impact upon your abilities. You've been through a lot, over the last few years, but you are perfectly capable and you have many good years left in you. I wouldn't be surprised to see you taking more of a leadership role in five years or so, if that's something that would interest you. Again, something to think about. After you have stopped worrying.'

Before their meeting drew to a close, Thomas felt comfortable enough to talk about his tears the previous month, how Monica had comforted him and how the weeping had initially felt overwhelming yet, in retrospect, seemed cathartic. 'It was a cleansing ritual, Thomas, and an important one.' Mrs Mendoza's dark green eyes stared piercingly into Thomas's. 'Tell me, when was the last time you had a really good cry? When your wife passed?' Thomas admitted that he couldn't remember. 'And did you cry much as a child?'

Thomas thought back, sifting memories both cherished and painful from the 1950s, his father often unapproachable while his mother was regularly busy with local volunteering activities, particularly with the church. 'I don't really remember crying at all, Mrs Mendoza. I suppose I must have done it sometimes, but I have no clear memory of doing so. I must have had a very happy childhood,' he said, although, in all honesty, he couldn't recall it being particularly happy.

'I doubt that somehow,' smiled Mrs Mendoza, 'and that is something which perhaps we can explore in more detail another time as I don't wish to overload you too much today. Of course, if you require me before our next loosely scheduled appointment in a few months, then I shall naturally make time for you and I shall implore Terry to conjure some fresher cookies. My advice at this point Thomas, would be to cry more. If you feel like doing so, then you must. Holding in your emotions may feel natural for a man of your age but you've seen how refreshed you can feel after the floodgates have opened. Monica is wise and she was right. It had been building up for some time; perhaps your whole life. Imagine sixty years' worth of tears collecting in a reservoir; the dam must burst eventually.' She reached over and placed a bony, long-fingered hand on his knee. 'Crying should never be a source of embarrassment. It should be a matter of relief. Of beautiful release. Like an emotion orgasm.' At this, Mrs Mendoza got a fit of the giggles, which proved somewhat contagious.

When he had recovered some sense of calm, Thomas thanked Mrs Mendoza and stood up, his left foot lightly brushing the small pile of books, which teetered alarmingly. The various squirrels portrayed on the walls of the room glared disapprovingly. 'Mrs Mendoza,' he frowned, 'why aren't you a full member of The Twelve? If you don't mind my asking.'

The rain had stopped and shards of sunlight were now appearing through small chinks in the low, grey cloud cover. The psychiatrist stood uneasily, her multi-coloured dress wafting voluminously around her thin frame, and took Thomas's right hand in hers, enveloping them both with her left. 'I was, Thomas. For five glorious years during which I had the most wonderful fun and killed the most horrible people. But I resigned. My skills are put to better use looking after all of you. It's not the Hotel California, you know,' she added, noting her guest's slightly shocked expression. 'You can check out at any time you like and you are genuinely allowed to leave.' She opened the door for him, smiled and stroked his upper arm gently. 'One more thing, dear. Look after Monica,' she said quietly. 'She is strong and she has the prettiest scars. They must not be reopened, if you understand me.'

13

'It's a distinctly odd thing to decide to do, isn't it?' Monica was rolling ideas around her head, deep in thought. 'Poison homeless people for no particular reason. Other than, perhaps, you really don't like people asking you for money. But even so, it's quite extreme. Unless there's some deeper reason for despising homeless people, for example, maybe he was homeless himself once and managed to find a way out but somehow harbours some pathological hatred of the person he used to be. This sort of thing doesn't tend to happen in Agatha Christie. I'm guessing, of course. Just throwing ideas into the wind.' Thomas and Monica were travelling east towards Upminster for what felt like the thousandth time, but which was actually only the sixth.

'Mrs Mendoza thinks not,' replied Thomas. 'She believes there is some sort of connection to the homeless community but that it's less obvious than simply someone who used to be on the streets. She doesn't know what it could be but she's mulling.'

November had offered up nothing in the way of sightings, intelligence or, thankfully, murders. It was fair to say that the journeys out towards Essex were becoming a little wearing despite the fact that the two friends were enjoying each other's company enormously and had, on many occasions, put the world to rights in almost every conceivable way.

Thomas was particularly surprised by how many of his own values were shared by this exciting, well-travelled, smart and inspiring woman. He had always assumed that, as happened often, his socialist, humanitarian tendencies would fade with age – but in fact the opposite was true. Monica shared his worldview almost exactly, and they would often tackle the important political and moral issues of the day from a broadly similar perspective as they immersed themselves in the joyful cacophony of languages and dialects which surrounded them on these inner-city journeys.

Now, in the earliest days of December, with no major advance or breakthrough in the case, their conversation was naturally drifting towards Christmas.

Thomas had, for the last few years, spent Christmas Day alone. He'd been annually invited to stay at Emily's, of course, but had always declined, partly because he didn't want to burden her young family even after her divorce. Emily would insist that he was always welcome, but, in truth, Thomas genuinely enjoyed the solitude of the day and the opportunity to take stock of the year gone by and to speculate on the one to come. Because of his only-child status, Thomas had never particularly feared or rejected his own company and had always used his time alone wisely, so when Monica asked about his plans for the holiday period, he was in two minds whether or not to spontaneously make up an imaginary day of family frivolity. Yet it was Monica, after all, and as he'd never yet withheld any truths from her, there seemed no sensible reason to start now. He explained about his Christmas ritual of the last few years and implied that this year would, in all probability, be no different.

'I understand completely.' She smiled softly, placing her gloved hand on his. 'I adore my own company. Goodness knows I've spent enough time alone over the last nineteen years. One's own space is wonderfully precious. However, if you do fancy a change this year, I'll be at home in St John's Wood with a good book and some fine wine. Probably no turkey – there's no point in a big bird just for one – but with enough cheese to stink out most of North West London.' Her deep brown eyes met his grey-tawny ones. 'I trust you like cheese, Thomas? I've never asked you before. An appalling gap in our knowledge of each other.'

He confirmed that he did. Despite his recent Christmas tradition, it was an enticing offer. He promised he would think about it, much to Monica's delight. This would be Thomas's fifth Christmas without Alice, but also his first as part of The Twelve. The pace of his life had changed somewhat since mid-October. He had felt a noticeable shift in his mood since that late lunch with Lexington. After many months of what often still felt like grieving but sometimes resembled something darker, Thomas had realised with relief that his recent thoughts were more often focused on the future than on the past, and this was a positive sign because the future was finally interesting.

Despite there being no obvious breakthrough, there was no shortage of social activity as the year drew to a close. Thomas found himself spending more time with Chris, sometimes joined by Monica and also by Anna Hopley, who was delightful company and had almost as many tales to tell from her career in forensic pathology as Chris did from his years in surgery.

'Monica's invited me over for Christmas Day.' Thomas had opened an expensive Japanese whisky, which Emily had bought him as a thank you for regularly looking after the twins. After a delightful evening at a local restaurant as a foursome, the two men had settled into armchairs in Thomas's warm, welcoming sitting room, facing out onto the trees in the square which had been brightly decorated with coloured lights.

'Then you should accept, my friend.' Chris swirled a single ice cube round his glass, chilling as much of the delicious-smelling auburn elixir as he could. 'She likes you. You like her. It could be enormous Christmas fun. Chin chin!' He raised the glass and took a sip.

'I know,' said Thomas tentatively, 'and she's wonderful company, but–'

'But what, exactly?'

Thomas took a deep breath. If he was going to open up, then he may as well do it completely. 'You have to bear in mind that my experience of women is fairly limited. There were a few short-lived girlfriends in the early seventies, but then I met Alice and that was that for the next forty years.' Thomas took a sip of whisky and let it meander around his mouth for a few seconds before swallowing, the gentle, oaky spice hitting the back of his throat with a pleasing slosh. 'It's fair to say that I'm not merely rusty but completely oxidised when it comes to matters of the heart.'

'As a chemist,' smiled Chris, 'Monica would no doubt appreciate your terminology, but going back to what you were saying before, do you mean to tell me there were no extra-marital activities at all?' Thomas shook his head. 'Oh well, never mind,' mused Chris with a look of admiration mixed with amazement. 'You're clearly more saintly than the rest of us. If you ask me, I think Monica is sending encouraging signals. "Good vibes", as my daughters would say. I've noticed the way she acts around you. Plus you two look good together. That always helps. But if you want any sort of advice, it's this: try not to take anything too seriously. At the age we are, you'd think that single people would want to settle down into the final lap, down the back straight, with a bit of stability, a steady pace. That's not necessarily the case. Take Anna, for example. I've stayed at her house perhaps a dozen times now. Sometimes I've stayed in the spare room. Sometimes Anna has wanted… close male company, shall we say. The simple warmth of another living body, if you like. And it has felt good.

Really good. For both of us. We've missed that intimacy. But she definitely doesn't want anything permanent or complicated and neither do I. Bear in mind also that her husband is still alive. Just. I suppose we've all grown used to having our space and some of us are, of course, still dealing with our ghosts. Monica may be the same, even after nearly twenty years. I don't know. Anyway, it's Christmas in ten days so we'll find out then, won't we? That's if you decide to go.' Chris winked, his gentle cajoling complete.

'I'll think I'll accept,' said Thomas. 'We're doing another trip out on the District Line in a couple of days so I'll let her know then. And I'll get her a nice present. I'll pop to Selfridges and get her a pretty scarf or something. This has been a helpful conversation, thank you. Another whisky before we turn in?'

'I should refuse but, frankly, why not?' Chris smiled, proffering his empty glass. 'I'll be up in the night, but the bathroom's only next door.' Thomas poured a generous shot and Chris took a long sniff. 'I have a feeling,' he said, raising his glass in a toast, 'that your Christmas could be the most interesting one for a few years.'

14

'I've been thinking about your kind offer for Christmas Day and I've decided to accept. That is, assuming you'll still have me.' Thomas was surprised at quite how nervous he had been during the evening's journey out to Upminster, as usual gleaning no useful information on the poisonings. Now they were on the third return into the city, he had decided to make his move just outside the faded glamour of East Ham station. The carriage was largely empty apart from an elderly couple three seats away, each reading the evening newspaper, and a scantily-clad young lady further down the aisle about whom Monica had commented, out of earshot, that she probably should have worn a coat. To Thomas's untrained eye, the girl didn't seem in the least bit troubled by the temperature and he strongly suspected she was a stranger to outerwear in general.

'Oh, that is truly wonderful news! I'm so happy, Thomas. Will you come for a spot of late lunch? Say, 1.30pm to eat at two. And please feel free to stay as long as you like. I feel sure there will be the usual panoply of cultural offerings on the radio or the television.' Monica clapped her hands delightedly, and her eyes sparkled as a broad smile spread across her face. The couple with the newspapers glanced over momentarily to see what the fuss was about. 'Oh, you've made an old woman very pleased. Thank you.' She gave him a warm kiss and Thomas felt that it was slightly closer to his mouth than her other kisses had been, bordering on his lips, but perhaps that was merely the bounce of the train carriage over-balancing her momentarily as it rattled noisily into the station.

As they parted company at Liverpool Street, Thomas was convinced that their friendly hug was tighter than usual and, as he watched Monica ascend the station steps to a taxi rank, he was sure there was a spring in her step. He meandered towards the Central Line to continue his journey home.

The following day Thomas took the bus to Oxford Street to buy presents. He decided to go early, knowing that London's busiest retail thoroughfare before Christmas was best avoided as the day wore on, but even at 10.30am it was reasonably unpleasant, thronging with flocks of braying shoppers.

Thomas had always been shocked at the number of homeless people on the damp streets and, particularly this year, he was glad to be able to give a note to as many as he could. He had not fully grasped the financial situation of The Twelve but knew that its coffers were deep and that his "salary" and expenses were far more than he ever could practically spend unless he suddenly and uncharacteristically acquired an interest in supercars. Giving to the less fortunate in the capital seemed a much better course of action, especially as he knew that they currently being targeted by a homicidal maniac, and a particularly devious and callous one at that. If he could somehow save a life by giving someone the means to get into a shelter early, then he would.

In Selfridges, after manoeuvring his way through an unseemly crowd outside the store, he enlisted the help of a friendly young shop assistant wearing a hijab. Together, they found a red patterned Vivienne Westwood scarf which he felt would go nicely with Monica's red beret. He then ambled into the Food Hall where he bought a selection of chutneys as an extra gift to go with the promise of cheese. Eventually, holding a selection of bright yellow bags of various sizes, Thomas left the store and took the bus back home. His successful Christmas shopping trip had lasted just under forty minutes.

Thomas was just passing a former retail arcade on Queensway when there was a text from Lexington. It had been decided that the District Line surveillance would end before Christmas unless there was any new intelligence between now and then. No suspicious activity had been spotted so far and there had been no murders since late October, therefore The Twelve's attention would be diverted elsewhere until there was a breakthrough regarding the timings of the attacks. Either that or they would enjoy a longer Christmas break and then regroup in the hope of further information from Suzanne or, less likely, from Dennis Burrows.

This was something of a relief to Thomas, as he imagined it was for most of the group apart from Martin, who seemed to be enjoying revisiting some of his old haunts. The line out east to Upminster wasn't the most enjoyable or inspiring, especially in the cold and dark, and he was often glad when his and Monica's regular journeys were finally complete. The east was a part of the city that he had never really frequented and as they had travelled out to the far reaches of the system and back, Thomas had often looked out across the flat landscape and the industrial rooftops towards the estuary and felt that if anywhere in London was a suitable location for festering crime, then it was here. He knew that Chris, Terry and Martin lived in different parts of the east so there was no rational foundation for his feelings of unease.

Perhaps he had simply watched too many gangland movies in his younger days.

Nonetheless, he always felt more relaxed when their train moved back into the apparent safety of the city after an evening's work. Sometimes he would share a black cab with Monica, always dropping her off at her door and watching her as she turned the key in her lock, before swivelling to blow him a kiss and then vanishing into the sanctuary of her home as he instructed the driver to please set a course for Colville Square.

The following day was Thursday and the final yoga session before Christmas. Once it was complete and everyone had recovered, Lexington asked everyone to stay behind for a few moments.

'As you all know,' he began, 'your regular visits to the eastern outer reaches of the Underground network have thus far failed to provide anything of use or relevance to the current case and so Suzanne has asked us to step back for a while. Whether our poisoner is particularly good at remaining undetected, whether his murderous appetite has been sated after October's fury of activity, or whether he has simply got bored, we cannot know. There are a couple of other cases which look potentially interesting, so I will research these over the next few weeks and convene a meeting perhaps in mid-January to let you all know which one we've decided to take on as our first case of the new year. Naturally, if there is another poisoning any time soon, we will reconsider our position.

'In the meantime, I hope you all have a glorious Christmas and New Year break and don't forget the first yoga class will not be until January 14th as a couple of people are away on holiday.' Lexington's phone started playing 'I'm Too Sexy' by Right Said

Fred. 'Sorry! My great niece again, fiddling with my phone, the little rascal.' He scrambled to answer it. 'It's the bank,' he whispered, placing his hand over the phone, 'just arranging your Christmas money.' He turned his attention back to the caller. 'Hello, yes? Mr Wheeler, so lovely to hear from you. Just one moment please, I'll go somewhere private.' He waved an excited finger at the group and gave David a wink. 'Let me just take this in the other room lest I spoil the festive surprise.'

'It's always exciting when Lexington talks to the bank before Christmas,' said Chris over coffee and pastries ten minutes later. 'This'll be my fifth Christmas surprise. I couldn't believe it the first time. I took everyone to Disneyland the following year, after I'd checked it wasn't a mistake, of course. The Florida one, not the French one.'

'Can someone please go over for me again how it works exactly?' asked Thomas. 'David tried to explain it but I'm not sure even he knew fully and it's all still a bit new to me.'

'You are so sweet,' said Monica. It was a red beret day, which had made Thomas smile, mindful of his present and anticipating Monica's reaction when she finally opened it. 'I can explain, if you'll indulge me in a short history lesson for just a minute. So, The Twelve was founded in the 1830s, as you know, 1831 to be precise, two years after Robert Peel started the Metropolitan Police. Originally the idea was for it to be connected to the police, staffed mostly by ex-military men, and something that the best of the nascent police force could do when they got older. That plan was discarded fairly quickly when a man called Edward Cartwright persuaded Peel that keeping the organisation secret would allow it more flexibility in terms of what could be achieved. Cartwright also wanted The Twelve to draw in talent from beyond the police force and, in fact, one of the inaugural members was a blacksmith named Morris... but I digress.

'It was set up with help from a small group of very wealthy

individuals who, at the time, created an investment fund into which every member of The Twelve could contribute when they died, if they wanted, or indeed when they were alive. Morris the blacksmith naturally didn't have much in the way of savings to give when he was alive, but since he had no relatives, when he died even he was able to contribute a tidy sum. They were very forward-thinking for the early nineteenth century. Anyway, in addition, after the First World War, because of the important undercover work of The Twelve during that conflict, a great many benefactors donated to the growing fund so that by around 1937, it was worth many millions of pounds. These days the fund is worth around £700 million, not including all the properties we own, and it keeps going up of course because we rarely take much out, just the £600,000 or so between the twelve of us annually, plus any extra miscellaneous expenses and charity donations. Collectively, we barely dent the lump amount. That's why, even in these difficult times with interest rates as they are, we can all get a bonus at Christmas without depleting the coffers too severely. The intention is always for the leader of The Twelve – Lexington in this case – to try to leave more in the pot for future generations. There's also a fair amount of "lost" art that belongs to The Twelve and that's also worth a fortune if anyone ever needs to sell it. You'll have seen it dotted about in places of safety, like the Jackson Pollock sketches in the Notting Hill house behind the cinema, for example.'

'I thought I recognised them!' said Thomas, exuberantly.

'One of The Twelve, Rosalyn Jones, was close friends with Jackson in the forties when she was living in America and the sketches were a gift. She joined The Twelve in 1956 and bequeathed the art to us when she died in 1975. They're worth around $80 million at auction, in case there's ever a need to sell them, but it's unlikely that will be any time soon.'

'Also,' added Chris, 'there has occasionally been a situation where a new member of The Twelve is brought in but despite having all the important qualities and talents which we need, they haven't necessarily got either the pension or the funds available personally, so the investment fund can help with tax-free gifts. A bit like if someone from a poorer background wanted to go to university and was smart enough but couldn't afford the fees. Plus, there are all the multiple charity donations to be covered and hidden. Usually when you read that a mystery donor has saved a riding school for disabled children, that'll be us. Lexington loves saving the odd riding school. Then there's the cleaning bill for all the properties, council tax, contents insurance, Martin's occasional parking tickets. It mounts up. Luckily there's cash to spare.'

Thomas nodded that he understood. His pension was fundamentally decent and he was fortunate enough not to want for money, yet the sudden arrival of £50,000 in his bank account a few days later from a mysterious 'Duodecim & Co.' temporarily threw him into a panic. Lexington's timely text arrived soon afterwards informing the group that they might wish to check their balances for their Christmas gift from the benefactor, Mr Duodecim – twelve in Latin, as Catherine Daniels had explained via text a couple of hours later.

With no District Line trips planned and no gatherings either, Thomas used the following days to catch up with family and other friends, some old work colleagues plus a couple of school friends he had retained. He felt that they looked rather older than he did and their outlooks on life were somewhat more downbeat in comparison with his own. There was little doubt that The Twelve had given him a new purpose in life. He felt revived, rejuvenated. Yes, that was the word. *Made young again.* And it felt good.

He spent Christmas Eve with Emily and the twins, baking mince pies for Santa and making sure that everything was ready for his and the reindeers' visit that night. 'Are you absolutely sure you won't join us tomorrow, Dad? There's plenty of food and plenty of space. We've got another friend over with her kids because she got divorced in September, so we're going to be six women around the table, but don't let that scare you off.'

Thomas smiled and gave his daughter a warm hug. 'I'll be absolutely fine. You know I will. I'll call you in the morning to wish you all a Happy Christmas. Oh, and I might go out in the afternoon for a walk to see a friend, so don't worry if you can't get hold of me.'

'A friend, eh?' Emily raised a quizzical eyebrow. 'All right, Dad. You just be careful. I love you.'

'I love you too, darling,' he replied, tenderly kissing her forehead, his mind already mainly focused on the following day. Thomas turned to the eight-year-olds, Flora and Lucy, already in their pyjamas at 6pm in anticipation of what Christmas morning might bring, and gave them a big hug. 'Now, I think we just need a carrot for Rudolph to eat and then everything will be ready, and we can all go to sleep and dream about what wonderful surprises Christmas Day has in store.'

15

Thomas woke late on the 25th, gratefully refreshed from a decent night of sleep, broken only once for a trip to the toilet. If there were dreams, he couldn't recall them. In midwinter, he tended to sleep later, often untroubled by light coming through the bedroom window until after eight. This Christmas Day was bright yet mild for December, so he decided he would walk to Monica's. That left the whole morning to himself until he would have to set off just after noon. Thomas prepared a light breakfast of scrambled eggs and smoked salmon with a cup of tea; he was uncertain what Monica would have in store for lunch so thought it safest to have a morsel or two for breakfast. He didn't want to appear rude by not tucking into her food, but equally he didn't want to arrive in St John's Wood ravenous and rumbling.

Most of Christmas morning he read his book, interrupted only by a brief but festive call to Emily and the twins at 9am to hear their exciting news of Santa's visit and the bewildering list of presents they had discovered in their stockings. Santa had been extra generous, perhaps in consideration of the difficult year the twins had had adapting to the break up of their parents' marriage. He considered calling Simon but settled for a friendly text –

Simon's reply was equally friendly but more businesslike, such was the current status of their father-son relationship. Thomas found that his morning reading was frequently distracted by random thoughts about poisonings and about previous Christmases with Alice, and he kept having to reread certain pages having taken in virtually none of the narrative.

At 11am Thomas started properly considering what to wear to Monica's. He didn't know why but there seemed to be an unusual level of importance attached to this style decision and, just as prior to their first meeting at St Pancras two months earlier, he discarded several options before finally settling on jeans, a black T-shirt, a dark blue V-neck jumper and a dark grey jacket. He wouldn't want to outstay his welcome and would most likely be back home around dusk; even if he was later, he could always hail a taxi. There would be no need to walk home in the chilly darkness so there was equally no requirement for a thick outer layer, and a quick check of his weather app indicated no rain forecast.

He left Colville Square at ten past twelve as planned and criss-crossed patiently through the streets north of Notting Hill, largely deserted apart from a congregation of amiable churchgoers leaving mass who all wished him a merry Christmas, and the odd couple out for a pre-lunch stroll. He made his way to Westbourne Park station before traversing the canal at the Union Tavern pub and veering left into Maida Vale, after which it was virtually a straight line to Monica's. It somehow felt strange that they'd never visited each other's houses before; the distance seemed so minimal now, the journey so straightforward on foot. She'd invited him in on a couple of occasions after their surveillance evenings, but he had always politely declined, owing to the lateness of the hour and his reticence to impose.

Monica's home was a spacious two-bedroomed flat on the top floor of a smart Victorian detached house on Hamilton Terrace a stone's throw from Abbey Road. Thomas rang the buzzer and waited. Seconds later, there was a metallic click and Monica's elated voice rang out, 'Welcome, my darling Christmas friend!' as the door growled mechanically to permit entry. Thomas climbed two flights of stairs and was greeted at the door to Monica's flat with two kisses, a festive hug and the smell of fabulous cooking mixed with that of an expensive candle..

A short hallway decorated with a variety of art from what looked like many different parts of the world opened out onto a large, sparsely-furnished, open-plan living area with a kitchen off to the left. From Monica's east-facing windows, Thomas could see the tops of some of the stands at Lord's cricket ground. Although there was a cello positioned in a corner of the large space, the music playing was a piano sonata, which Thomas guessed incorrectly was Mozart – 'It's Schubert, but an excellent guess. Slightly later than Wolfgang and a bit less busy.'

'Do you play?' asked Thomas, gesturing towards the cello.

'I do. And the piano. Sadly, we couldn't get a piano up the stairs or through any of the windows when we bought the place, so the cello it must be. And although I don't practise quite as often as I should, it's always good to have something to keep one's fingers nimble, don't you think? Especially in later years.' Monica's dark eyes twinkled mischievously. 'Luckily the walls and the floors are thick, so the neighbours don't complain, and I'm fortunate that the old lady on the ground floor has a grand piano and lets me have a tinkle on that from time to time.'

Despite it being Christmas Day, the apartment was noticeably unfestive with the exception of a wreath of holly hanging over Monica's marble fireplace with one expensive-looking gold bauble attached; a solitary nod to the season. Thomas wondered whether she might have had even a small tree but supposed that, like him, Monica tended to feel that it wasn't worth the bother.

They exchanged presents – Monica adored her scarf and her

chutneys and Thomas received a beautiful leather wallet engraved with his initials and some expensive Scotch whisky – and chatted while Monica finished the cooking.

Monica's idea of a light Christmas Day lunch was a spectacular array of dishes which she had apparently spent the morning preparing. They included a light, spicy fish curry, which Monica explained originated in Goa; some delicate spinach, pea and potato cakes; fried paneer and green peppers marinated in herbs and served on wooden skewers; and a Parsi dish of chicken cooked with mango and chilli, of which Thomas enjoyed three portions. His tastebuds were purring by the time his plate was clean.

———

Thomas helped to clear away the lunch debris into the dishwasher and the two of them settled into the seating area with a glass of wine each, Thomas on a soft brown leather sofa facing the window and Monica on one of two comfortable-looking red leather armchairs with patterned mauve cushions.

'It's so lovely to have company for Christmas,' smiled Monica, 'I don't mind being on my own, as you know, but I'm actually surprised at how much more enjoyable it is this year. If I'm honest, I can think of no one I'd rather spend it with, Thomas. I've so enjoyed getting to know you over the last few weeks. I feel like you're a true friend.'

Thomas blushed slightly and looked out of the window into the pale London sky illuminated now by weak December sunshine. 'I've certainly been enjoying The Twelve a lot more than I thought I would, thanks to you. I'm glad you volunteered me all those weeks ago. I mean, Martin and Terry are lovely chaps, don't get me wrong, but they're not my ideal companions.

I'm not sure I could have travelled up and down various Underground lines with them for weeks on end!'

Monica sipped her Pinot Grigio delicately. 'Martin is a dear. And very cultured, which surprised me initially. You know his history, do you?'

Thomas shook his head. 'He's a chatterbox but he doesn't really reveal too much about himself apart from odd snippets. A typical cabbie, I suppose. Although we did go to the theatre a couple of weeks back and I know he loves that and music.'

Monica shuffled slightly to make herself more comfortable. 'He won't mind me telling you the story, I'm sure. Martin doted on his wife. They were teenage sweethearts. He married Pauline at eighteen and neither of them ever had eyes for anyone else. It was one of those relationships. He did The Knowledge and became a cabbie while she became a dinner lady. They bought a little house over in Wanstead and watched as the East End transformed around them. The cranes went up followed by the skyscrapers. The old wharf buildings to the south of them turned into plush flats. The world moved on, but they remained Martin and Pauline. Pauline and Martin. Like me, they never had any children, but it didn't bother them. They were a self-contained unit, just the two of them, spending any spare money on theatre trips, which is where he got his love of the stage. In many ways it was the perfect marriage, according to Martin.

'Then when Pauline got to her late fifties she found a lump on her breast and by the time they got a diagnosis it was too late to do anything about it. The cancer had spread, as it so often does, and although chemotherapy gave her an extra year, there was little that could be done in the end, apart from make her comfortable as the polite euphemism goes. When she died, he was a broken man. Completely crushed. He threw himself into cab driving because he had nothing else, but his heart wasn't really in it. Some days he would drive the whole day and couldn't recall a single detail about where he'd been or who he'd picked up. Everything was on autopilot. Luckily, once you've got The Knowledge, it never leaves you, so he was able to simply switch off and drive like a robot. He worked fifteen, sixteen hours a day sometimes; he simply didn't want to go home because Pauline wasn't there, so he preferred to just drive. He quite often slept in the cab to avoid opening the front door to an empty, silent house.' Thomas nodded in recognition. 'He did that for three years, barely speaking to anyone apart from the basic pleasantries with passengers. Can you imagine? And then one day he got a call from Margaret Wilmot who was the leader before Lexington.'

'Sounds like he got the call just like I did. When I was ready.'

'Exactly. And me. The Twelve had had their eye on Martin since before Pauline died. Not only was he one of the best cabbies in the business but he also had the right temperament and was an incredibly good driver. No violations or anything in over forty years. Not even a speeding ticket or a parking ticket until he joined The Twelve. Not many cabbies can say that! Plus he's got a bit of ancient history with The Twelve, apparently. Anyway, Margaret waited patiently until she felt the moment was right and enough time had elapsed since Pauline's death, and she basically rescued Martin from his life, or what his life was becoming, at least. More wine?'

Thomas realised that he'd finished his glass of Australian shiraz rather quickly while listening to Monica. 'No, I'm fine, thank you. Is that how you view what The Twelve does for its members? Rescues people?'

Monica looked down at the polished wood floor. Somewhere in the near distance, a car alarm started and then stopped abruptly. 'Sometimes it does, of course. It rescued you, didn't it? Just as it rescued Martin and Chris and Anna and Belinda. And me.' She took a deep breath, looked up and her eyes met Thomas's. 'You've noticed the one solitary bauble, I suppose. The gold one on the fireplace. It's my one Christmas reminder of Patrick. He loved this time of year so much and this place always used to be absolutely covered in decorations and cards and what have you. The Christmas after he died, I couldn't bear to put anything up so the place was completely bare; you wouldn't even know what day it was. I didn't even open the cards. A couple of cards arrived addressed to both of us, clearly from people who didn't know him that well and somehow hadn't heard what had happened, unbelievably. I mean it's not as if it wasn't in the bloody news.' Monica closed her eyes, fought back a tear, sipped her wine and took another deep breath.

'As soon as the new year came, I crazily gathered all the decorations that we had collected together over the years and I gave them to charity. *I'm finished with Christmas,* I thought. *Forever.* A few weeks later, I regretted what I'd done, but by then it was too late. Thankfully, the gold bauble must have fallen out of the box when I was rushing around in a frenzy. It had ended up under the bed, which was where I found it. We'd bought it together from a little shop down a narrow lane in Florence in 1998. Clearly it didn't want to be cast out like all its friends. It too wanted to be rescued. So now it's a Christmas reminder of good times past and I smile when I place it, rather than cry as I did for many years.'

Thomas pondered this for a moment. He could sense that the atmosphere in the room had changed subtly but he couldn't pinpoint exactly how, so elected to slightly change the subject. 'So where were you when you got the call from Lexington?'

'I was exactly where you're sitting now,' said Monica, moving a strand of hair away from her face. 'That very sofa. It was 2013, Valentine's Day of all days, and I'd been retired for about a year, I suppose, maybe slightly less than that. After Patrick was killed, I did the same as Martin. I submerged myself in my work; it was the only thing I could think of to keep me from crumbling completely. For the first six months or so, I would wander around this flat in a daze. I would put on Patrick's jackets, convinced that I could still detect some essence of him, until one day I realised that was utterly ridiculous and I took everything to the same charity shop and dumped it. Then I immediately regretted that too. I felt so stupid. I should have learned from the Christmas decoration fiasco but my mind was still all over the place. At least that time I went back and bought one of his favourites for £10 – it's still in the wardrobe somewhere. The charity shop people must have thought I was completely barmy. There's that crazy old Indian woman again. Work was the only way to stay sane or even to stay alive. Don't forget I was only fifty when the Towers fell but I felt that my life was over, certainly in terms of love. I knew I'd never find that beautiful connection again. I'd never find that deep, consuming passion again. So, work would have to do. I needed to have a sense of purpose to balance the sense of emptiness, so I worked. I barely socialised for the first five years and when I did, I'm sure I was abysmal company.'

'Oh, I feel sure that you weren't,' protested Thomas, unconvincingly.

'I seriously was, Thomas. God, I even bored myself. By about 2008, there were a couple of perfectly nice gentlemen circling around but they didn't really interest me that much. They were both chemistry professors so it was a bit like being at work when we went out on dates. Neither lasted very long. A few weeks at best. Even the sex was functional as opposed to desperate and passionate. I guess there was no chemistry, ironically. I retired in 2012 and I had this vague idea to join some sort of reading club or something to occupy my time. Needless to say, I didn't get round to it. I pottered around here a bit, the archetypal widow at a loose end for about nine months, and then in February I was sitting on that sofa and my mobile rang. I didn't recognise the number but something made me answer and it was Lexington inviting me to lunch to discuss what he described as a "late career opportunity". I asked whether he needed my CV and he responded by rattling off my entire work history there and then, in the most charming and eloquent way. He pretty much knew more about me than I did. I should have been unnerved but the way he explained it was so charming that I was intrigued. Lunch was inevitable.'

Thomas leaned back into the softness of the leather. 'It's interesting how The Twelve finds broken people right at the point where they're...' he fumbled for a word, 'ready, I suppose.'

'It's a science,' explained Monica. 'I'm learning it myself at the moment. As a relatively senior member of the team now, Lexington and Owen are training me to recognise potential recruits. One day, some fortunate souls may be getting a life-changing call from little old me! Can you imagine? We've got our eye on around twenty people right now. They won't all end up in The Twelve, of course, but a few will. Maybe five or six of them, maybe fewer. There's some very interesting talent out there but I'm having to learn not only to identify the right individuals, but also to assess precisely the right time to approach them. Get that bit wrong and you could end up in a rather tricky situation. Stop me if I'm talking too much, won't you?'

'Heavens, not at all,' mumbled Thomas, slightly spellbound. 'Are all of them broken? The potential people.'

Monica rose from her armchair, carefully put down her wine glass and glided over to the sofa to sit next to him. Thomas could feel his heart rate increase as he took in her now familiar scent. She had positioned herself with her right leg crossed so that it was touching Thomas's knee. He decided not to move it away although he became suddenly and acutely conscious of the ground shifting gently under his feet.

'Everyone who is remotely interesting is broken in some way or another, Thomas. It's how you deal with it that determines where your life leads you next. Now,' she leaned in and kissed

Thomas lightly on the lips, caressing his cheek with her right hand while gazing deep into his eyes, 'it's nearly three o'clock on Christmas Day and the two of us are faced with an interesting dilemma. We can either watch what Her Majesty has to say to the nation, while eating the cheese that I promised you, or I can lead you to my bedroom and we can see what unfolds there. With the greatest respect to Her Majesty, I know my preference.'

16

Thomas lay motionless in Monica's bed with its crisp white sheets and snuggly, matching duvet, staring at the ceiling while she snoozed, peacefully curled up with her head on his chest. He felt like he was soaring through the air without any form of safety net. The experience was both exhilarating and terrifying at the same time. Considering it had been almost twenty years since he had last been naked with a woman, Thomas was somewhat surprised and delighted that the afternoon's activities had evolved quite as well as they had. He struggled to remember the last time he had been in anything resembling this position. Alice had died in January 2015, almost six years ago, yet before that there was her illness and before that even, the slow demise of their physical marriage, which had dwindled sometime around the early part of the century when familiarity had bred quiet comfort. That, in turn, had led to forgetfulness of what had once been so pleasurable for both of them. Maybe it had been merely the natural passage of time, advancing age and its attendant changes in priorities. The incremental, strategic retreat from intimacy.

Monica stirred and smiled as the slow realisation dawned that she had company. 'What time is it?' she murmured sleepily.

'It's just after seven on Christmas Day evening,' said Thomas, leaning up slightly so that he was in the right position to check the large wall clock behind Monica. *So much for being home around dusk,* he mused to himself. 'Did you have a good nap?'

'Wonderful, thank you.' To Thomas, she somehow seemed more radiant than usual, even while yawning. 'You absolutely wore me out! My goodness, that was a quite gorgeous surprise. A bit fiddly at the start but that's to be expected.'

'I think you were the one who surprised me!' Thomas smiled, choosing to ignore the comment about fiddly. 'You certainly aren't shy at coming forward, are you?'

Monica stretched, wide-eyed, and then settled back to her former position on Thomas's chest, although her right hand now wandered down his torso and began to stroke his hip bone and the loose fold of flesh above it. He took in her honey-coloured skin. 'The young people have a handy term for it,' she explained. 'YOLO. You Only Live Once. And therefore I believe it would constitute criminal negligence not to enjoy oneself while one can. Which, by the way, I did. Very much. Enjoy myself.' She kissed Thomas on the lips. 'And particularly at our age, I would consider it a moral duty to use whatever quality time we have left in pleasurable pursuits. None of us have any idea what's around the corner, especially in our line of business. Anyway, I'm going to make a decaf coffee just to perk myself up just a little. It's too late for caffeine. Would you like one?'

Thomas watched as her naked body extracted itself from the cotton duvet. Monica walked casually and confidently over to the door where a white silk dressing gown with a blue bird motif was hanging, fully aware that she was being admired from behind. She reached up to gather the gown and then, having a different thought, turned and placed her hands on her hips so that Thomas could fully see her nudity. 'Not too bad for nearly seventy, wouldn't you say? The odd sag and wrinkle here and there but nothing too off-putting, I would hope.'

Thomas certainly couldn't remember an occasion when a woman had quite so proudly displayed herself to him, not even in the early years of marriage to Alice who had tended to put on a nightdress after their lovemaking. 'I don't think "not bad" really does you justice, Monica. You're beautiful.' She blushed but stayed in her position, exhibiting herself to him as if it were the most natural thing in the world before slowly moving her right hand toward her pubis and gently stroking the fine, grey hair. 'Yes to decaf coffee, by the way, and then I should probably be on my way.'

'Oh dear, darling. Won't you stay? Please. The night is young.' Monica was finally wrapping the white silk loosely around herself.

'I'll pop to the bathroom if I may and then we can talk about it.'

Thomas put his underpants on and went into the huge black and white tiled en suite bathroom with its walk-in shower and separate bath. By the time he returned to the bedroom, Monica was back in bed in her dressing gown with two cups of coffee on coasters on a side table. The gown was so loosely wrapped now that Thomas could make out the edges of her dark, small nipples.

'I suppose we'll never know what Her Majesty's message to the nation was about,' he said, conscious that it was now him and not her standing almost naked in a bedroom in St John's Wood. He looked around for another gown to put on but there wasn't one. *Why would there be?*

Monica sighed contentedly. 'She's happy about the new additions to the family, she says that we should all have faith in God during times of hardship and wants the nation to embrace the diversity within society, particularly when it comes to educating children. I checked online while the coffee was brewing. Won't you get back into bed? It's getting chilly without you.'

In an effort not to appear self-conscious, Thomas slipped into the king-size bed, still in his underpants. He wasn't sure whether to get close to Monica but it didn't matter because, sensing his reserve, she turned towards him and snuggled close. 'I'm very much enjoying this Christmas,' she announced. 'More than I have in a very long time. And, call me selfish if you like, but I'd very much like it to continue. So will you stay the night? Please. I don't snore, as far as I know. We can have more wine or we can find a movie to watch. Or,' she smiled and moved her right hand to just inside the elastic of Thomas's pants, 'we can just stay here and talk until we fall asleep again.'

Thomas weighed up the situation as he thought he understood it. On the one hand, he didn't really have any pressing need to get back to Colville Square. He wasn't expecting to see anyone until the day after Boxing Day when he had arranged to meet some old friends for drinks. In addition, the bed was very comfortable, he was enjoying Monica's company enormously and she seemed to be enjoying his. Furthermore, their afternoon had, after the initial sense of surprise had worn off, been extremely passionate and he felt reasonably confident that enough time had elapsed for him to be able to muster a repeat performance if that were required. In fact, if he wasn't mistaken, Monica's hand had now moved inside the elastic and her fingers were creating something of a perceptible stir. He attempted, futilely, to balance a counterargument where he got dressed, politely said goodnight and went home to an empty house but no, there was no point in even attempting to weigh the options, distracted as he was by what was already happening in his underwear.

'I'd love to stay. If it's all right with you? Although I don't have a toothbrush or anything.'

Monica grinned widely. 'I'm so pleased, darling. Don't worry,

I have travel toothbrushes and airline wash bags by the bucket load. All virgin – some of them, um, Virgin! And anything else you need, just ask. Now, our coffee's getting cold but,' her face assumed an expression of pretend shock because, like Thomas, she had noticed that his penis was reacting to the gentle persuasion of her nimble fingers, 'I strongly suspect I'm simply going to have to make a fresh pot in about half an hour.' She sat up, pulled off her dressing gown and tugged playfully at Thomas's underpants. 'I don't think you or I will be needing these naughty clothes for a little while.'

17

Awakening after a glorious night's sleep, Thomas found he was alone. However, the smell of fresh coffee infused with some sort of bready, doughy aroma, plus the low-level sound of jazz piano from elsewhere in the apartment, indicated that Monica was pottering about in the kitchen. He retrieved his underpants from the floor where Monica had theatrically thrown them the night before, added a shirt and ambled into the bright Boxing Day light which, to Thomas, felt like an entirely new world.

'Good morning!' beamed Monica. 'I'm an early riser and I didn't want to wake you. You looked so peaceful. I have fresh coffee and cinnamon buns. I part-make them when I have time and then freeze them for baking whenever suits. I hope that's all right. There wasn't time to make fresh ones this morning. They take about five hours usually.'

'I can't remember the last time I slept so well.' He blinked as Monica embraced him and planted a long kiss on his lips. 'Your bed is very comfortable.'

'Well, you did have a rather busy and, if I may say, deliciously active Christmas Day; a change from the usual, I'd think.' She uncoupled herself from the embrace but not before taking the opportunity to gently stroke Thomas's back. 'Take a seat and I'll bring over some breakfast. I hope you like Bill Evans. This is one of his LPs from sixty-eight, I think. Live from Montreux.'

Thomas had never heard of Bill Evans but nonetheless positioned himself at the marble table, which could seat twelve but was laid for two, and glanced to his left at another large wall clock. It was just after 9.30am on what looked like an overcast but breezeless day outside, the sky white and unthreatening. Despite the warmth of Monica's morning greeting and the undoubted mutual pleasure of the previous night, he wasn't entirely sure what was going to happen next, his uncertainty arising from simply never having been in this position before. He wondered whether to broach the subject and, on balance, decided that he ought to.

'You seduced me,' he began, tentatively, frowning in feigned confusion. 'I think. At least, that's what it felt like. And, for the avoidance of doubt, I'm glad you did. I liked it very much.'

'Okay, you caught me,' replied Monica, beaming unrepentantly. 'I seduced you. And I also liked it very much. I'm sorry for pouncing but I felt that we'd been pootling around the edges of something interesting for a while and I wasn't sure whether you were going to make the first move so I took the initiative. I'm that sort of woman.' She had positioned herself next to him at a corner of the table so that they were at right angles to each other and she could caress his left hand with her right. 'And just in case you were wondering, yes, this is something I would like to happen again, if you would be willing and interested, of course. Nobody's going to make you do anything against your will, least of all me. Perhaps not tonight but certainly in the foreseeable future.' She lifted his hand and kissed it gently. Thomas was conscious that he was still wearing his wedding ring, but it didn't seem to deter Monica.

'Okay,' hesitated Thomas. 'Yes, um, I was wondering but

that's good. And yes I would be willing and interested too. Thank you very much.' He smiled and returned Monica's hand kiss. Both of their phones buzzed simultaneously, indicating a Twelve communication.

'It's from Lexington,' said Monica, studying the text. 'He's made a last-minute decision, he says, to have a select soiree on New Year's Eve in Pimlico and everyone's invited. He says cars will be provided for those who require them both there and back. He also says he has "an announcement". It might be about retiring from The Twelve. I know he's been considering it for a while.'

Thomas tucked in to a freshly-baked cinnamon bun. 'Does that mean you would take over as senior partner, as it were?'

Monica was deep in thought as she sipped her cappuccino. 'I don't know. Maybe. Either me or Owen or maybe Catherine, although she's quite young still, but very ambitious, in a good way. Owen joined before me but he's always said he's not really that interested in Lexington's job because he never really enjoyed the admin side of things when he was at MI5. But Lexington's news could be something else entirely. He might be getting married, for all I know. Or coming out. Or getting a puppy. "Announcement" could mean pretty much anything where Lexington is concerned. It could be about the case, although if it were anything truly urgent then he would have called us together sooner.'

They finished breakfast and Thomas helped to clear and tidy everything away. Then they showered, together – Monica's idea, naturally. Thomas had never showered with anyone else before and found the experience hugely enjoyable, despite initially struggling to avoid knocking over Monica's shampoo bottle with his elbow. After getting dry, they made love again and dozed off in each other's arms, finally waking around lunchtime, at which point Thomas decided that he really had better be heading home. 'Why don't you come round to mine on New Year's Eve?' he suggested, somewhat bravely he thought, under the circumstances. 'We can spend the afternoon together and then go to Lexington's in the evening. If you're not busy, of course.'

'I think that's a splendid idea. May I bring an overnight bag?' asked Monica, wide-eyed, hopeful, questioning.

Thomas smiled. 'Of course you may. I would like that,' he nodded, 'very much.'

———

Between Boxing Day and New Year's Eve, Thomas busied himself with non-Twelve activities and was grateful not to receive any updates on the poisonings; it appeared that even serial killers wound down their activities for the festive period, although Thomas also deduced that most homeless people would be in charity shelters over the holidays owing to the scarcity of donors in London or on the tube network, and that was more likely to be the reason for the lack of murders.

He spent a quiet evening alone on the 29th going over the events of Christmas Day and Boxing Day morning. Thomas recalled another morning almost exactly six years earlier, which he had spent by Alice's side at the hospice, watching the life slowly drain out of her. It was a process that, from Boxing Day, would take three further harrowing weeks until the brutal annexation of her body was complete and at last she could rest.

Monica hadn't supplanted Alice in his mind. He was sure that would never happen, could never happen. Yet she had begun to occupy a tiny, brightly lit corner far away from the shadows. It was a sanctuary that Thomas realised he enjoyed spending time in during those quiet moments when he could allow his thoughts to drift.

The last day of the year was breezy and cold, a biting winter wind chicaning through the streets from the north east. Monica arrived at Colville Square by taxi at just after two o'clock in the afternoon. 'This is nice,' she said, entering the long hallway with its wooden floors and rich, russet walls, and greeted Thomas with a lingering kiss. 'Someone has an eye for style.'

'Most of it will have been Alice. I haven't done an enormous amount to the place since she passed.' Thomas took Monica's overnight bag, which was navy and leather and looked expensive, and then decided the subject needed to be changed. 'How have you been since last week? Anything fun going on?'

Monica found her way into the living room and settled in one of the armchairs. 'Not a huge amount. Did some more personal research on the poisonings. Went to the opera with friends. Met up with Anna and Graham for a drink on the 28th – they can't make the party tonight as they've gone skiing together. It's lovely and warm in here, by the way.'

'Are they a couple now?' asked Thomas, ever fascinated by the apparently complex relationship permutations within The Twelve.

Monica's tone was playful yet definitive. 'Good Lord, no. No, not at all. You know Graham is with Owen. And occasionally Catherine, of course. He and Anna are just good friends and both of them happen to like skiing, while nobody else can be bothered with it, not even Chris. Anyway, so I met up with them,' she bit her lip gently, hesitantly, 'and I might have possibly let slip about our little Christmas adventure. Not the beautiful details, you understand, more the general gist. I hope you don't mind. They dragged it out of me because they said I was smiling too much. They were delighted, not only because it was such a glorious story but also because it was tremendous gossip. They both love a gossip. I swore them to secrecy, but it'll probably have telegraphed its way to a few of the others by now. Owen, Chris, Belinda, I expect. You don't mind, do you? I've been slightly terrified that you might have wanted to keep us under wraps.'

Thomas wasn't overly sure what he felt. He stood in the doorway to the living room and rattled the information around his mind for a few seconds before deciding that by far the most important word that Monica had said since arriving in his house was "us". He smiled. 'Are we an "us", then?' Monica stood up, quickly assessed that his mood was one of approval and not disappointment, ventured over, wrapped her arms around his waist and kissed him.

'I've been thinking about it a lot and I very much hope, Thomas, that Christmas night wasn't a one-off. A one-night stand, as we used to say in the seventies; I've had quite enough of those, thank you very much. Obviously I don't know exactly how you felt about it but I'm sixty-nine years old and I know by now when something feels special and that,' there was a pause while she stroked the side of his face, her fingers tracing the lines that ran down his cheek, 'felt special to me. Now, I'm not saying that we shouldn't take things slowly; maybe we should, I don't know. I haven't figured that out for myself yet, although of course, as I say, I've given it some thought. I'm also not saying that we should be making long term plans because one never knows at our age. But what I *am* saying is that I enjoy your company and I sense a connection and I would like us to explore where this takes us for however long it takes us there. Does that sound as if it could be something you might find agreeable? At least for now? Sorry to rather throw this at you when I've only just arrived but it's been on my mind, and as you know, I tend to act rather impulsively at times.'

Thomas was silent for a few seconds while outside the wind picked up, whistling round the square. 'I like the idea of being an "us",' he announced finally, gently repositioning a strand of hair behind her ear. 'And I don't mind who knows it.' He kissed her forehead and gave her hand a gentle squeeze. 'Now, we have a few hours before the car arrives to take us to

Lexington's. Would you like a quick tour of the rest of the house?'

———

Lexington's home was a three-bedroom apartment on the tenth floor of a new-ish building with views over the river towards the American embassy and the shell of the old power station at Battersea that was awaiting redevelopment. Lexington opened the door wearing a tartan smoking jacket and carrying a large brandy. Behind him, Thomas estimated that around thirty people were chattering away in small groups of three and four, while some classical music that Thomas didn't recognise played quietly in the background. 'Welcome, friends!' he greeted them warmly, then lowered his voice slightly. 'Just so you know, everyone here this evening knows about The Twelve so there's no need for secrecy, although I wouldn't go blabbing too much about the current project just in case. Simone couldn't make it, sadly, because it's a busy night at the restaurant, but otherwise it's a full house. Most of them you'll know but a few you won't, like the lady in the corner and her husband.' He gestured to a small but formidable-looking woman with black, curly hair wearing a tight, magenta dress. 'She's the new London head of the CIA. I'll introduce you later. I was frankly surprised she could make it at short notice but according to her husband, who is something big-cheesy in computing apparently, she was delighted as it gave her a solid excuse to decline an invitation from the Secretary of State for Health who is a frightful bore, as you know. Suzanne is here, of course, with her husband.' They all waved at the commissioner who fluttered a hand serenely in response. 'He's a former cricketer so you should have a lot in common, Thomas. And apart from those already well known to you, the rest are mostly people who have half an eye on a role within The Twelve when they retire. Some of them haven't got a chance in hell, like him for example.'

Lexington pointed out a tall, bearded man talking animatedly to Owen, whom Thomas recognised immediately as the Foreign Secretary in the previous government. 'The Twelve doesn't really go for former career politicians, as you know. Their qualifications aren't generally up to the required standard. But it's adorable that he's interested and he's a fascinating source of Westminster tittle-tattle. Did you know the current Home Secretary has a love child and he apparently has a thing for wearing frilly knickers under his suit when he does television interviews? What an absolute scream! I won't be able to keep a straight face next time he's on *Question Time*. Anyway, let me get you a drink. What will you have? There's a rather splendid 1974 St Emilion open if that entices you? I'll fetch a couple of glasses.'

Armed with fine wine, they joined Chris who was in deep discussion with Catherine and the commissioner whose husband had been reluctantly dragged into a conversation with the ex-Foreign Secretary. Chris gave Thomas a subtle wink. 'Good Christmas?' he asked with a knowing grin.

Monica clasped Thomas's hand firmly. 'I did warn you,' she whispered. 'Sorry.'

'Outstanding, thank you, Christopher,' said Thomas, not rising to the bait. 'Santa was most generous. And you?'

'Pleasant. Probably not as active as yours,' he glanced towards Monica with a smile, 'but I can't complain. A few days doing the rounds of the various daughters. A couple of days with Anna before she went off skiing. Let's just say I kept myself busy and broadly out of trouble.'

'By way of explanation,' said Catherine, 'and so that Suzanne isn't completely in the dark, Thomas and Monica are now a couple.'

'Oh, how lovely! Congratulations!' beamed the commissioner.

PETER BERRY

'Love flourishing at Christmas time. What could be more romantic?' She gave them both a hug and raised her glass in a toast. Thomas had never been embraced by a commissioner of the Metropolitan Police before and yet he took it in good heart. He was quickly getting used to new experiences late in life. 'Now that everyone's here, I suppose Lexington will make his announcement. Do you have any idea what it might be?'

Monica sipped her wine before raising her glass to David who was waving from the direction of the balcony, where he appeared to be deep in conversation with Mrs Mendoza, resplendent in a flowing scarlet smock. 'I have an inkling, but I can't be totally sure. It's either retirement or a puppy. Those two particular horses are where my betting money would go.'

'It *could* be retirement,' said Suzanne. 'I know he's been thinking about it. That would mean a step up for someone – and also a space within The Twelve, of course.' She glanced at Monica almost unconsciously. 'It's far too early for me, I'm afraid. I still have another eight years or so behind a desk before I'm finally done with the Met, and that's if I survive that long. You never know in this job. A new mayor or a home secretary who doesn't see eye to eye with you and suddenly you're out. Consigned to the public speaking circuit for eternity, telling your career stories to groups of bored businessmen and women in glamorous places like Burnley. No offence to Burnley, of course.'

'Other vacancies will become available in time, you can be sure of that,' said Chris. 'Natural wastage and all that.' Thomas noted that Chris had positioned himself closest to the table where the canapés were plated, allowing him to snatch one every thirty seconds or so. 'Have you got any more information on this poisoner, by the way? It's been a bit of a dead end of late. Obviously things tend to slow down a bit around this time of year and I'm grateful for the chance to relax, but we'll need to speed up a bit soon. I can't help but feel we need a breakthrough.'

144

The commissioner took a deep breath. 'Well, we've done a lot more work over the last few weeks with criminal psychologists and they've drawn up a new profile but it's largely inconclusive and there's not much we didn't already suspect. Loner, psychopathic tendencies, probably an only child although not definitely, abused as a kid, in a menial job, that kind of thing. Probably gives the appearance of being very ordinary. The banality of evil, as they say. Also compulsive, so that explains why there's an order to the locations as we know, but there will almost certainly be an order to the timings too… but we haven't worked that out yet.'

'I've given that some thought over Christmas,' said Monica, 'but I've so far drawn a blank.'

'The only strange element, which is actually quite concerning,' continued the commissioner, 'is that most psychopathic murderers either like to watch their victims suffer or like to take a "trophy" from them. This one doesn't, as we've discussed before. To this chap, it's enough for him to assume that the victim has been poisoned and will die. He doesn't feel a need to see it happen because he simply doesn't care and that's very unusual.'

'A psychopath who's squeamish perhaps,' suggested Chris. 'I mean, it's unlikely but not impossible.'

'Maybe,' muttered Suzanne unconvincingly, 'but this sort of detachment is quite rare. It's almost as if he's killing not for the pleasure of killing but just as something to do. To pass the time, alleviate his boredom. A hobby, like stamp-collecting or whittling. The fact that the human mind can do that is actually scary. That might also mean that the dates don't have any pattern at all. He simply kills when he feels that enough preparation has been done.'

'That would go against the two October attacks in the same week,' said Monica. 'Unless he deliberately planned two in short succession to see if it could be done. No, I still believe there's a pattern and if we can figure out what it is then we've got a much better chance,' said Monica. 'I'll give it some more thought over the next week or so and I'll have a play with some algorithms. If there's a system, we'll uncover it eventually.'

———

It was just after eleven when Lexington finally decided to make his announcement, standing in front of his balcony doors, the lights of South West London twinkling expectantly behind him.

'Ladies and gentlemen,' he began. 'First of all, may I say that it's so wonderful to be able to host you all on this New Year's Eve and at such terribly short notice. Either my humble abode holds a strange and magnetic draw or you are all so fundamentally and profoundly unpopular that you had nowhere better to go.' A ripple of laughter passed around the room and Martin exploded a party popper accidentally. 'As you'll all know to varying degrees of detail, I have been a member of a quite fantastically secret organisation for almost eighteen years and erstwhile leader of it for five, an enormous privilege which I don't take lightly. That it remains secret is a testament to all of you, plus a handful of others who cannot be here, and I would like to take the opportunity now to formally thank you all for your trustworthiness and your frankly remarkable skills of concealment.

'As you know, I shall be eighty-two years young this coming year, July to be precise, and I can feel that I am quite definitely slowing down and that the rate of deceleration is increasing. Yes, the yoga helps but one reaches a point where one simply feels like taking more of a back seat. In addition, my knee isn't in the finest state, my prostate is being rather a beastly nuisance of late and dear old Chris,' he glanced toward the former surgeon who raised an eyebrow, 'advises me that I could well do without all the gallivanting around that this job entails. So I should like to give you all fair warning that I shall retire after the current case, whenever that may be, or on my birthday in July, whichever comes first. Naturally I hope that the case is resolved sooner rather than later but, if it does rattle on, then I shall have already handed over to my replacement who will be notified in good time.' Thomas noticed that Catherine Daniels was looking at Monica and smiling. Monica's gaze, meanwhile, was fixed on Lexington.

'In addition, there will naturally be a vacancy within The Twelve and I have little doubt that the lucky person to fill that space is currently in this room.' He cast an eye around and settled on a blonde-haired woman who was standing with Martin. Thomas recognised her as a former television newsreader who was also famous for fronting one of the many programmes about antiques which seemed to have proliferated across the schedules of late, none of which particularly interested him. 'Again, that person will be notified in the fullness of time, after all of the relevant checks have been completed. It just remains for me to thank you again for your company and your support over the last few years and, of course, this evening. Thank you for allowing an old man to annexe your New Year plans. And don't forget to ensure your glasses are filled for the chiming of the bells in just under an hour. You'll be able to hear them rather well from here.'

Chris began the round of applause, which lasted a good minute or two before Suzanne tapped her glass. 'I think we can all agree that Lexington has led The Twelve with extraordinary skill, exceptional calm and quite astonishing effectiveness. I personally have no doubt that his time as senior partner will be remembered as something of a golden age and I only have two regrets. One is that I didn't get to know him sooner. The other is that I'm currently too young to join.' Gentle, polite laughter filled the room once more.

'Your time will come, Suzanne,' smiled Lexington, jovially. 'I feel sure of it.'

'I also have no doubt that this current case, challenging though it may currently be, will be completed long before July and so we shall simply have to treasure every day we have left with you, Lexington. A toast, if you'll join me. To Lexington Smith!'

18

From one end of Lexington's balcony and by leaning out ever so slightly, it was just possible to see the Queen Elizabeth Tower at the Palace of Westminster as well as hear its famous bell. As January was heralded in and the familiar sound of inebriated revellers drifted up from the street, Thomas and Monica kissed and embraced while those around them shook hands and hugged and welcomed in the new year with the traditional smiles and warm greetings. 'I wonder what this year will bring,' mused Monica. 'Personally I have a pretty good feeling about it.' She looked into Thomas's eyes and sighed.

'I think it'll be interesting,' said Thomas. He was thinking as much about Lexington's announcement and what it might mean for Monica as he was about their own embryonic relationship. 'Some changes, of course. Good ones, mostly. Maybe *all* good ones. It's certainly started on an upward swing.' He kissed her again as the slurred, mis-sung lyrics of 'Auld Lang Syne' spluttered to a close around the streets of SW1 below, cups of kindness having been drunkenly taken in abundance.

'Hello, um, I'm sorry to butt in.' It was the former newsreader. She was slim and brown-haired with a wide smile and was wearing a lemon yellow dress with a silver necklace and matching bracelet. 'Veronica Madison. You must be Monica and Thomas. Terry has been telling me all about you.'

'Terry's here?' asked Thomas. 'I haven't seen him.'

'He's in the kitchen doing the canapés and having his own private party with a couple of Lexington's old friends from the diplomatic service – I think one of them used to be our ambassador to Japan. He's quite the gossip for a locksmith, although, thinking about it, I suppose I've never been in such a lengthy conversation with a locksmith at a New Year's Eve party before, or in fact any party. Happy New Year, by the way.'

'Isn't he just!' agreed Monica in a friendly tone. 'It's lovely to meet you, Veronica. I've seen so many of your programmes. The one with the old lady and the teddy bear made me cry. When she talked about it being the only toy she managed to rescue from a house fire during the Blitz, I was bawling.'

'Oh, me too!' shrieked Veronica. 'We had to do five retakes of that show because my mascara kept running. I spend most of the filming for that show in emotional turmoil, especially when it comes to the very old people.'

'It's lovely to meet you, Veronica. How do you know Lexington?' asked Thomas, changing the subject in an attempt to avoid revealing that he hadn't watched any of Veronica's televised output for around ten years. Since she'd given up reading the news, in fact.

Veronica explained that she knew Catherine first, after the journalist came to interview her around fifteen years previously, before she became an editor. Unusually, the interview situation led to a firm friendship with regular dinners at each other's houses. When Veronica's long-term partner died in 2018, Catherine had been a source of great comfort and, after a year, had introduced Veronica to Lexington as she knew they too would become good friends.

'I'm so sorry,' sympathised Monica. She squeezed Thomas's hand. 'About your partner. Was it sudden?'

'Short illness. She was ten years older than me. She had a bad stroke and never really recovered. Catherine helped to keep the worst of it out of the papers and for that I'm forever grateful to her. Nobody knew I was gay until then. One rather kept it under wraps until a few years ago. Even these days, in terms of telly folk, the closet remains a bit of a cramped space, if you understand my meaning… but it's getting better, thankfully. You just have to be careful on social media otherwise you come in for all sorts of abuse. Still. Anyway, when Lexington told me about The Twelve, I was most intrigued. Slightly shocked at first, I'll admit, but the more I thought about it, the more it made total sense. A group of older people, wiser people, with varying skill sets, collectively a force to be reckoned with and a force for good. I suppose I've kept the secret for about a year now. Lexington believes I'm a potential member, maybe not this year but some time.'

'Well, there's going to be a vacancy and I'm sure you'd fit right in,' said Monica. 'Oh, here comes Catherine. Your ears must have been on fire.'

The former newspaper editor sashayed across the room to join them, ostentatiously squeezing Veronica's bottom as she did. 'What do you think of our two new lovebirds, V?' she grinned. 'Sweet, aren't they?'

'Adorable,' agreed Veronica, gripping Catherine around the waist. 'We've been having a lovely chat. So tell me, what happens now in terms of a replacement for Lexington? Is there a vote or something? Are there rules? Different coloured smoke from a chimney? That much I don't know.'

'Traditionally,' explained Catherine, 'it's Lexington's decision to start with. The outgoing senior partner nominates their personal preference and, unless anyone has any alarming objections, that's that. Very straightforward. So far, in almost 200 years, nobody has had any major concerns so that's the process. A bloodless transfer of power and all very amicable. I suspect Lexington will either choose Owen or Monica, although Chris is also in with a shout despite only being a member for four years.'

'And you, Catherine.' Monica added brightly. 'You have an excellent chance with all you've achieved in a relatively short time.'

'You're very kind to say so, but in all honesty, any of us would be perfectly well-equipped. We all know the ropes by now, apart from Thomas of course, no offence. And Lexington will be around to advise from the sidelines. He won't be able to simply step away. He lives and breathes The Twelve. It's like he's back running an embassy, but with less bureaucracy and more fun.'

'Did I hear my name?' Lexington, Owen and Belinda had been within earshot and had shuffled into the widening group which now occupied a significant corner of the apartment.

'We were just talking about your retirement and subsequent coronation process,' said Catherine. 'Veronica was asking and I imagine Thomas hasn't been aware of quite how it works either.'

Lexington stretched and then winced slightly, his knee clearly grumbling at all the activity. 'It will be what it will be,' he mused, cryptically. 'And I shall take my time to come to the right decision as you would all expect. The important thing at the moment is to make a breakthrough in this terrible case. Suzanne thinks she has a half-decent photo of the chap from one of the platform cameras at Theydon Bois. He's got a cap on and his face is looking down as usual, but you get the lower half, so it might be something to work with at least. Belinda is going to take it to the East Europeans who run the begging empire on the Metropolitan Line and ask them to keep a look out. She speaks both Romanian and Bulgarian, you know.'

'Fac,' said Belinda, unassumingly.

'Pardon me?' Veronica looked mock-shocked.

'I do. In Romanian. Fac is "I do" in Romanian,' explained Belinda, to Veronica's noticeable relief. 'Romanian is similar to Latin so in the present tense it goes, Fac, Faci, Face, Facem, Faceti, Fac. Understand?'

'Not really,' said Thomas, confused. 'Anyway, I thought he was due to target the District Line next?'

'That's theoretically correct,' said Lexington. *'if* he's following a logical clockwise progression. He might not be. Suzanne and her psychoanalysts believe that we can't presume. Equally, we can't monitor all the lines at the same time, so we've decided to try to enlist help from one of the communities who operate a successful, and of course illegal, begging system on one of the lines that hasn't yet been targeted. It won't be easy to gain their trust but if we explain the danger then they may be interested. At the very least, we should be able to just ask them to keep a casual eye out and let us know if they see him. We know that each episode is carefully planned so he'll be doing many reconnaissance trips before he strikes, checking the best exits from stations, working out where the CCTV cameras are, figuring out the optimum time. We're closing in, slowly, especially as Owen thinks he may be making some progress within the dark web.'

'Oh really?' asked Monica, excitedly. 'Do tell.'

The former surveillance expert raised a hand as if to temper expectations. 'Only possibly,' he began. 'It's still early days but I managed just before Christmas to trace some purchases of poisons. They were all using stolen credit cards so the trail went a bit cold. However, there was a name, or more correctly, a pseudonym that kept reappearing in chat rooms where poisoning was being discussed – GKS14. Over the last couple of days, with Graham away skiing, I've had a bit more time to myself and so I've spent a good few hours just dipping in and out of various chat rooms and two days ago I came across GKS14 again in a group talking about mass shootings in America. His argument seemed to be that shooting was fairly inefficient because the gunman always got caught or took his own life and that you had to be more subtle if you were going to achieve a greater number of fatalities over the longer term. He rarely spends long in the chat rooms but if I can find him again then I might be able to trace the email address which created the GKS14 identity and from there possibly identify our suspect.'

'Have you told Suzanne?' asked Monica.

'Yes, about twenty minutes ago,' replied Owen. 'I've also asked whether I can use some slightly illegal cyber software to cloak my own identity for the next few weeks. If I'm tracking him then there's a good chance that he'll begin to do the same to me and that could scare him off. Suzanne is happy for me to do whatever is necessary to get a breakthrough, which is refreshing. It sounds like GKS14 is our man, or at least is connected to our man. Whether those are his initials, I would doubt… but the pseudonym is almost certainly relevant. This isn't over. He's planning. Or hunting.'

19

A week after the party at Lexington's, as the fifth anniversary of Alice's death began to loom, Thomas, as usual, became more introspective. This year, however, the geometry of his feelings felt different, somehow less sharp-edged, and he was in no doubt that Monica was the benign catalyst. They had spent New Year's Day together and he had also enjoyed a wonderful couple of nights in St John's Wood during the early days of the infant year. She had noticed his mood shift incrementally and, understanding why, asked whether he would like her to stay with him on the night of the 12th so that they could wake up together on the 13th.

Thomas had had to consider this invitation very deeply, anxious that perhaps it was too soon or that he was in some way tarnishing Alice's memory. Ultimately, however, he remembered what she had told him, quite firmly in fact, during one of the darker days they spent together at the hospice; Alice didn't expect or want him to "mope about" and she was very firm that if he could ever be happy again with someone new then he should absolutely grasp that opportunity if and when it came, so long as he didn't forget her. Thomas, lovingly caressing her weakened fingers, had promised that he never would.

So it was decided.

They climbed into bed around eleven. Despite the hour, neither of them was especially tired so they lay in silence, simply enjoying the warmth of each other's bodies. Monica kissed him, softly. She knew his mind was elsewhere, as hers was every September 11th. 'Tell me more about Alice. What did she most enjoy doing?'

Thomas was lying on his back, staring at the ceiling. 'Probably motherhood, I would say. She just loved being with the kids more than anything. She would have had more than just the two if money and space had allowed. She was always trying to figure out ways to make their lives better. Trips out. Adventures. We were forever going to museums and galleries and places like that, educating them by stealth. Even when it was cold and raining outside and they didn't want to leave the house, there would always be some sort of indoor adventure to embark upon. Alice was highly inventive when it came to keeping them active. It's a good job they didn't have mobile phones in those days. She probably would have banned them from the house.'

'She sounds wonderful,' said Monica, snuggling closer and relieved that her strategic gamble of getting Thomas to talk about Alice on this particular night appeared to be making him happier rather than sending him into a downward spiral. 'Tell me more. What would she be doing if everyone was stuck in the house on a rainy January day?''

Thomas smiled, searching out the memories, winkling them from the recesses. He was glad the two of them were clothed. He didn't want to feel aroused when talking about Alice, not that Monica was doing anything to suggest that she wanted anything other than his warmth. 'She was always coming up with games but with an educational aspect to them. I suppose that's why the kids both ended up at university and in good jobs; one of the reasons anyway. One of her favourites,' he chuckled at the recollection, 'particularly if it was an all-day rainy day, was that you could choose a letter of the alphabet in the morning and then you'd have to go and research an animal and a plant and a country that began with that letter. We had plenty of books and encyclopaedias and things in those days. Then over dinner you had to tell the family what you'd learned. That way, we all developed our knowledge. I could tell you everything you need to know about tapirs.'

Monica smiled and hugged him tighter.

'And another favourite Alice trick was that she used to research famous people whose birthdays were the same as the kids' and they had to guess their ages. So, for example, Emily's birthday is May 4th which is also Audrey Hepburn's birthday and Graham Swift's birthday. They used to guess their ages and then go and research the lives of those people, so that too was a learning game, as well as a bit of fun. This was before the internet so they had to go to the library or root around in the book shelves. I remember one day, they happened to be showing *Roman Holiday* on the television so we all watched that and Emily was so excited because Audrey shared her birthday. She loved that movie. She probably still does. I'll have to ask her.'

Thomas felt Monica smile into his chest as he welcomed the forgotten memories now cascading back. 'Oh yes, and one day, this will make you laugh, my son Simon came home from school and he was in such a state because they'd been doing a project on the Second World War and the lead-up to the outbreak – this must have been when he was about ten or eleven – and he'd found out that his mum shared her birthday with Joseph Goebbels, Hitler's propaganda chap. He was so sad when he told Alice, but she said it was okay and that sharing a birthday didn't mean there was any similarity between them. She had to take them to a cafe for tea and cake to take Simon's mind off it.'

Thomas suddenly noticed that the tightness of Monica's cuddle had loosened considerably. 'What's the matter? Are you okay? Have I upset you?'

Monica sat up rigid in bed, deep in thought, before reaching for her phone. 'I'm fine,' she said, concentrating hard. 'I just need to…' She tapped away for a couple of minutes as Thomas waited. He hoped that all this talk of Alice hadn't somehow made Monica feel uncomfortable or even angry, but decided that was unlikely. He'd never seen Monica in a bad mood, and she didn't seem to be in one now, so clearly something else that had distracted her. *Perhaps she'd forgotten to do something earlier and talk of tapirs had somehow reminded her.*

Finally, Monica collapsed back onto the pillow with a broad grin. 'Alice,' she announced, 'brilliant woman that she was, has solved the puzzle with the dates. The dates of the poisonings. They all fit with the birthdays of prominent Nazis. The first victim Daniel was June 13th, which is the birthday of Anton Drexler. The next one when Sean died was October 7th, which is Heinrich Himmler's birthday. Then October 25th for Nabil, and that Gary bloke which is Klaus Barbie and finally the 29th, the day that Lenny and Pongo were poisoned, which is Joseph Goebbels' birthday. As well as Alice's, of course. Sorry about that.' She stroked Thomas's face delicately. 'Anyway, it can't be a coincidence, so it's got to be the link. That's how he's choosing the dates and that's how we catch him.' Monica's tension had given way to intense excitement. 'I've been trying to figure it out scientifically or mathematically when I should have been thinking historically. I've had those dates in my head for so long that I know them off by heart. I should have realised sooner.'

Thomas, who had begun to feel sleepy during his reminiscence, was now fully awake. 'So is there a likely date for the next one? We can work out how long we've got to make a plan.'

Monica did further furious tapping. 'Okay, obviously it depends on which particular high-profile Nazis our suspect considers worthy of his specific attention but,' she placed her hand on her temple as if in pain, 'shit. It's Herman Goring's birthday on the twelfth of January, today. I'd expect any self-respecting right-wing fanatic to want to mark that date. So if we're right,' she looked at her watch and her excitement evaporated almost as quickly as it had arrived, 'then the next victim is already dead.'

20

'Good evening, Monica. I trust you are well?' Lexington didn't sound remotely infuriated. He never did. *His calm and analytical mind would be missed when he retired,* thought Monica. In that moment, sitting cross-legged in the pale, corner armchair of Thomas's bedroom, she pondered whether she might be able to persuade him to somehow reconsider his decision, although deep down she knew his choice was the correct one.

'Lexington. Sorry to call so late but we think,' she hesitated. 'Sorry, I think.' She hesitated again, catching herself and remembering that Lexington knew that she and Thomas were a couple and were likely to be together. 'Sorry. I'll start again. *We* think that we've worked out the pattern for the dates of the poisonings and, if we're right, the latest one has happened earlier this evening. We believe the poisoner is commemorating the birthdays of leading figures in the Nazi movement in 1930s Germany. The first one in June was the birthday of Drexler, then in October there was Himmler, Barbie and Goebbels. Today was the birthday of Herman Goring. The targets are all people a far-right extremist would probably consider unworthy of living and so deserving, in his warped mind, of being exterminated. That's why the homeless are being targeted.'

Lexington was silent for a moment while he calculated whether it was worth calling Martin to see if he could get down to the District Line sharpish to attempt to locate anything of interest, but, on reflection, decided that the odds of one man finding another in such a vast arena of possibilities made the thought easy to dismiss. 'This is splendid news. Obviously not for the victim, whomever he or she may be, but it gives us more of an opportunity, I hope, to prevent any further incidents. I shall call Suzanne immediately and we shall doubtless all reconvene for another look at our strategy. Thank you, Monica. You were right to call. Now, I assume Thomas is with you. Do please pass on my condolences for the anniversary of his wife's passing. I suggest we all get some sleep. Goodnight.'

Monica uncrossed her legs, stretched them and got back into bed where Thomas had been waiting. 'He's very happy,' she relayed. 'He's going to talk to Suzanne now and convene a meeting to decide next steps. He thinks it's a significant breakthrough. He sends condolences for tomorrow's anniversary, by the way.'

Thomas put his arm around her shoulder and pulled her close. The thought of someone being brutally poisoned that night had somewhat changed the atmosphere in the house. 'I'm not sure I'll be able to sleep for a while,' said Thomas. 'Do you want to listen to the radio or something?'

Monica snuggled tighter to him. 'Yes, I'd like that. I'd just like to lay here with you. We don't need to talk. I'm sorry for jumping away from you earlier. I was just so excited and so proud of us, of you, for making this breakthrough. And we should also thank Alice. She's part of this team too, by association.'

Thomas turned on the digital radio next to the bed. The volume was already low but they could both make out the delicate undertones of a culture review show discussing current and upcoming films. 'We should go and see a film,' whispered Monica after a while, her eyes closed. 'Can I take you?'

'Why don't I take you? I'll find something we can both enjoy.'

'Good plan.'

It was during the next programme, a documentary about the history of Lent, that Thomas became aware that Monica's breathing had shifted into the slow, rhythmic pulse of early sleep. Because of her position on his chest, he was unable to turn off the radio and so it was well past the Shipping Forecast before he finally dropped off himself, only to be woken a matter of hours later by a newer, marginally adapted Shipping Forecast as the low around Southeast Iceland and Faroes had deepened overnight and was now threatening Hebrides with severe gales as opposed to the more serene variety. Monica had rotated so that she was now facing away from him but was still sleeping peacefully. He took the opportunity to turn the radio off and then turned back to Monica to study her right shoulder, slightly exposed from the twin sheaths of both nightdress and duvet and visible in the dim glow of one of the streetlamps in the square. It was a very attractive shoulder, he decided. The yoga and general fitness had served Monica well.

Thomas considered the last three weeks and how different he felt now, both emotionally and physically. He felt more confident; that was Monica's doing. He felt more energised; that too was Monica's doing. It had been a long time since he'd experienced anything quite like this, and of course he could be mistaken, but, could it be the beginnings of love? At his age? Thomas had forgotten precisely how this feeling manifested itself, it had been so long, but some distant memory suggested that it might just be what he suspected. Or, on the other hand, he might be mistaken, his memory playing tricks.

He kissed the shoulder gently, like a small bird settling on snow. Monica didn't stir. It wasn't quite 5.30am and yet Thomas was wide awake. Alice battled her way into his mind, infiltrating the cracks. She was happy for him. 'You deserve this', she was saying. Did he really, though? Coruscating self-doubt was making its uncomfortable, occasional early morning presence felt, not as a flood as sometimes, but as an annoying trickle like a tap left half-on in a remote unreachable corner of the house. Thomas didn't know what to do about it, so he lay back on the pillow, closed his eyes and attempted to use a yoga technique to calm his mind. Before long, he too was asleep once again.

Monica woke around 8am and checked her phone. *Nothing from Lexington yet.* She nuzzled into Thomas's body and felt his warmth which made her smile as he began to stir. He opened his eyes sleepily and immediately met hers. 'Good morning,' she beamed. 'I have to admit that I do rather enjoy seeing your face first thing. I could quite easily get used to it.'

He kissed her cheek and looked deep into her eyes where Monica's pupils were expanding subtly. Again, the thought barged its way in. *Was it love?* Maybe he was just being a sentimental old fool on the anniversary of his wife's death. He decided it was too early. If this feeling was going to develop then it would do so in its own time. Sooner or later. Neither of them was likely to be going anywhere soon.

They showered separately and took their time getting dressed. Thomas was aware that this was the first time they had spent together since Christmas when they hadn't made love, but it didn't seem to be a problem. They were both simply being respectful. At just before ten, they left the house and headed to a small cafe on Westbourne Park Road for breakfast, avoiding the Wednesday morning rush of torrid commuters ebbing tidally toward the Central Line for their jobs in the West End and the City.

They had just sat down to coffee and toast when Lexington texted the group and they both sat in silence as they digested its contents. As predicted, there had been a person poisoned on the Underground system the night before. Less predictably, the victim had been neither homeless and nor had the murderer used the District Line as anticipated. Instead, the commemoration of Herman Goring's date of birth had taken place on the Jubilee Line at Canons Park station, and had involved an inebriated football fan named Mark Root, who had been reported missing by his frantic mother when he hadn't returned home from a Tuesday night cup replay match at Wembley. According to the Met's early information, Root's friends had described him as "cheerful and a bit tipsy" when they put him on the northbound train at Wembley Park just after 9.30pm. Sadly he was pale and a bit dead by the time the station staff found him slumped in a seat on a train at Stanmore less than an hour later. CCTV at the previous station, Canons Park, had shown the poisoner, in trademark cap and a scarf to obscure even more of his face, disembarking the train, exiting the station quickly and disappearing into the residential streets where there would be no cameras to track him. Toxicology reports were yet to come in but would have been finalised by Friday and so a meeting had been called for 3pm that day. Suzanne would attend to give a full briefing and so would Dennis Burrows. The meeting location would be communicated within hours.

Monica finished reading the message and placed her phone on the table in front of her. 'A different sort of target,' she noted. 'I wonder why.'

'My guess,' began Thomas, 'and it is only a guess at this stage, would be simple opportunism. He's a psychopath so maybe he just doesn't like people who drink alcohol. Or Spurs fans. They have a big Jewish following so maybe it has something to do with that. And maybe this Root chap felt he needed something to soak up the alcohol before he got home and jumped at the chance of a free sandwich.'

Monica was thinking. 'And why go anti-clockwise? Back to the Jubilee Line. It was meant to be somewhere out east. That's where the surveillance was taking place. That's the way the pattern was going. It feels like we've gone forward a square and then back a square.'

'Again, I'm surmising from the little information we have,' said Thomas, 'but maybe he's worried that the police, or whoever, are getting close to catching him. Possibly he noticed that someone, Owen to be precise, was watching him in the dark web. Maybe he's now picking lines at random and the first few just happened to be in an order. He's had to sacrifice his system to avoid being captured so he can somehow complete whatever appalling mission he believes he's on.'

'Yes, I think that's plausible, but I suppose we should keep our minds open.' Monica sipped her latte and Thomas was struck, for the second time that morning, by how lovely she looked doing something completely mundane like drinking coffee. She reached out a hand. 'You know, I appreciate it sounds a little forward, but I'd rather be with you than without you at the moment, if you know what I mean. There's something in the back of my mind that tells me this poisoning case could be more dangerous than some of our previous cases and I suppose that's why I want you close, Thomas. Am I making any sense?'

Thomas stroked her fingers, wondering fleetingly whether this was the right time to unveil the L word, but he decided again to hold back. 'I understand completely,' he smiled. 'Would you like me to pack a bag for a few days and come to St John's Wood tomorrow and stay for a bit?' Monica's eyes sparkled and she leaned forward to kiss him.

'Yes please,' she smiled, 'if that's okay with you?'

'Bless. Young love!' said the cafe owner from behind the counter, causing Thomas to blush.

They were walking on Hampstead Heath, arm in arm on the Thursday afternoon, both invigorated by the morning's first yoga session of the year. Thomas decided to broach the subject as they sat for a rest on one of the wooden benches near the mixed bathing pond. The weather had turned colder and windier and both were wrapped in coats, gloves and scarves to suit the season.

'When did you decide that you liked me?' As soon as the words were out, he felt like an awkward teenager as opposed to a man in his late sixties, but Monica appeared genuinely enthused by the question.

'Let's see,' she thought for a moment and looked out over the expanse of the city, the taller buildings occasionally glinting as sunlight appeared from between the fast-moving clouds. 'Almost immediately, to be honest. There was an instant physical attraction, for me at least, but I thought that jumping on you immediately might be out of order and besides, that foursome business with Owen and Graham and Catherine was still in the back of my mind. So, I decided in that moment that I needed to take my time and not suddenly jump into anything, but by pairing with you on the surveillance trips I could get to know you. I invited you into my home a couple of times after surveillance but you always politely refused so I took that to mean either that you weren't interested in me or simply that you were focused on your first case and didn't want any distractions. Inviting you for Christmas was more or less my last throw of the dice. If you'd said no, I would have probably assumed that was that and we were just going to be firm friends and nothing more. As it turns out, we've become *amitié amoureuse*.'

'Which means? Sorry, I was never brilliant at languages.'

Monica squeezed his gloved hand. 'It's a French term, which means friends who also love each other in a romantic way. And it's what we've become very quickly. That and the astonishing sex, of course.'

'Does that mean you love me then?'

Monica was about to speak when both of their phones pinged with the WhatsApp message about the meeting the following day. It was to be at the Clarges Mews base in Mayfair, a place Thomas had never visited. 'Don't worry,' assured Monica. 'We'll go together from my place. It's a nice location. You'll like it. Nothing to write home about from the outside but glorious once you're in. And we can go to Fortnum's or somewhere for tea afterwards if you like. I'll buy.' She pulled her coat tighter around herself. 'However, that's tomorrow. Right now I think we need to get indoors and find an activity to warm us both up. My poor cheeks are starting to freeze up in this wind.'

Thomas was wondering about his earlier question but, as usual, Monica was way ahead of him. 'And I hadn't forgotten,' she said with a grin. 'Yes, I do love you.'

'I love you too,' replied Thomas as they walked briskly in the direction of St John's Wood. He hadn't said those words in a romantic sense for over six years, the last time as Alice was taking her final breath.

21

Anyone accidentally happening upon Clarges Mews would find a small and unprepossessing alleyway secreted away in a venomous corner of the expensive yet styleless neighbourhood of Mayfair. Here, taciturn, high-class escorts of various nationalities rubbed shoulders, and more, with loud, burly and besuited men, themselves with little more to do than to move dirty money around the globe using transactions into which no one with an ounce of sense would consciously delve. At the end of the mews was an inconspicuous grey door, seemingly leading to nowhere but an equally inconspicuous grey building but which is, in fact, one of the first meeting places purchased by The Twelve in 1857, following an inheritance bequeathed by widower, former sea captain and Twelve member, Jack Green, whose only son had been lost in action in the Crimean War, and renovated after bomb damage during another less localised war over eighty years later.

Beyond the grey door, accessed using the triple-lock system developed and favoured by Terry to prevent the high-class escorts from accidentally finding their way inside in the event that the pressing need arose, was a soundproofed corridor leading to a very large, windowless but well-lit meeting room, stocked with the latest presentation technology, comfortable suede chairs of various colours and – at Lexington's request – a fully equipped drinks cabinet. Fine art hung on every wall and now that Thomas had been made aware that The Twelve was in possession of a pretty decent collection, he recognised some of the pieces as being most likely the work of great artists, although his knowledge of art sadly didn't allow him to decipher which. He was reasonably sure there was something by John Constable, but only because he could just make out the signature.

Unusually for Twelve meeting rooms, this one had an oak table, hewn from one very large and very ancient tree, around which up to twenty people could sit, with a screen at one end and the various paraphernalia for transmitting pictures at the other. Suzanne was manning the audio-visual equipment and was outlining the latest position on the poisonings to the group which, as expected, also included Dennis Burrows, already tucking into the cheap, supermarket own-brand biscuits Lexington had brought along since Terry had been otherwise occupied on family matters and couldn't easily do any baking.

'This is Mark Root,' stated Suzanne, tapping a keyboard. The photograph which appeared on the screen was of a smiling young man, possibly on holiday and probably without sunscreen judging by his bright pink face, garish shorts and white T-shirt with the letters COYS in blue across the front. He had dark brown hair and a rather rat-like appearance, which didn't endear him particularly to Thomas or indeed to anyone else around the table. 'Twenty-four years old. Unemployed. He lived with his mother and four sisters in Hatch End. He was an avid Tottenham Hotspur fan and had a criminal record for GBH – he got into a fight with some other football fans three years ago and was sentenced to six months on remand. He's behaved himself ever since although, according to his mum, he enjoys "banter" and getting into "scrapes". Her words, not mine. My words would be "irritating" and "hooligan", but that's between these walls only. Incidentally, we managed to tidy him up before formal identification so his friends and family believe he simply had a heart attack. Luckily, or unluckily depending on which way you look at it, he had a diagnosed heart condition.

'One of the more interesting things about this one, over and above that fact that Mark wasn't homeless, is the toxicology report. It appears that Mark was poisoned using a substance called batrachotoxin, which I suspect may be as unfamiliar to most of you as it was to me, but not to all of you.'

Anna Hopley took in an audible breath and glanced at Monica, who returned the pathologist's look of surprise. 'Unsurprisingly, I see I was right,' continued the commissioner, wearily.

'Now where on earth could he have got that?' asked Monica, more to herself than to anyone in particular, but audible to all.

'Is it rare?' asked Catherine. 'I've certainly never heard of it.'

'It's not especially rare,' explained Monica, 'provided you happen to live deep in the Amazon rainforest and have access to a steady supply of Golden Dart Frogs. In north London, on the other hand, it would certainly be one of the more challenging substances to track down unless you've got a very clever chemist friend to create a synthetic version of it for you. It's one of the most poisonous toxins on the planet. The indigenous tribes in remote areas of the rainforest harvest it from the frogs and use it to put on the ends of their spears and arrows because it'll kill pretty much anything in seconds and you only need a tiny amount.'

'It's not a very big frog,' added Anna, helpfully. 'But it is brightly coloured. Not that that necessarily helps on this occasion.'

'So we're looking for an Arsenal fan who's into poisonous

frogs,' suggested Martin, darkly. 'Shouldn't be hard to track down.'

The commissioner frowned, her concern clear. 'We currently have no idea how, let alone why, anyone would get such a substance into the UK without considerable difficulty. However, this is what it did to the unfortunate Mark.' She clicked forward onto the next photo. The smiling young man was replaced by an image of what looked like a statue in a particularly painful state of contortion, the arms and hands rigid and at angles and the face etched with unendurable agony. Belinda looked away and covered her face.

'How does the poison do that?' asked David, mildly horrified.

'Nerve cells are very sensitive, fragile things,' said Anna, gently. 'This particular poison stops them from allowing the muscles to relax and basically everything goes into a state of being extremely clenched, as you can see. Relatively harmless if you're, say, a finger muscle. Somewhat devastating if you're a heart muscle. Everything basically shuts down. It would have been horrifically painful for Mark for about five minutes. Hopefully less, for his sake.'

'Another interesting element to Mark's death, of course,' continued Suzanne, 'is the location, which is not what we were expecting. We anticipated east on the District Line because that was the pattern we believed was being followed before Christmas. But the pattern has now changed so we can't be completely certain yet where the next attack will take place.'

Lexington was leaning back in his chair, ingesting the new information. 'We do, at least, have a reasonable idea of *when* the next attack might occur, though, thanks to a bit of ingenuity from Monica and Thomas.' He looked at the couple approvingly. 'The middle week of March will be of particular importance to our killer if our recent calculations are correct. The Tuesday of that week sees the birthday of Josef Mengele, which I doubt will be allowed to pass uncelebrated, although, as it is Mengele, I shudder to think precisely *how* it might be marked. Then on the Friday of the same week, we have a double opportunity for *kuchen und ballons* as both Albert Speer and Adolf Eichmann get to blow out the authoritarian candles. The big birthday after that, as I'm sure we are well aware, is April 20th. I believe it is imperative that we stop our man long before we get to that inauspicious date as there seems little doubt that he will already be planning something very big and something very ghastly.'

'On that note,' began Owen, softly, 'I've worked out that GKS14 almost certainly signifies Gertrud Kolmar Strasse 14 which, as many of you will know, is the location of Hitler's bunker in Berlin... so it looks like we do have a very clever, very fanatical individual who will be working towards late April as his *pièce de résistance*. I've started to notice him more regularly in one particular chat room more than any other. He seems to feel more comfortable there. At the moment, I only dip in and out as I don't want to arouse suspicion but with any luck, and if I'm careful, I should be able to have a name for you within a couple of weeks unless he goes to ground completely in advance of these March dates.'

'That would be incredible if you can, Owen,' added Suzanne. 'In the meantime, I think it is fairly safe to assume that either the District or the Metropolitan Line will be next as they've not yet been targets, and that we shall need as much surveillance as possible on both lines. We may also need to work with the homeless community – as subtly as possible, of course – to obtain their help as amateur eyes and ears on the ground.'

'I already intend to talk to the East Europeans on the Metropolitan,' said Belinda. 'Lexington and I talked about it at New Year. They're generally quite insular but if they believe they're in genuine personal danger then I'm pretty sure they'll cooperate. I'll have to be more open with them than I was hoping to be, but I think it's necessary. I'll take the photograph from Theydon Bois, although it's not the best.'

Monica had also been thinking. 'It's entirely possible, if there are two dates in the same week to commemorate, that he'll be doing reconnaissance on both lines over the next few weeks. He won't want to mess this big week up. We should have a far better chance of catching him than we have had up to this point.'

'Very true,' said Lexington, casually eyeing the drinks cabinet from a distance, 'but we also have to come up with two separate plans to ultimately deal with the problem and there may not be much time to finesse them. I suggest that you and Thomas work on a Metropolitan plan with Terry, Chris, Martin and Belinda. The rest of us will develop a strategy for catching our man on the District. We'll share these plans by the end of February so that everyone knows what's what. Is everyone happy with that? Dennis, you're unusually silent.' He lifted an eyebrow suspiciously at the rotund official who was sitting in the darkest corner of the room away from the main conversation. 'I do apologise if my shop-bought biscuits are not up to scratch. They are M&S.'

'Perfectly acceptable, Lexington,' said Burrows, nonchalantly, his thoughts clearly elsewhere. 'And an excellent plan. You know where I am if you need me.'

'I'm getting the feeling that Dennis isn't really that interested in major and horrific crimes committed on his patch. I have to say that I find that a little strange.' The meeting had drawn to a close. Monica and Thomas had decided against a trip to Fortnum & Mason and instead decanted to a quiet cafe in Shepherd's Market with Catherine, Chris and Lexington.

'He's always been a bit odd,' said Catherine, skimming froth off a latte with a teaspoon. 'I remember when he was appointed, there was surprise in the police force and surprise in the media too. Unlike Suzanne, he appeared to have minimal people skills, which you'd think would be fairly key for a person in his position. We did a bit of a background check on him when I was at the newspaper to see if there was anything dodgy but there was nothing really to speak of. Wife is a bit of a religious nut who does a lot of charity work, but nothing too drastic. There's a stepson who's off travelling the world or something and a stepdaughter who works for a local council in Surrey somewhere as far as I can remember, although it was a while ago so she may have moved.'

'I like that room in the mews,' announced Thomas, distractedly. 'Is all the art genuine?'

'It is,' confirmed Lexington. 'As well as the John Constable, there are a couple of Vermeers, a Gabriel Metsu and a Jan Steen from his late period, so around 1675 I think. It's a bit of a Dutch treasure trove, to be honest, but don't tell the Dutch or they'll be banging on the door before you can say "little mouse with clogs on"! I'm not sure why, as the paintings were in position long before I was; since the fifties, I believe. Somebody smuggled them out of the Low Countries at the start of the war and they ended up here.'

He lowered his voice to a whisper as everyone eased into the centre of the table to capture every word, Thomas and Chris both leaning their jowls on their knuckles in readiness for a juicy tale. 'As you'll know, there are twenty different bases for our little organisation all over this fine city. They are, of course, largely unknown to most outsiders – even people like Suzanne only know about a handful. Now, apart from the one in Beckton, which is a bit of an exceptional case in many ways not least because the home contents insurance in that area would be extortionate, they all contain works of art, sculptures, antique furniture, bits and pieces of value that your comrades over the years have acquired in one way or another.

'In the seventies, an enterprising old chap named Alan Dunbar, who used to work for Lloyd's before retiring and joining The Twelve, did a rough audit of everything and worked out that if The Twelve were a country, it would have slightly more wealth than Wales. Not GDP, you understand, but ready cash and assets. It's not bad for a gang of oldies.'

Chris leaned back in his chair and considered ordering one of the tartes Tatin which were calling to him from the cafe counter. 'So, we have a few weeks until March,' he announced, clawing the conversation back to business. 'We're into a planning phase at long last. I'll accompany Belinda to make contact with the East Europeans and we'll let you know what they say. We'll do that this week.'

'Do you need help?' asked Thomas. 'Monica and I are available and willing.'

'No, don't worry,' reassured Chris. 'We'll be okay. I think the fewer of us that confront the East Europeans initially, the better. It might take a little while to win their trust as they're not used to people engaging with them. It's more usual for them to be ignored or abused, as I understand it. They'll be suspicious of us, just as many of the commuters are suspicious of them. It's the default human condition, I'm afraid, to be wary of strangers.' He paused for a moment and got up from his seat. 'It's no good,' he announced. 'There's a big slice of tarte Tatin that has my name on it.'

22

As they had anticipated, it took Chris and Belinda a few days to connect in any useful way with their targets. While travelling back and forth on trains between Watford at the most northerly point on the line and Wembley Park halfway down towards the city, the usual parameters of the East Europeans' dominion, they encountered someone from the Slavic community on almost every journey. In each case, a different dark-haired woman would either place cheap packs of tissues on the seats next to them in the hope of meagre payment or, in some cases, simply beg for change apparently without the sufficient grasp of English to get beyond the most rudimentary pleas for help.

The women were all thin and fairly young, and possessed of the same drawn, haunted look. Each of them gazed in bemusement at Belinda, even when she addressed them in a familiar language which, by a brief process of trial and error, turned out to be Bulgarian with what seemed to be a strong regional accent. It was clear that these women were at the very bottom of the food chain when it came to decision-making, but both Chris and Belinda felt certain that at some point, news of the two strange old British people, one of whom spoke "posh" Bulgarian, would filter upwards.

After five days of journeys, during which they had begun to receive the occasional wary but encouraging smile from a couple of the women, a breakthrough. It came on a cold, bright morning just outside Northwick Park station as they travelled south towards the metropolis, winter sunlight gleaming off the stadium at Wembley to the west where Mark Root had unknowingly spent his final evening. Belinda and Chris were facing the front of the train in a seating pattern which catered for four when they became aware that one of the friendlier women had, for the first time, placed herself opposite them alongside an imposing figure they had never seen before.

'My name is Nikola. I understand you have been trying to contact us. How can I help you?' The voice was deep and rhythmic and belonged to a tall, muscular man with dark hair and piercing green eyes bordered on two sides by thick, black eyebrows. He was wearing jeans and a tight leather jacket and Chris couldn't help noting that although he was smiling at them – most teeth white, one incisor gold – he did not offer his hand. 'I can speak in English,' he addressed Belinda with a heavy accent, 'because I hear that your friend may not speak Bulgarian but if you prefer to change, then please just let me know. If you are in danger, for example.' This last line was delivered in Bulgarian. The gold tooth glinted in the winter sun, shining low over the suburban rooftops to the east, as Nikola eyed Chris with suspicion.

Belinda reached out a hand. Nikola studied it cautiously for a few seconds and tilted his head, watching the linguist with a mixture of fascination and wariness. She slowly withdrew. 'Don't worry. Chris is a friend. But thank you for your concern. Is there somewhere we can talk more privately?' she began, conscious of the fact that although it was mid-morning, the carriage was still reasonably full and with the knowledge gleaned over the previous days, it would become busier when they stopped at Wembley Park. 'It is rather important. It affects the safety of your community.' She looked over at the young woman who remained stony-faced, perhaps not fully understanding the discourse.

'My community can look after itself, thank you.' Nikola smiled defiantly, stretching his broad shoulders. 'We have been a travelling people for many centuries. We fight to survive wherever we go. We fight for food, we fight for home, we fight for survival. We always win. With respect, British people do not need to be concerned about the safety of my community. Particularly old British people.' He stared once more at Chris who was beginning to feel uneasy.

'That may be so and I have no reason to doubt you,' agreed Belinda, aware that this was a delicate piece of international diplomacy but one which badly needed to work sooner rather than later, 'but there is a new danger on these trains which has already killed six innocent victims and one of your friends may be next.' Her voice was now no more than a whisper and she leaned toward Nikola so that the other passengers wouldn't hear, staring deep into his eyes as she did so. 'Your people cannot fight it alone. My name is Belinda. This is Chris, as you know. We aren't travelling on this line for fun. We want to help protect you. I beg you to please trust us.'

Nikola paused briefly while he contemplated the conversation, then looked at the woman sitting next to him, leaned over and whispered some words of Bulgarian with a strong dialect, although Belinda managed to make out the words for "danger" and "trust". The woman whispered back, glancing cautiously between Belinda and Chris, but Belinda couldn't clearly make out anything that she said. Finally, Nikola straightened up. 'We leave at Wembley Park in two minutes. We have coffee together. It will be quiet so we can talk.'

At Wembley Park station, the overwhelming majority of departing passengers tended either to veer right towards the famous arena for music concerts and conferences, or troop under a tunnel towards the glowing arc of the iconic stadium. Belinda, Chris, Nikola and the woman turned left and soon found themselves in a less celebrated area of North West London that was littered with payday loan premises and betting shops. 'We go here,' said Nikola, stopping by an independent cafe that seemed to be called Ratko's although the font in which its name had been written made the letters unclear. There was only one other customer; an elderly man nursing a strong coffee at a corner table near the counter where he was hunched over a foreign newspaper, which Belinda noted was Turkish. He peered over his newspaper at the new arrivals for a split second before returning, unconcerned, to his reading.

Nikola ordered four coffees and they sat at one of the yellow Formica tables in the window, as far away from the old man as possible. 'This is Mirela,' he said. The woman nodded and smiled but remained silent. 'Her English is not so good but she understands more than she speaks and she is strong. She will fight. She has fought me before and I do not wish for it to happen again. She – what's the term you use? – kicked my butt. Literally. I had bruise for days.' He complimented Mirela in her native language and she giggled, her plain face brightening. 'Now, tell me more of this "danger".'

'What we're about to tell you, Nikola, must remain completely secret,' Belinda began. 'Of course you must do all you can to protect your community, but equally it is very important that knowledge of what is happening is restricted to as few people as possible. When we tell you, you will understand why.'

Nikola sniffed casually and took a slurp of his coffee. 'I understand. Please. Carry on.'

Belinda lowered her voice further. The Turkish newspaper rustled in the corner. 'There is a murderer operating on the London Underground system and he is deliberately targeting the homeless and begging communities with some of the nastiest and most effective poisons on the planet. He laces sandwiches and bread rolls with the poison and gives them to desperate, hungry people late in the evening when the tubes are quiet and there are few – if any – witnesses. He's killed six so far, on different lines, and we believe the Metropolitan Line may be next, which means that your people, like Mirela, are in terrible danger.'

'Mirela does not work evenings.' Nikola shrugged.

'But someone does,' whispered Belinda. 'We've seen them. We know your community works in shifts. Morning until around 2pm and then a break, and then different people in the late afternoon into the evening. That's to get more money and also to trick people into thinking the beggars are different when in fact you're all part of a team. We know that.'

'You are police?' Suddenly Nikola's face was etched with concern and at the sound of the word, Mirela started scouring the street outside the window with agitation, like a cat ready to bare its claws.

'Do we look like police, Nikola?' asked Chris gently. 'No, we're not. And you won't get bothered by the police either, I promise. We simply want your help to catch this killer.' He took a sip of coffee, its bitterness making him wince. Mirela noticeably relaxed.

'Who are you then?' Nikola's tone was warmer but still with an undercurrent of deep suspicion.

Belinda made the snap decision that, as Nikola seemed to be more receptive to her than to Chris, she would wrestle back the initiative. 'Nikola, put very simply, we're a small group of retired people who help to keep danger off the streets.' She smiled, hoping to look as though she was pleased with herself for completing a triple word score in Scrabble.

'Like Neighbourhood Watch!' he beamed, excitedly.

'Yes. If you like.' Belinda was enjoying the burgeoning sense of international camaraderie which was gradually developing across the small table and was also somewhat relieved that it looked like she wasn't going to have to reveal much more about The Twelve's secrets. 'Admittedly with a more direct approach to crime-fighting but I can see the similarities.'

'Good!' exclaimed the Bulgarian. 'I like Neighbourhood Watch. Where I live, near Harrow, they keep the troublemakers away.' Chris and Belinda shared a look that suggested the irony of this statement wasn't lost on either of them, but Nikola chose to ignore it. 'What would you like us to do?'

Belinda breathed out, relieved. 'We need you to please keep an eye out for anything unusual. There are more of you than there are of us and the more eyes we have on the ground, the more likely we are to catch this murderer before he strikes again. I'll give you my number so you can call if any of your people notice anything. We know he's a young man, tall, wears a cap that can be pulled down to shield his face from CCTV. Sometimes smartly dressed but not always. I'll text you the best photo we have so far. It's not brilliant but it might help. We know that he makes reconnaissance trips to check out the best places to strike so you'd be looking for someone new to the line, who travels up and back quite often, but not like a normal commuter. He's likely, for example, to get off somewhere near the end of the line and then go in the opposite direction and at various times of the day and evening. Unusual behaviour like that is what we're looking for. And whatever you do, please, please make sure your community don't eat any food taken from him. It's always wrapped in foil. We don't believe he plans to strike again until mid-March but you need to be on your guard just in case. Is that clear?' Nikola nodded that he did. 'Now, which number can I use to text you?'

Nikola read out his number and Belinda carefully added him to her contacts before texting him one of the grainy photographs from the security camera at Theydon Bois. The Bulgarian stared at the photograph intently. 'I don't recognise,' he said finally, and showed the photo to Mirela who shook her head. 'But we will help. I am trusting you. You can trust Nikola. If we see him, I will call you.' He held out his hand to Belinda. She gently reciprocated and he shook it firmly but warmly before turning to Chris who, though still struggling with the taste of the coffee, accepted this belated greeting. 'We will walk you back to the station. The coffee is on us. We have money.'

I'll bet you do, thought Chris, trying to mask his mild discomfort at having to join forces with someone who made his living from organised begging. They rose to leave and Chris was just about to open the door when the newspaper rustled again and a low, breathy voice came from the table in the far corner. 'Wait.'

The old man had turned to look at them. 'Please. Will you show me your photo,' he wheezed, his accent definitely Turkish. Belinda moved across to the far table, sat down opposite the stranger and held out her phone on which was the CCTV photo, blurry but with the distinguishing smart suit and incongruous cap. A wrinkled hand gently touched Belinda's and drew the phone closer to a similarly furrowed face with watery eyes, which studied the picture intently. After a short silence, the old man slowly pushed Belinda's hand away and a smile formed. 'I have seen him,' rasped the voice. 'More than once. I can help you.'

23

'His name is Mehmet Durak.' Belinda was sipping gingerly from a still-slightly-too-hot mug of tea. 'He worked for the Turkish police in Istanbul for thirty years before becoming a private detective in the nineties, not for the money apparently, but more because he simply enjoyed focusing on the crimes he wanted to solve as opposed to being given a huge pile of cases and told to get on with it. He did, however, make a small amount of money, enough to move here in 2004 with his wife who sadly died two years ago. He currently lives alone in Harrow but he likes to get out and see the city while he can still move without too much discomfort from arthritis. So he travels the Underground, usually down to Wembley Park or sometimes Finchley Road but sometimes north as far as Eastcote or Pinner, wherever there's a decent coffee shop which lets him sit and people-watch for a few hours and has a clean toilet. He's very particular about hygiene.'

'A man after my own heart, Belinda,' smiled Lexington. 'There are few things as beastly and disappointing in life as a dirty lavatory, especially in one's old age when the need may arise quite suddenly. And believe me, it does! I usually pop into a hotel these days if I need to spend a penny.'

He had called an emergency meeting of The Twelve with no outsiders, to discuss the findings of the discussion with the Bulgarians. Their location was a snug mews house in Marylebone owned by The Twelve since the 1950s and often used as a place for members to stay if they had an early start in the West End. Over the years its decoration had altered regularly and it was currently a very plush space with lots of wooden flooring, comfortable chairs and, as usual, a wide selection of expensive-looking art including an early Kandinsky, which took pride of place above an artificial fireplace.

'He has a preference to travel in the middle of the day when there are fewer passengers and he likes to engage with people, which is why he remembered the suspect,' Belinda continued. 'Apparently Mehmet tried to talk to him a couple of weeks ago when they were sitting opposite one another, but our man didn't even respond. He just stared from under the cap. Mehmet remembered that and decided not to bother him again. Interestingly, and somewhat surprisingly I thought, he had heard rumours about The Twelve when he was in Turkey but dismissed them as pure fantasy dreamed up by crazy British people. He couldn't conceive how such an organisation was possible let alone successful. He was most excited to find out that we were real and he understands the need for utmost secrecy. Anyway, the important point is that he's seen our target three times in the last two weeks, on each occasion going north on the Metropolitan Line. Twice, Mehmet has got off at Harrow and because the line splits he doesn't know what happened after that. However, on the most recent occasion Mehmet saw him at Pinner, getting on the northbound train as Mehmet was getting off to go for coffee and a cake.'

'That probably means he's checking out where best to make

his escape,' mused Chris, noisily slurping a freshly made coffee. 'Figuring out where the CCTV is patchiest.'

'And the Bulgarians?' asked Lexington, intrigued. 'Were they full of the spirit of joy and Slavic *bonhomie?*'

'Not initially,' explained Belinda, glancing at Chris with a smile, 'but they warmed up. And after Mehmet got involved they really started to pay attention. Their leader is a chap called Nikola. I have his number and he has mine. He's going to ask all of his people working the lines to look out for the suspect, without going into the details as to why, and in addition to that, he's going to keep an eye out for Mehmet and make sure he's okay. Mehmet doesn't have a phone so he can't tell them when he's going out but, as I say, it's usually the late morning or early afternoon when it's quieter.'

'Should we get him a phone?' asked Terry. 'It's easily arranged.'

'It's a lovely thought,' said Belinda, 'but he's eighty, not in the best of health and the last mobile phone he had was a Nokia about twelve years ago. I suspect giving him a smartphone now would be counterproductive. I shudder to think what would happen if he happened upon Twitter, for example.'

'Good,' exclaimed Lexington with delight. 'Progress is rapidly being made all of a sudden. We know which line he's focusing on and we know which date he's working towards, which is March 16th. We can plan properly from here. It's now mid-February so we should work towards contact with him by the first week of March.'

'When you say "contact"', asked Thomas, sitting on a two-person sofa squeezed next to Monica, 'are you suggesting capture or disappearance?'

Lexington eased back in his leather armchair. 'I think we should leave those options open for now. Capture would be ideal and then to leave him somewhere for Suzanne's teams to pick him up, yet we should also be prepared to act swiftly where necessary. Needless to say, we shall all need to take shifts on that line to glean as much information as possible, but I wonder whether additionally I might ask David, Terry and Owen to please venture out of the stations from, say, Pinner northwards, in order to establish any possibilities for a potential disappearance. Sadly I don't think it will be possible to use any of our usual locations as they are too central. We shall simply have to improvise on this occasion. It wouldn't be the first time.'

'We'll start today,' said Owen. 'We'll do two stations and their surroundings every day so we'll be done in around a week. I'll continue my work on GKS14 in the evenings, which is when he tends to be more active anyway.'

'Thank you.' Lexington nodded, thoughtfully. 'I'll let Suzanne know but apart from her, I think this information should be kept secret until we have rather more of a strategy. We're getting close to the denouement and we can't risk any mishaps. Belinda, do you think our friend Mehmet can be trusted not to try anything, um, heroic if he sees the poisoner again?'

The linguist sighed. 'Not entirely, I would say. He's a lovely chap and he's still sharp mentally. He's a little less able physically but I get the impression that there's a fair bit of the old police detective have-a-go spirit still in there somewhere. There's a reasonable chance he might decide to do something rash if the opportunity arose.'

'That's what I feared,' mused Lexington. 'Do you think you could impress upon him, the next time you see him, the importance of keeping a distance. If the target cottons on that he's being observed, then he'll go quiet and we'll miss our best chance. And we cannot risk that. We may not get another. Now, in other news, today is David's seventieth birthday.' The plumber put his hands to his cheeks in mock surprise. 'Terry has appropriately baked a cake so perhaps it's time to put the kettle on.'

―――

Over the following week, it became clear that Mehmet's travels on the Underground had conveniently fallen into some sort of rhythm, as a result of which it was relatively easy to keep track of him. Whether this was because Mehmet felt he now had some degree of function to serve the investigation, or whether the unseasonably high temperatures for late winter meant that his mobility had improved, could not be determined. Anna and Graham first noticed him on a sunny Wednesday as he arrived at Harrow station just after two in the afternoon, making his way tentatively but purposefully down the stairs, holding the handrail and using a cane, and then travelling south to Finchley Road before disembarking, crossing to the Jubilee Line and one stop to Swiss Cottage, which allowed him to then travel north without any additional stairs. The old Turk would then change back onto a Metropolitan Line train at Finchley Road – again, no stairs required – and travel either back to Harrow or sometimes, if he felt strong enough, to one of the stations further north, which had a convenient lift from platform level.

During these journeys he would open a book but generally not read a page, instead covertly surveying all around him for new passengers to speak with, and for one in particular whom he knew would remain silent.

'That's what Belinda was saying about the old policeman still being deep inside,' smiled Lexington when he heard the news. 'He's on his own personal stakeout, as they say in American cop movies.' He was sitting at a table outside an old workman's cafe in Euston having a late breakfast with Anna, Graham, Thomas and Monica. The day was again bright and the group was enjoying the unusually warm late winter sunshine.

'At least it means we can easily keep an eye on him,' said Monica. 'Dear old fellow.'

'May I remind you that he's younger than I am!' exclaimed Lexington, playfully.

'Yet not quite as fit,' added Thomas, cutting a cinnamon bun in half to share with Monica. 'What's the latest from Terry's end, by the way?'

Lexington stretched his shoulders back and gave a satisfied grunt as something muscular clicked. 'Good. As ever where Terry is involved, there's a methodical steadiness to the process, which David rather admires and which mildly exasperates Owen in equal measure, and yet, between them, they are making excellent progress. Owen tells me they have scoured everything from Pinner to Watford and identified and logged every available scenario for capture. They're now working through the other branch of the line and expect to be finished by March 3rd. As a result, we can all meet on the 4th, which I believe to be a Thursday, and finalise our plan as far as it is possible to do so at that point. They've been assisted rather by the fine weather we've been having, although I'm told that's threatening to change at the weekend.'

Lexington was correct. By Saturday a fierce winter storm had blown in off the Atlantic, which meant that all sensible people were holed up indoors, out of the constant driving rain. Thomas awoke early in Monica's bed to the familiar cadence of the wind harmonising around the eaves and corners of the building. Beside him, the soft body of his lover was snoozing peacefully.

Thomas spent the next hour listening to her gentle breathing and thought how extraordinarily fortunate he had been to meet such an inspirational woman at his stage in life. His thoughts shifted to Alice and the mornings they had spent together both at the beginning of their marriage and towards the end. Thomas had loved Alice completely but, he supposed, in a very different way. Alice would rarely want to spend the morning cuddling and making love, even when they were younger. She was much happier being out of bed and getting on with her day, busying herself with chores.

It would be interesting to see how his children would react to this new relationship. Emily would be fine, he suspected; relieved probably, and delighted that he had found some late life happiness, and the twins would love Monica with her elegance and style and verve for living. He imagined the girls as teenagers going clothes shopping with Monica and smiled, realising that he wanted Monica to be part of his long-term future.

Simon, perhaps, would be more suspicious. He had never had the closest of relationships with his son. They were very different people and, now he thought of it, Thomas couldn't even remember the last time the two had spoken, either by telephone or in person. Thomas decided that he would need to put in the effort with Simon, once this case was out of the way.

He could feel Monica stirring. It was still early for her, so he kissed her forehead gently and she purred, turning to nuzzle into him in her drowsiness before returning to her dreams, her breathing becoming slow and deep, her head now on his chest, her arm wrapped around him like a silk bow around a precious gift.

After about twenty minutes, Thomas was drifting back into shallow sleep but became conscious that Monica's hand had moved and was now caressing his thigh gently.

'You're awake,' he said softly, and kissed her delicately on the lips.

'I am,' replied Monica, moving her hand sideways, 'and by the feel of things, Mr Quinn, so are you.'

By Monday the Atlantic storm had passed through, leaving a thick film of mulchy dampness on the pavements and in the gutters and there was a noticeable chill in the air as the westerlies had veered into northerlies. Monica and Thomas were scheduled to take their shift monitoring the line for sightings of both the suspect and, for now, Mehmet. They rose late, brunched at an Italian cafe on Marylebone High Street and were at Baker Street by 1pm for the first of many northbound excursions that afternoon and evening. Just before two, they decided to wait at Harrow to see whether Mehmet would maintain his informal timetable and, sure enough, just after the hour they spotted him. He was wearing a smart but dated suit and an old raincoat in case of sudden showers, which were stealthily circling the capital like watchful hyenas, and was making his way, cane in hand, with great care down the stairs to the southbound platform. As he did so, Thomas and Monica were able to take a convenient tunnel and still reach ground level before him with three minutes to spare before the next train.

As Mehmet had never met either Monica or Thomas, they were able to sit in reasonable proximity without arousing his suspicion. From the corners of their eyes, they watched intently as the old man extracted his book from his pocket and then pretended to read it while casually scanning the carriages, then, placing his book on his lap, Mehmet reached into his other pocket and pulled out a disposable camera.

'That's new,' whispered Thomas, leaning close to Monica, 'and a little worrying. He must have bought it over the weekend.'

'He's probably hoping to photograph the poisoner,' surmised Monica, 'but let's hope he doesn't get too close or it'll arouse suspicion. Those old things can make a hell of a click. Nobody really uses them anymore because most people can take better pictures on their phones, but of course Mehmet probably doesn't know that.'

Thomas pondered momentarily the wisdom, or otherwise, of providing Mehmet with a smartphone but decided, as had been agreed at the meeting the previous week, that the disadvantages outweighed the benefits. 'Do you think we should say something?'

'We can't,' said Monica. 'Not yet. We just have to hope and pray that he's careful. Or that he doesn't have the need to use the camera today.'

Mehmet carefully wound the camera spool until it was ready to take its first picture, then lifted the light plastic carapace up to his eye, pointed it in the vague direction of Monica and Thomas and clicked. The noise was just audible over the hum of the rails, which helpfully blanketed and muffled most of the sound. All of them realised that when there were more passengers, it was likely that Mehmet could potentially carry out his plan unfettered. Without looking at his photographic subjects, he smiled, placed the camera back into his pocket and continued not reading his book.

They travelled down to Baker Street where Mehmet disembarked to visit the toilet, and then back up to Pinner and then down again, all the time keeping an eye out for anything unusual.

Just before 4pm, when the carriages were transforming perceptibly into mini mobile discos for small groups of noisy but friendly secondary school children, Mehmet's body language changed and it was immediately obvious to Monica and Thomas what had been the cause; a few metres away, the bustling students had been joined at North Harrow station by a tall, smartly-dressed man wearing a cap. He was staring silently into the carriage, oblivious to the laughter and mobile phone examination around him.

Mehmet reached for the throwaway camera but this time, rather than raising it to his eyes, he placed it on his lap, pointed towards the man in the cap, and waited, all the time watching out of the corner of his eye, conscious that his moment would eventually arrive. After a couple of stops, the carriage had emptied out somewhat, although there was still enough bustle and activity to muffle any sound softer than a heavy footstep.

'We're going further north than he's used to,' said Monica, anxiously, as trees replaced rooftops as their window vista. 'He's out of his comfort zone but hopefully he knows what he's doing.'

As the train slowed into Moor Park station, the man in the cap got up and turned in Mehmet's direction towards the door of the carriage. 'Click'. The sound could be heard by Monica and Thomas and, for a moment, the poisoner turned in Mehmet's direction, alerted by something out of the ordinary. Mehmet, however, had already shielded the camera using his book and was now looking down at his knees pretending to doze.

'Oh, he's good,' nodded Thomas, sagely. 'He's still got it.' The doors opened and the tall man pulled the cap further down over his eyes and left the train purposefully. Once they were moving again, Mehmet lifted the book and placed the camera back in his pocket. 'We'd better make contact,' said Thomas, rising from his seat.

'Mehmet?' began Monica, her voice low in the emptying train. The old man turned slowly, as if expecting them. 'Hello, it's nice to meet you. We're friends of Belinda and Chris. We're here to help. My name is Monica and this is Thomas. And we saw him too. What you did was very brave. Did you get a photograph?'

Mehmet held out a bony hand. 'It's good to meet you too,' he said. 'I knew you were part of The Twelve because it is unusual to be travelling up and down the same line without a purpose. I noticed you about an hour and a half ago but it was necessary to stay quiet, as I'm sure you understand. Did I get a photograph? I think so. I've been practising over the weekend with other cameras to get the angle right from my lap. I'm not sure if he noticed. I hope not. It is definitely him. Now, can you help me, please? There's a one-hour photograph place in Pinner just near the station that I was using on Saturday. If we can get there by five, they can develop what I have. If we go to the end of the line, we can get the train back without any stairs.' He raised his eyes to look directly at Monica. 'Stairs are the enemy of the old,' he warned.

As it turned out, the place in Pinner was unable to turn the developing process round before closing time but promised to have the photos ready by ten the next morning; three copies, enlarged to show the 'detail', one for Mehmet, one for The Twelve and one to pass on to Nikola.

Monica and Thomas were at the shop just before ten and Mehmet was already there, studying his work with interest. 'I believe this will help us,' he smiled, proudly handing over four of the 10 x 12 prints. Two of the pictures showed a quiet carriage with a scattered seating of travellers including, in one corner of the frame, Monica and Thomas looking troubled. The other two photographs had a couple of chattering schoolgirls in the foreground but, of more relevance, a tall, gaunt figure behind them, moving towards the camera, his face clearly visible under a baseball cap.

24

'That is excellent news.' Thomas had called Lexington immediately from a sheltered spot under a pine tree in some woodland conveniently close to Pinner station, while Monica contacted Nikola from a car park nearby. 'I shall gather everyone tomorrow afternoon and include both Suzanne and Dennis this time, provided their diaries allow. It's important to bring them up to speed with both our good progress and our plan.'

'We'll await your text,' said Thomas. 'Now, before you go, would you like a quick word with Mehmet?' Their companion was sitting on a bench, surrounded by tall conifers, watching the morning dog walkers, and dogs, go about their business.

'I think that would be both appropriate and necessary under the circumstances,' agreed Lexington.

Thomas handed the phone to Mehmet who looked at him with a bemused but joyous expression. 'He wants to talk to you,' said Thomas. 'Don't worry, he's very friendly.' Mehmet took the phone and stared at it as if it were primed to explode before carefully lifting it to his ear; Thomas moved a few steps away so that the senior man could have some privacy. From his distance, he could surmise that the conversation had begun tentatively, certainly on Mehmet's side, but after a couple of minutes there was a lot of smiling and even laughter, so much so that Thomas became slightly concerned that the Turk might drop the phone into the fallen pine needles during a fit of hysterics.

'Nikola is on his way,' said Monica, crunching towards him through the winter leaves. 'He was just up the road, conveniently.' She kissed Thomas and nodded towards the Turk. 'Lexington?'

'Like a house on fire,' smiled Thomas. 'Apparently.'

Ten minutes later, after Lexington had hung up, Mehmet returned the device to its owner. 'You seemed to get along well,' enquired Monica in a friendly tone.

'It seems we have mutual friends, myself and your Mr Smith. We have arranged to meet after his retirement and share stories.' Mehmet's face suddenly developed a look of horrified concern. 'Oh my! I do trust you know about the Mr Smith retirement and that I have not opened the bag of cats?'

'It's fine,' said Monica, to Mehmet's obvious relief. 'We know. The cats are already in the wild.'

'Look at you, all good friends together!' Nikola and Mirela were walking up from the direction of the station and greeted the group warmly – kisses for Mehmet from Mirela, handshakes for everyone else. 'It is good to see you again, old man. And you must be Monica and Thomas. Belinda has told me all about you. I am very happy to meet you both.'

'Likewise,' said Thomas, somewhat surprised at the Bulgarian's amiable demeanour, considering his reputation.

'Please,' continued Nikola, 'pass on my personal apologies to Belinda and to Chris for my early behaviour towards them. You understand, I hope, that I cannot be too careful, and my people are not generally used to major acts of kindness because of our line of business. But as soon as I realised the truth of the matter, you all became my good friends. Now, I understand you have a better photograph.'

Monica handed over the picture with the poisoner in the background which the Bulgarian studied closely, frowning as he turned it to get better light. 'I still do not recognise,' he said finally before showing the print to Mirela and speaking briefly in their native language. Mirela shook her head once again and shrugged her bony shoulders. 'She still does not recognise. I will show this to the group and maybe we will have some news later. I will call Belinda. Thank you again for everything you are doing.'

He shook hands with Thomas and Monica and then gave Mehmet a big hug which almost crushed the old man, whispering something inaudible in his ear. 'You are my favourite,' said Nikola, decoupling his embrace. 'You remind me of my father. Maybe you will meet him one day, if he ever decides to visit London for a holiday. I try to persuade him every week but he is scared of flying. He has never left his village in the mountains except to go to the market in the next village to buy and sell chickens, so you can perhaps understand why he is reluctant. We are not cuts from the same cloth, as you would say. My father and I.'

———

A short, brisk walk from the upmarket bustle of Sloane Square is Minera Mews, a tree-lined cul-de-sac with the quiet sophistication of a place where you could, should you so wish, get lost in the centre of one of the busiest parts of the capital, forgetting you are a hefty stone's throw from Harrods and the King's Road.

Halfway down the mews is a house where the heavy curtains are always drawn but the occupants are rarely seen. The residents of Minera Mews occasionally spot one person, usually a man, enter the property but have never seen him leave. However, those who have lived in the mews for a number of years remember a curious day – it was a Thursday – back in 2007 when a group of twelve elderly people arrived at the house early one afternoon and were joined shortly afterwards by an individual in a chauffeur-driven car who, it was discussed at the time, bore a striking resemblance to the then Defence Minister.

A meeting of the Minera Residents' Association was rapidly convened to get to the bottom of the matter, and the chairwoman of the Association, a retired army widow named Mrs Eunice Clatworthy, tried on a number of occasions to make contact with anyone inside the strange house to invite them to attend the gathering, but without success. As a result, the meeting descended into a farcical series of progressively fantastic conspiracy theories, one involving the Russians and another more far-fetched option centring around people from Battersea, but not before a motion was passed agreeing that the police should be contacted to see whether they might enter the property just in case any funny business was going on.

The required call was duly made the following morning and the emergency operator promised that an investigation would be forthcoming. However, when two weeks had passed without any noticeable progress, the chairwoman called the emergency services again. This time, to her surprise, Mrs Clatworthy was immediately put through to Scotland Yard where a woman claiming to be a detective chief inspector informed her that a thorough search of the property had already taken place and that no further action was required.

When Mrs Clatworthy stated that she had personally been keeping a beady eye on the property every day but had thus far seen neither hide nor hair of a uniform, not even a shiny button, she was politely informed that the search had occurred during the hours of nightfall between 1am and 5am the previous Tuesday; and when Mrs Clatworthy mentioned that she felt it was rather an unusual time of the day or night for a routine police search, she was slightly less politely informed that such timings were entirely normal under these particular circumstances and that the matter was firmly and most definitely closed as far as the police and all other relevant authorities were concerned.

'Do you know,' said Suzanne Green, reclining in one of the mews house's comfortable sofas with a mug of late afternoon tea, 'it's the funniest thing. This is my first visit to this particular house but I do remember about ten or twelve years ago having to deal with a very nosy and quite rude lady who lived opposite. I was a DCI in those days and she was insistent that something suspicious was going on. I remember her case going all the way to the top. I ended up taking a call from her and having to explain in no uncertain terms that she should mind her own business. Clatworthy, I think was her name.'

'It was,' smiled Lexington, matter-of-factly. 'And you'll be relieved to hear that she no longer lives across the road.'

'Oh, did she move away?' asked the commissioner casually, placing her mug carefully back on a side table.

Lexington smiled quietly to himself as well as to anyone else who happened to be watching. 'Oh no, she died, poor thing. A ghastly accident. She kept getting squirrels in her attic, apparently. Every time the pest removal people got the buggers out, within days new ones would creep back in. Eventually she decided to tackle them herself and went up in the attic with a pistol that her late husband had acquired in case of burglars. It seems that whilst waiting in the semi-darkness, poor Mrs Clatworthy was startled by something, probably a spider, fell back, pulled the trigger and the bullet blew half her brains out. Nasty business. Bits all over the tiling. They're clever things, squirrels. They won't enter a space if they can't see an alternative exit so you need traps with two doors, one at either end, and a tempting snack in the middle.' Thomas was reminded of the pictures in Mrs Mendoza's room and began to wonder. 'Mind you, a lovely young couple lives there now with their delightful toddler. She's something big in the city and he's a house husband who runs an online bakery business on the side, so all's well. They have far less time on their hands than dear old Mrs Clatworthy.' He scratched his nose, knowingly, as the front door opened. 'Ah, here are Belinda and Chris, so we can begin.'

The linguist and the surgeon had phoned ahead to say they would be slightly delayed as they had received a call from Nikola relaying news that one of his community had spotted the man in the cap that day and had followed him, at a safe distance, north to Moor Park station where, again, the poisoner had left the train. On this occasion, the train had been held in the platform, which gave the Bulgarian amateur surveillance operative the chance to see his target emerge on the opposite platform, walk up and down as if noting the positions of cameras, and wait for a southbound train.

'This would strongly suggest,' said Belinda, 'that Moor Park is his chosen station for completing the next murder and escaping, probably because the CCTV is relatively easy to avoid.'

'And also,' added David, 'if anything were to go wrong, there's a lot of land outside the station where someone could easily vanish. It's basically the countryside up there. There's even farmland with cows and things.'

'How do you mean, "vanish"?' asked Dennis Burrows. The transport police chief had managed to wedge himself tightly into an armchair marginally too small for him and was fidgeting uncomfortably like a small and agitated dog attempting to settle on a beanbag.

David eyed him suspiciously. 'As you'll doubtless know, chief constable, many of the stations on that particular line are in fairly suburban areas with shops and houses as soon as you leave the station. Moor Park, on the other hand, has a considerable amount of grassland, a couple of golf courses and a moor running down to a canal. We've done a broad sweep of the area ourselves and if you wanted to disappear quickly, you would have a number of options from that particular station. In fact, it's probably the best place for doing so, simply because of the local geography.'

Burrows shuffled awkwardly, managing only to dislodge a mauve cushion onto an adjacent table and nearly knocking over Anna's mug of coffee before she speedily reached out and rescued it.

'On the positive side,' continued Terry, 'if he has chosen Moor Park then it plays very conveniently into our hands. Yes, there is a lot of open land but there are also a handful of secluded structures we can use for our plans. Outbuildings owned by the Underground system; deserted cottages; even a small, disused storage shed. We've checked them all out. I can get us into them without any trouble so it'll be fairly easy to develop a couple of strategies for how this saga might be finally concluded to everyone's satisfaction.'

'I'd like to explore those a little now if we may,' suggested Suzanne. 'It would be helpful for Dennis and I to know whether we need to tentatively begin to engage our own teams to bring this case to a close.'

'Personally, I don't believe you do, commissioner,' said Lexington, 'but let's hear what David and Terry have to suggest and we'll make an informed and collective decision.'

'Thank you,' said David with a nod. Burrows made a huffing sound as if some air had been rapidly let out of him. 'We have about two weeks until the 16th, which is when we anticipate the next attack will be. Moor Park station is situated between two golf clubs. The closest one to the station is of little use to us because it's all just greens and fairways and light woodland, but the one slightly further away has more dense clumps of trees as well as a disused outbuilding, as I've mentioned, which we can adapt to our needs.' The plumber looked towards Burrows. 'With your permission, of course.'

Burrows attempted to move but realised he was stuck fast and decided it was wisest, particularly in this company, to brave it out for fear of another cushion mishap. 'What sort of adaptations are you considering, sir?' he asked, although it was clear to everyone that he had forgotten David Latham's name.

'We believe there are two distinct choices within the available timescale. The first is to convert it into a temporary prison cell of sorts. That's relatively easy. Terry and I have talked it over and we just need a bit of help transporting raw materials. Martin has agreed to assist with the cab, and we'll hire a van if we need to move anything big, although I don't think we will.'

The ex-cabbie saluted ostentatiously. 'Thank you, Martin,' said Lexington. 'And the second option?'

'The second option is trickier, and far from ideal, but it is possible. You remember the makeshift place we created over in Westminster a couple of years back where we temporarily borrowed the property with the artesian well and dropped that drug dealer down it?'

Lexington took an anxious sideways glance at the Metropolitan Police commissioner who winked casually. 'Wilcox,' said Suzanne. 'How could I forget? His family is still campaigning for us to investigate his whereabouts. Happily, they know as much about that as they do about how he made his absurd amounts of money for the last umpteen years, but there you are. Sometimes people just don't want to admit what's staring them in the face. Isn't that right, Dennis?'

Burrows huffed again and seemed to sink even further into a chair that appeared to be incrementally yet purposefully devouring him whole.

'We could rig up something similar,' continued David. 'There isn't a well on this occasion but there is a toilet in the outbuilding. I've looked at the survey and because the land is low, it's only a few metres to the sewer. We could create a temporary well and put the toilet back afterwards. The reason it's not ideal is that the deceased body will end up somewhere eventually, because there's no easy way to mince it or dissolve it. We simply don't have the time to build the necessary equipment. However, by the time the body would be found, the likelihood is that there would be nothing tracing it back to the outbuilding. He would just be some unfortunate fellow who drowned in the river.'

'And we could cover over any discrepancies with the forensics team, of course,' added the police commissioner, definitively.

'Essentially,' concluded David, 'you'll need to decide whether this is a capture, in which case option one is far more preferable and easier, or a death by misadventure where the cards are stacked in favour of option two.'

Burrows had managed to partially unwedge himself although with minimal subtlety and a lot of squeaking. 'How do you propose to move the suspect from the station to the outbuilding?' He smirked, the implication being that if there were flaws in the plan, he would be the man to find them.

'An excellent question, chief constable.' It was Chris Tinker's turn to use his expertise. 'And one that we posed to ourselves early on. He's a tall fellow but slim so relatively light – we estimate around twelve stone, maybe even a bit less. Three of us should be able to transport him easily but we plan to have six on hand for backup. As soon as he makes his move, I'll inject him with a strong tranquilliser, ketamine probably. The amount will be enough to put him out for an hour or so but not do any lasting harm. We'll get him off the train and wait until any commuters have departed, then we can carry him down the stairs and out of the station where two of us, probably David and Terry, will be waiting with golf buggies to transport us all to this outbuilding. Then it's just a waiting game until he wakes up. If you decide on option one, we'll let you know and you can pick him up alongside the evidence, which he'll doubtless be carrying. If it's option two,' the surgeon took a deep breath, 'then we'll be prepared to use more ketamine to finish the job – as well as whatever plumbing wizardry David has managed to create out of thin air.'

Burrows was straining himself so hard to unearth a chink in this armour that he was turning slightly purple. 'And how do you propose getting close enough to the suspect to administer this injection?' A look of quiet satisfaction once again crossed the chief constable's porcine face.

'That's easy,' said Chris. 'I'll be the target for the poisoning. I'll pretend to be a homeless old man and I'll almost certainly be the only one because we'll make sure Nikola's people finish their shifts early. Sorry, I should explain that Nikola is a senior member of a Bulgarian begging group whom we've befriended to help with the case. There are hardly any other homeless people on that line because the Bulgarians have a bit of a reputation for being protective of what they consider their patch. Monica and Thomas will monitor from a distance in case anything goes wrong and they'll both be armed with syringes too.'

Burrows looked crestfallen.

'The plan isn't one hundred per cent there yet but that's the bones of it,' said David. 'But we need to know today which option you all prefer because if it's option two then we'll need to start work pretty sharpish to get the outbuilding into the right shape. I should also point out that if I have to convert the toilet then it probably shouldn't be used for its designed purpose so anyone responding to the call of nature will need to go outside.'

Still desperately hoping to find some weak spot, Burrows coughed and interjected, 'Okay, but how do you know he's about twelve stone?'

'We've seen him,' replied Monica, 'as you know. And we also have a new photograph taken by a friend of ours.' She reached into her bag and pulled out a large, brown hard-backed envelope from which she pulled Mehmet's picture of the killer and handed it to Suzanne, who studied it intently.

'That's far better than anything we have from CCTV,' said the commissioner, handing the photograph to Burrows who miraculously managed to lean forward far enough to reach it. 'I'll run it through the police database when I get back if I may.'

'Of course,' said Lexington who then turned towards the chief constable. Burrows' face had lost its earlier colour and he was looking, if anything, like he might vomit. 'Is everything all right, Dennis?'

Burrows pursed his lips and was silent for a moment. 'Yes, I'm fine. Thank you. But I have to leave, I'm afraid. There's an urgent meeting I have to attend about signalling technology.' With difficulty, he managed to lever himself out of the chair, dropped the photograph in Belinda's lap and hurried for the door. After a couple of seconds, from the direction of the exit came noises of predictable fury as Burrows again failed to escape the building.

'I'll go,' said David. 'Terry's triple lock mechanism strikes again.'

25

Once Terry had returned from his latest impromptu rescue mission, the remaining thirteen sat in silence for a few moments until Monica finally voiced what everyone was thinking. 'He doesn't have a signal technology meeting, does he?'

'Not according to the calendar, which I can access,' confirmed Suzanne. 'I checked it this morning in case this one overran.'

'And it seemed as though he might have recognised the man in the photograph.'

'I got that impression too, Monica.'

'So, what now?' asked Thomas. He had been becoming more uneasy about Burrows but couldn't fathom why. Now, the feeling had intensified considerably.

'I think,' began Suzanne tentatively, 'that we all need a little time to consider our options while at the same time progressing the ideas you've been working on already. We don't want to fall behind. I suggest that in terms of the outbuilding David and Terry start work on the basis of a capture at this point as that sounds the least labour intensive. I also think at this stage that we keep Dennis out of the meetings and planning communications just in case. I'll see if I can get some one-to-one time with him to find out what's going on. Maybe it's someone he used to work with in the criminal underground before he worked for Transport. Owen, are you any closer to identifying the poisoner through the chat rooms?'

The former surveillance officer reported that he was using some new, experimental software which should be able to make a positive identification the next time the poisoner was active during the chats. 'It's like a trap. All it takes is one message, one press of any key on a phone or a computer and I should have all the information we need. It's just a waiting game.'

'A slightly scary thought,' said Lexington, calmly. 'I shall push my keys with more care now that I know such things may be done. Thank goodness I still maintain my landline.' He smiled warmly at Thomas who immediately understood the reference. 'Now, just to let you know, I may be a little quiet for a while as I have some urgent negotiations of my own to conclude over the next day or so and I will be in touch about those as soon as possible. I have a surprise for all of you. A pleasant one, I hope. In the meantime, we should draw the meeting to a close although if anyone would like a brandy or a port before they go, the drinks cabinet here in Minera Mews is quite exceptional.'

Tucking himself deep into Monica's duvet that night in St John's Wood, Thomas was untypically restless. 'What do you think Lexington meant by "urgent negotiations"? Does he know something that we don't?'

Monica's right hand delicately traced the furrows on his brow. 'If I've learnt one thing about Lexington over the last few years, it's that he's always at least one step ahead. It's something I'm trying to master myself. He'll be plotting his chess moves for every eventuality, or at the very least, he'll be shoring up his non-Sicilian defence.'

Thomas frowned. 'You will be okay, won't you?' Monica's head rose gently from his chest and kissed his shoulder. 'With this plan involving the syringes? I know I'm silly to worry, but this poisoner sounds particularly unhinged. He could lash out if he's cornered. Like an angry tiger. Or worse, a furious tapir.'

Monica giggled and nuzzled deeper into him. 'I'll be fine, darling,' she said. 'Lashing out spontaneously doesn't seem to be his style, so far at least. He's more into methodical, planned execution. Anyway, Chris is in more danger. I'm just backup on the train and we'll be together too, so I'll feel more secure. Besides, we may not even need to get to that point, but it's sweet that you worry and I love that about you.'

Thomas lightly kissed her forehead, taking in her aroma. 'It's just that I've grown so close to you so quickly. If anything happened to you, I really don't know what I'd do.'

Monica eased herself up onto her outstretched arms before reaching down to caress Thomas's face, and kissed him gently on the lips. 'You'll be fine because I'll be fine. I'm also worried about you Thomas, but we're a team and I've been in dangerous situations before. Yes, I know it's your first case and it's unusual not to be in a familiar part of the city and yes, we're relying on a number of unknown factors, but the plan will work. And if not, the backup plan will work. And we shall look back in two weeks' time at a job well done. You, me, all of us. It's good to be out of our comfort zone for a change. It sharpens the senses.' She smiled and kissed him again, more passionately this time, and then assumed a playful stern look. 'No one's taking my man away from me. And certainly no one's taking me away from my man!'

Their phones buzzed simultaneously. It was a message from Owen to the group.

'Poisoner identified in chat room. His name is Michael Burrows. Stepson of Dennis Burrows.'

26

The following Monday dawned cold with a biting east wind scything through the city via the conduit of the river and extending its icy talons seemingly around every street corner. The Twelve's meeting place was changed at the last minute to a new venue at an address no one had ever heard of, a detached house in Harrow. It was much further north than usual, in a pretty tree-lined avenue just down the hill from a church whose imposing spire could be seen from a distance as the various members approached either by road or by rail. Almost all of them were late.

'It's new,' chirped Lexington excitedly as he greeted the last of the arrivals in the doorway, which was surrounded by cascades of flowering yellow winter jasmine on neat wooden trellises. 'I bought it last week for cash and furnished it over the weekend. I hope nobody minds. It was rather a rushed job with the interior design, I'm afraid. I had to involve a couple of old friends in the legal and conveyancing business, but I intend to sell it within weeks anyway and so I was thinking more about its next owners, whoever they may be, than about us and our immediate requirements. There's a fabulous little shop down the road called IKEA and they delivered everything on Saturday. I found a pair of willing friends of Nikola's to put it all together on Sunday – told them I needed it for a birthday party and it's amazing what the promise of hard cash will achieve. Anyway, I believe this chair is intriguingly called *Strandmon*.'

He pointed to a large, grey armchair, one of three in a spacious living area which, despite needing a lick of paint, did appear surprisingly homely for somewhere until only recently unoccupied. 'Why it's called that is anyone's guess but it is remarkably comfortable. Some of these cushions are curiously named *Ullkaktus,* by the way, which to my ears sounds like something spiky but I can assure you these aren't anything of the kind. Aren't they simply delightful?'

'Well there's certainly enough room for everyone,' said Owen in admiration. 'How many bedrooms?'

'Four doubles!' announced Lexington, proudly. 'It seems the place had been on the market for a little while and there's no chain, so when I enquired about a cash buy, the dear estate agent was ecstatic virtually to the point of delirium. Whizzed through all the legal nonsense in no time. My logic was that we might need somewhere up this neck of the woods, even if temporarily; it'll help with the planning. People are welcome to stay if they wish although I stress it isn't mandatory. Feel free to move in for a week if you like, or a couple of days as you prefer. I appreciate this part of the city is a bit of a trek for some of you, and we're not getting any younger. Would anyone like a coffee?' Lexington began to move purposefully in the direction of the kitchen and continued talking over the sound of crockery being moved and a coffee machine performing its intended business. 'I'll be mother. The cups are mostly called *Strimmig,* somewhat alarmingly, but don't let that deter you. There are biscuits too, although not Terry's home-baked, regrettably. Suzanne is arriving with Dennis in about half an hour. He knows that we know about Michael so expect him to be a little downbeat. I thought we could all have a more private catch-up first.'

Once everyone had settled in and been caffeinated, Owen explained how he had been waiting in one of the chat rooms, occasionally dipping into a volatile conversation about Islamic extremism, when GKS14 appeared. He was present for less than a minute, during which time he had typed a short message advocating prison sentences for all Muslims found guilty of any crime, however minor, but it was enough time for Owen to identify an email address which GKS14 was using. That address in itself was no help as it had only been registered that day, but by hacking into the network where it originated, Owen was able to quickly access emails and data, which in turn led to an IP address for a computer owned by Michael Burrows two years previously. 'After that, a quick search of social media and I knew it was him. He hasn't posted anywhere for well over a year but you can see from old photos that it's the same person as the one in Mehmet's snap. I'm using military grade encryption, by the way, so he won't be aware that we're onto him.'

'Excellent work, Owen,' said Lexington. 'Although this knowledge makes our lives somewhat trickier. How's the backend of the plan going, as it were?'

David explained that he and Terry, along with Martin and Chris, had spent recent days making alterations to the outbuilding which had included changing the locks temporarily so that no one else could gain access from the outside; bringing in a few comfortable chairs as well as one uncomfortable one to which they could safely fasten Michael Burrows securely; making sure the toilet still worked properly – in fact, said David, it now worked better than ever thanks to some fancy adaptations to the closet bend – and they'd also installed a kettle and a mini fridge because Terry felt certain they would all need a cuppa at some point during the night. He might even bake if he had a spare hour during the daytime on the sixteenth.

In addition to his work in the chat room, Owen had befriended the secretary of the nearby golf club who had given him a tour of the greens and shown him the shed where the buggies were kept overnight. A further investigation under cover of darkness by Owen and Terry had revealed that getting hold of up to four buggies would be very straightforward as the shed was protected only by the most rudimentary of padlocks, something Terry felt that he would need to politely address with the secretary as soon as this Burrows escapade was over.

'Later today, we'll do some tweaking,' said David, and we should be ready for a complete test run tomorrow.

'Outstanding work, gentlemen,' nodded Lexington. 'Chris, how are you feeling about the sharp, pointy end of the plan?'

The former surgeon sipped his coffee thoughtfully. 'I've liaised with Nikola and he's going to stop his people working from 4pm on the relevant day. They don't tend to work as much during rush hour anyway because it's impossible for them to move around easily and the chances of getting caught by the transport police is higher.'

'Ironic,' mused Monica.

'So, if I start around 7.30pm after the busiest bit of rush hour has passed, I should be the only potential target for the next three or four hours. I've bought an outfit from a local charity shop and I won't wash for a few days to get a bit of authenticity. I'm rather glad you've bought this place, Lexington, as I didn't fancy travelling up and down from east London as I get progressively more fragrant. Anyway, Nikola's team have been extremely helpful with monitoring and they say that the poisoner, Michael as we now know, has been travelling later, always to Moor Park, never further, but often not starting out until 9pm.'

'And the method of incapacitation?' Lexington noted that a

car had just pulled into the driveway and that the doorbell was imminent.

'All acquired,' assured Chris. 'Enough to do the job many times over. I'll work with Thomas and Monica over the next few days so they can operate the spare syringes if anything happens to me. I'm sure Thomas will pick it up in no time and I know Monica has visited this rodeo before, but a bit of stabbing practice never goes amiss, as I used to tell the first-year nursing staff.'

'They're talking in the car, by the way,' said Graham, peeping through the net curtain.

Lexington quickly explained that over the weekend Catherine had done some research into Michael Burrows and, unusually for a young man, he had virtually no social media presence at all, 'apart from those four or five posts that Owen found from way back, and nothing in the last year'. It was almost as if he had decided to no longer exist, although quite clearly that was impossible. Everything pointed to him being assisted or manipulated by someone else, or a group of people, who allowed him access to the internet under an assumed identity until Owen's software cleared through the obstructions.

One thing Catherine did mention was that in interviews with Dennis, his daughter was often referenced but never Michael, as if he had been deliberately written out of the family history. There was even an at-home feature in one of those celebrity magazines with Dennis and Fiona showing the readers around their detached Highgate house. In the background of one of the accompanying pictures, there was a photograph of Dennis and Fiona Burrows with their daughter, but no sign of Michael anywhere. In addition, Catherine had contacted a couple of Dennis's former colleagues in the Transport Police, both of whom had suggested that Dennis had something of a ruthless streak. Underneath that apparently harmless, almost buffoonish exterior there beat a heart of ambitious cruelty. Perhaps Michael, once he'd become a difficult teenager, had somehow stood in the way of Dennis's plans to get to the top and had to be manoeuvred out of the picture with unknown but devastating consequences.

Two car doors closed, one quietly, the other with a purposeful bang. This was followed by a period of silence which was in turn followed by the metallic tap of the door knocker.

'Your new bell doesn't appear to work,' said Suzanne in a friendly tone as the front door opened. 'Although, as you've only been here a couple of days, I suppose it's understandable.' She embraced Lexington warmly. 'How are you, Lexington? All ready for the big push?'

'I'm well, Commissioner, thank you for asking.' He turned to Burrows, whose head drooped like a dog who knows it's in trouble. 'Of more relevance to today, how are you, Dennis?'

The chief constable lifted his head and smiled somewhat unconvincingly. 'I'm okay, thank you,' he offered, wearily, all prior arrogance diminished. 'It's been a difficult couple of days, as I'm sure you can imagine, but I think we're bearing up. Fiona was very upset at first, when we found out, and I think she's very concerned about how it will all end. I didn't tell her about your option two. I didn't think it was wise. She's also very anxious about where he might land, prison-wise, and what might happen to him when he gets there. He was always a bit of a solitary child and so being around large numbers of other people is going to be challenging.'

'I understand. And you were right not to mention the second option,' agreed Lexington, placing a comforting hand on Dennis's shoulder. 'We've dismissed that rather grim alternative anyway. Do please reassure your dear wife that we will do all we can to avoid harm or undue discomfort.'

'Even though he's a mass murderer?' Dennis's face was beginning to crumple again, his jowls quivering.

'First and foremost, he's your stepson. That must always be a consideration. Now, why don't you both make yourselves at home, join the group and we'll run through the plans as they currently stand.'

'This is rather nice,' said the commissioner as they moved into the living area where the others were already seated on various newly constructed chairs and sofas. 'It's different to what you're used to, I'll say that about it. Not necessarily in a bad way. Just… different.'

'I bought it last week,' Lexington explained once again. 'Furnished it sparsely over the weekend, but I think I've managed to get all the fundamentals in, somehow. I thought it advisable to have a temporary base up here to save time over the next few days. I'll sell it or something when we no longer need it. The market being what it is, I may even make a few hundred pounds, although of course we don't need the money. I'll decide when the time comes. Dennis, come and sit in the *Gronlid*. It's one of the most comfortable.' The former diplomat ushered Dennis to the large, dark red chair while Terry made fresh coffee and Monica retrieved a stray Allen key from the floor.

'Now, Dennis, I'm afraid the first point on our makeshift agenda must be to interrogate you gently. First of all, when we last met together, you recognised Michael from the photograph, didn't you? That's why you left so rapidly. Might I ask why you didn't mention anything at the time?'

All eyes were on Burrows as he moved his hands towards his head and methodically began massaging his temples. He was silent for about a minute, all the time sensing his own vulnerability, his isolation. 'I know what it looks like,' he whispered, finally. 'But there are some things which you need to understand.' He inhaled slowly, the air reverberating as it crossed the narrow gap between his lips. 'Michael is not my son. When I met his mother Fiona I hadn't anticipated the problems that might be caused. You don't, really, when you start a new relationship.

You're caught up in the moment, selfishly thinking about nothing outside of the two of you.'

Dennis leaned forward in his chair as far as he was able and stared at the floor for several seconds before raising his ruddy face to engage again with the assembled group, looking at each in turn. 'I suppose in some ways this is my fault,' he faltered. 'I arrived on the scene when Michael was fourteen, and deep down I knew it would be difficult with a boy that age, but even so I tried hard to be his friend. I knew I couldn't replace his father but I suspected he didn't want me to.'

'What do you mean by that exactly?' asked Monica, compassionate rather than enquiring.

'Michael's real father beat him from an early age. It was one of the things that led to the break-up of Fiona's first marriage. He beat her too, but as we all know, sometimes people are afraid to leave abusive relationships for a variety of reasons. Anyway, I knew when I started seeing Fiona that Michael would be suspicious of any new man in his mother's world. I may only be a policeman but I know a little about child psychology. So, after Fiona and I had been seeing each other for a while, I tried to be Michael's friend and to provide reassurance, but almost immediately the shutters came down. Yes, there were occasions in those early days when we were a happy family unit but they were few and far between.

'By the age of about nineteen, Michael was very much regressing into his own world. He seemed to be constantly on the internet or gaming, those violent fantasy world games where there's lots of fighting and killing. We would try to talk to him over mealtimes but we generally either got silence or we ended up having an argument because he'd seen some crazy conspiracy theory online and couldn't accept that we were too "blinkered" to see that it was what he regarded as the truth. He seemed to be consumed by a different obsession every week, always something completely absurd but in his mind it became totally serious and absolutely believable. He became very manipulative, trying to get his sister to back him up all the time, but luckily she was too sensible to be taken in.'

'What happened to Michael's real father, Dennis?' Lexington had sensed that Burrows would respond better to sympathy rather than interrogation, however gentle. 'And do let Terry know if you need a top-up of coffee. Please, carry on.'

'He died. Three years ago. Heart attack. Michael seemed unaffected by it but I realise now that we could have done more to try to talk to him about it and how he felt deep down. We found out a couple of years ago that someone had defecated on his father's grave. I suspect that was Michael, although I can't prove it.'

Monica was listening intently to the chief constable's words. 'I'm sorry to have to ask you this, Dennis,' she murmured softly, 'but did you ever hit Michael?'

Dennis sighed. 'No,' he said abruptly before retracing his steps, sorrowfully. 'Actually yes. Just once. I've tried to block it out of my mind but this weekend brought it all back. It was a couple of weeks before we threw him out for the last time. I came home late; it had been a particularly challenging day because of the number of passengers coming into the city for the January sales and there were lots of signal failures and a couple of suicides, as there often are at that time of the year. Anyway, as soon as I opened the door, I knew that something bad had happened. Fiona was in tears and had a bruise on her face. Michael had hit her for no reason, just out of the blue. They'd been talking about her charity work and suddenly he had just lashed out. My first thought was to comfort her and make sure she was okay but then I could feel my anger coming to the boil.

'When Fiona went to the bathroom, I went to Michael's bedroom to confront him. He didn't seem to think he'd done anything wrong. He was completely dismissive. I remember at one point he said his mother deserved it for being weak and helping those less fortunate. I just went for him. I'm ashamed to admit it now. I desperately wish I could turn the clock back. Soon afterwards, Fiona and I decided he had to go. We had talked about it for hours. I thought he'd plead with us to stay but he seemed perfectly happy to get out. He said he'd found a "better place" to live where people understood him. That was the last we saw of Michael, until that photograph. We told friends he was travelling whenever they asked.' He took another deep breath and flopped back into the chair. 'So, I suppose the short answer to your question is that I was in denial. I didn't want to believe it was him. I couldn't bring myself to concede that he was capable of doing something like this. I was terrified about what it might do to Fiona and about what it might do to us as a couple. Selfishness again, I know. I was afraid. That's the truth.'

The room was still as The Twelve and Suzanne weighed the importance and gravity of Burrows' honesty. Martin reached for his mug of tea but then thought better of it, not wishing to shatter the silence with slurping.

'Fiona works for a homelessness charity, am I right?' asked Catherine. Dennis confirmed that she did. 'So, it wouldn't be too far-fetched to assume that part of the motive for the types of attacks and their locations would be some sort of warped revenge on both of you.' Dennis nodded solemnly, unable to find words without fracturing.

'I see,' said Lexington, relieving the chief constable of the need to talk. 'Thank you Dennis, for your candour. I appreciate that this cannot have been easy. Whether it helps us significantly is questionable, but you never know. Now, may I turn to David, Chris and Terry for their update.'

As everyone ingested Dennis's outpouring, the former plumber, the ex-surgeon and the sometime locksmith ran through their strategy for the following Tuesday as well as explaining how Owen could ensure that the CCTV on that section of the system would be adapted temporarily so that no one in the control rooms would notice anything unusual.

'When you say "adapted", Owen, am I to believe you mean "hacked into"?' asked the commissioner with a mock raised eyebrow.

'Yes, of course,' said the former surveillance officer, 'but rest assured that it will be both temporary and limited in area so it's unlikely that there will be any adverse effects other than the one which we require.'

Dennis, who had been listening intently to everything that was being said, adjusted in his chair with a high-pitched squeak. 'If we know roughly where Michael is going to be and when, wouldn't it just be easier if my staff, or indeed yours, Suzanne, took over from this point and used armed officers or tasers to bring this sorry business to a close?'

Not only did silence fill the room yet again, but Martin, who was in the process of lifting his cup to his mouth for the final, stronger dregs, stopped midway and sat statuesque and agape. Thomas briefly imagined the possible unpleasantness which might result from a group of heavily-armed police officers boarding a commuter train, albeit during a relatively quiet hour on a peripheral part of the network. A soft hand squeeze from Monica trawled him back into the silent room.

It was the commissioner who broke the spell. 'Dennis, as we've discussed previously, it is a long-standing, unspoken agreement with The Twelve that once they've embarked on a case, they should be allowed to finish it unless they decide that outside help is required. This agreement has been in place for well over a century and so far not only have they never required the aforementioned outside help, but neither have they ever failed. Furthermore, if you cast your mind back to the last time firearms officers were used on the Underground system, I think you'll agree that it ended rather badly for all concerned, and I for one am not comfortable with recreating the conditions for something similar to happen again. Certainly not in suburban Middlesex, or wherever we are.'

Martin's cup finally completed its journey mouthwards as the background noise assumed a more relaxed tone. 'Hertfordshire,' he corrected between swigs.

'I understand,' said Dennis, defeated, 'but is it worth maybe having some people on stand-by? Just in case. Some professional people.' Martin's sharp intake of breath was audible and there was an unpalatable sense that voices may end up being raised if the line of conversation continued.

'Dennis,' began Monica, calmly, although even her own sympathy for the chief constable was rapidly evaporating. 'Please trust me when I say that we know what we're doing. We'll run through it again and again over the next few days and we will call you when Michael is safely incarcerated. After that, you can do as you wish, but please allow us to complete this job as we've completed so many others. We know from experience that the more outside…' – she was about to use the word 'interference' but checked herself and instead settled upon something softer – '…involvement in these cases, the more chance there is of something unusual happening. And unusual is quite often bad.'

She exchanged a look with Lexington whose face was a picture of quiet admiration. Thomas thought he noticed the suggestion of a wink and he playfully nudged Monica in the shoulder when the conversation resumed and the focus had passed elsewhere.

'All right,' said Dennis, bruised and defeated but actually relieved to be so. 'But if you change your minds, you know where I am. Also, if anything happens on the day which is unexpected and needs clearing up, just let me know. I have a desk at an office in Wembley so I can be nearby if necessary.'

'Just try to avoid any signal failures or unplanned engineering work,' quipped Anna.

'Thank you, Dennis,' said Lexington. 'We will, of course, keep you informed at every available opportunity. Now, if you'll excuse me, I require the bathroom. Luckily this house has two on the ground floor as well as two upstairs if anyone else is similarly indisposed.' Lexington placed his hands on the arms of his chair, lifted himself slowly to standing and walked steadily but with a mild limp down the corridor to the toilet, whistling cheerfully to himself as he did so.

'He's amazing for his age,' exclaimed Suzanne. 'I hope I'm as nimble in my eighties.'

'It's the yoga,' said Monica. 'It keeps us all strong and flexible. Although he is slowing down a bit. He knows he is. And his knee hasn't been the same since the Cooper job this time last year. Hence the retirement.'

'Maybe he bought this as a retirement home,' said Dennis, hopefully.

'I suspect not,' said Graham. 'It doesn't feel very Lexington. Plus, why would anyone of sound mind swap Pimlico for Harrow?'

———

Before going their separate ways, one of the final decisions made was that the main actors in the case would move into the Harrow house the following day so that covert rehearsals could begin as soon as possible. As a result, and knowing they would need to be more well-behaved while staying in a house with other members of the group, Monica and Thomas decided to spend that Monday evening and night in the comfort of St John's Wood. It wasn't that they didn't enjoy being together in Colville Square, but simply that Monica's flat had more space as well as a more relaxed feel to it. Besides, some of Thomas's clothes and toiletries had already trickled conveniently to NW8 so there was no pressing need to return to his house to pack. He would buy anything urgent in Harrow as required.

Monica had picked up some monkfish from the local fishmonger as a treat and was in the kitchen transforming it into a delicious-smelling curry with coconut milk and an array of aromatic spices which filled the air in the flat along with, they suspected, most of the nearby apartments too. A bottle of Domaine Matrot Meursault 2017 had been opened and was sitting, half-full in the fridge while the other half was slowly being consumed from two expensive glasses which Monica liked to keep for special occasions.

'It's going to be a bit strange being together in a different house,' said Monica, her voice straining ever so slightly over the whirring sounds from the cooker fan. 'We shall have to behave a bit better than usual. That will mean pyjamas and nighties for a start. I don't want to be wandering about looking for the loo in the nude and bump into Terry. Or Martin for goodness' sake. Can you imagine?' She giggled at the thought.

Thomas agreed that he couldn't but he also had the distinct feeling that Lexington, who was the sort of man never to leave anything to chance, had already considered every eventuality. Everything about Lexington screamed precision and know-how, and he wouldn't have bought a house on the spur of the moment without first reflecting on every requirement from the point of view of all the potential residents, however temporary they might be.

'It's only for a short while,' he smiled cheekily. 'I'm certain that if you can struggle into a nightdress then I can cope with pyjamas. By the way,' he took a sip of the white wine, one of the most delicious he could remember; Monica was so good at wine pairing, 'has Lexington given you any further indication on where his thoughts are concerning his replacement?'

A cloud of steam rose from the kitchen as Monica plucked the lid from a pan of sticky rice which had been assimilating boiling water for the last few minutes. 'He's still thinking about it, and obviously this case has rather taken a lot of his energy of late on account of it being a slightly tricky one, and particularly with these recently added complications.' She dished the rice onto two large white bowls decorated with blue swallows and then delicately added a ladle full of golden curry before a final flourish of chopped, fresh coriander. 'That said, he has intimated that I'm in with a good chance. In his noncommittal, Lexington-ish way. You saw the look he gave me earlier? In the meeting?' She glided over to the table, lay the bowls at their places, not opposite each other but at right angles, as usual, and kissed Thomas on the cheek before lowering herself sedately onto the seat next to him.

Thomas, hungrily digging in, agreed that he had. 'Would you want the job, though? With all that comes with it? This curry smells wonderful, incidentally.'

Monica smiled and, with her middle finger, carefully wound some stray hair behind an ear. 'Of course. Who wouldn't? Yes, there's the responsibility and all the knowledge and a bit of politics, but we're all grown-ups. Most of us could handle it. Oh, and there's a fair bit of admin, apparently. What with all the art to keep insured and various bits of household maintenance to be delegated. Council tax for all the properties, although luckily no mortgages to worry about as they're all owned and freehold. Lexington says he has a secret trick to getting it all done but he's not going to tell me quite yet.'

'I'm not sure I could handle it. I'm not certain that I'd want to.'

'You could, Thomas. Easily.' Monica ruffled his hair in a way that she hoped was amorous as opposed to condescending. 'You're very smart and capable. Perhaps not right now as you're new to The Twelve but I've no doubt you could do it after a few years.'

Thomas looked down at his bowl thoughtfully, his nagging fear of losing Monica had resurfaced. 'If you get the job, though, I wouldn't want to do it in a few years because that would mean something terrible had happened to you and I wouldn't want that. Ever.'

'You're so sweet.' She picked up her wine and took a sip. 'But even if I get it, which I may not, nothing's going to happen to me so there's no point in being concerned about it.' Monica looked up and saw in Thomas's eyes that her reassurance hadn't had the desired effect. She put down her glass and gently cupped his hand. 'What's worrying you about this case, Thomas? I can assure you that it'll end well, just as they always have.'

Thomas couldn't put his finger on it but for the last few days and nights there had been a nagging feeling that all was not as it should be. Perhaps it was the lengthening of the days which had caused a change in his mood, or maybe it was simply that so much was new in his life. It sometimes felt overwhelming and, at moments, he felt submerged by thoughts of impending disaster, irrational though he knew these to be. A few months before, everything had seemed much easier, but not now. Thomas had even wondered about trying to persuade Monica to leave The Twelve with him so that the two of them could spend their final years doing what normal people of their age would do – cruises, city breaks, nights out. He had remembered Mrs Mendoza's words about leaving any time he wanted and wrestled with whether to tell Monica, but then at every meeting of The Twelve, Thomas had looked round at the faces of people he now considered his friends and he knew that no decision would be straightforward and certainly couldn't be taken until after the Burrows case.

'It's nothing,' he said, tucking into his curry. 'I'm just being over thoughtful as usual. You're right. It'll all be fine.'

Monica touched his face, drawing two fingers gently across his lightly stubbly cheek. 'You'll tell me if I can do anything to help, won't you? I don't want you losing sleep unless I'm the cause.' Thomas smiled and promised that he would. 'Now, there's a good film in half an hour so I suggest we eat up, finish the wine in front of the film, and then use our last opportunity for a pyjama-less night for a while. Does that sound appealing?'

Thomas replied that it did but that there was something he needed to do first. He took Monica's hand and gently led her to the window where he wrapped his arm around her waist and together they looked out at the rooftops and the darkness, freckled with the city lights illuminating a thousand urban stories. A crescent moon was rising beyond the cricket ground and Thomas realised that being around Monica meant that he was noticing more of these sparkling fragments of everyday beauty which he had previously taken for granted. They stood embracing in silence while London got on with the business of the night. Eventually, Monica turned and kissed Thomas on the shoulder. 'Come with me, you gorgeous man,' she purred. 'I think we can give the film a miss tonight and I can always warm up the leftovers later when we get peckish.'

27

At least one of Thomas's suspicions from the previous night had proven to be true. Lexington had chosen the house not merely for its convenience to where their operation was due to take place, but also with the specific personal needs of each of its temporary inhabitants in mind. Each bedroom had an en suite so there would be no nocturnal wandering around landings; there were twin rooms for David and Terry and for Chris and Martin as well as one for Lexington, which he would share with Owen, plus a large and extremely comfortable-looking king-size double for Monica and Thomas, conveniently located away from the others down a short corridor at the rear of the house. Their privacy for these few, unusual days had been taken into consideration, with typical and meticulous Lexington attention.

During the preceding twenty-four hours, he had also arranged for both the fridge and the larder to be well-stocked as well as, naturally, the drinks cabinet with everyone's personal favourites plus a selection of fine wines to be enjoyed as and when they were required. There was no compulsion to stay in the house but Lexington had conspired to make the place so welcoming and homely in a short space of time that, once settled, no one had any pressing desire to leave.

By the time Monica and Thomas arrived in Harrow at two o'clock in the afternoon, having woken late and enjoyed a leisurely brunch, the others had already settled in and the living area was empty apart from Terry and Lexington as the others were either reading or taking naps in their rooms. To Thomas, the casual atmosphere made it resemble a student house, only with extremely mature students. 'We'll make our way to Moor Park in about half an hour,' said Lexington, 'just so we can all familiarise ourselves with the layout and walk the route, as it were. Then we can come back and decide on any tweaks and changes and have a nice dinner together. I think a couple of the others might also pop over. Chris and Terry are going to make a vegetarian paella.' He smiled at Terry who raised an imaginary hat in response. 'I imagine the Spanish might take issue with the concept but, as they aren't here, I anticipate few complaints.'

After a ten-minute amble to the station, Lexington using a stick as he had been for a few weeks on longer walks, the eight of them travelled north together for the first time, although of course everyone bar Lexington had, in their smaller groups, made the journey on many occasions before. 'What a fascinating part of the world,' said Lexington, wide-eyed, as he watched the suburban landscape of rooftops, chimneys and satellite dishes melt into a rural idyll of fields, trees and quaint cottages. 'Do people actually commute from here?'

'Loads of the buggers, Lexington,' answered Terry, who had been travelling the route at various hours during recent days and was familiar with the congested unpleasantness of the same journey some three hours later than the one on which they had embarked. 'You'd be surprised. Like that old Sunday newspaper, all of humanity is here to observe if you pick the wrong moment.'

Pulling into Moor Park station, Thomas explained the

probability that Michael would be in the middle section of the train, as this would allow him to get to the exit quicker. As a result, that would be where he and Monica would position themselves, one slightly ahead and the other behind, ready for Chris to make his move. 'There's one CCTV camera just by the door here,' said Owen, pointing out the security as a fast train sped by on a nearby line, 'so it's possible Michael will be a few seats further down the train so he can get off in between cameras. I'll hack into the system and have them all out of action for the duration, so it won't matter anyway, but Michael won't know that. I'll also be in this waiting room as it's easier for me to disrupt from here. Plus, it's warmer. Martin will be with me as an extra pair of hands getting Michael down the stairs, so there will be five of us in all. More than enough bodies even if he's heavier than we anticipate.'

Lexington nodded approvingly. 'This all looks under control at platform level. We should move on. Now, I may need a bit of time getting down those stairs myself,' he said. 'Legs not as decent as they were, I'm afraid, so you'll have to indulge me just a touch. I'm rather glad I'm not an active participant in this one. The current cold snap doesn't help matters.' The group took their time moving down to ground level, Lexington quite gingerly, where Terry explained that he and David would be waiting around the corner in golf buggies for the signal to move. This would only come when the area was clear of the usual passengers. David had assessed the pattern over many nights and concluded that the residents of the surrounding area either walked home briskly, especially in cold weather, or were rapidly collected with precision timing in expensive cars by brash wives or grumpy husbands. In all likelihood, the place would be deserted by the time Martin, Thomas and Monica had transported Michael down the stairs and out of the station.

'Another advantage of the time of night,' said David, 'is that after a certain hour this station is only manned by one person during the week and he's almost always in the office watching pornography. He does it every evening after the other chap knocks off, if you'll excuse the term, at seven, so he's unlikely to be distracted by a group of oldies like us. He seems a nice enough fellow so I daren't let on that I know his secret. Everyone has their little hobbies.'

Owen grinned wickedly. 'I'll make sure his broadband connection is behaving particularly well. He'll experience no buffering issues on the night.'

Terry then outlined the route that the golf buggies would take to the outbuilding. 'We won't go there now,' he explained, 'because it's too far to walk and the terrain isn't great… but if you want to pay a visit later in the week, perhaps after dark on Thursday when it's dry, then I can organise that. It'll be a good idea to practise on the buggies anyway. We were planning a couple of trial runs before next Tuesday as it is, just so that everyone can get a feel for the buggies and how they operate on different surfaces.'

'Splendid!' said Lexington, relieved at not having to walk any further than necessary. 'Let's do that. I've never travelled by buggy. Golf never appealed. I wonder, will I require a robust cushion?'

'Already arranged for you, Lexington.' Terry smiled, gripping him firmly on the shoulder. 'As well as a blanket, if needed. You're not the only one who thinks of everything, old boy.'

That evening, back in their Harrow basecamp, Chris and Terry served up a feast of Spanish rice flavoured with paprika and saffron and adorned with fresh peppers, peas and asparagus. The former surgeon had also made *patatas bravas* and, for good measure, had hunted down some Iberico ham for the meat eaters. Lexington had lightly chilled a few bottles of a Tempranillo from the 2010 harvest, which he explained had been one of the best in recent years owing to the spectacularly warm summer, even for Spain; and Belinda had joined as she had been in the area seeing friends, in addition to which, she had news.

'Michael was on the line again today, according to Nikola. He called me earlier.'

Lexington looked anxious. 'Did he say what time?'

'Yes, he got on at Baker Street shortly after three and went to Moor Park. He would have got there around twenty to four or thereabouts. You would have left by then, otherwise you would have seen him yourselves. Nikola says that one of his associates followed Michael as he crossed over onto the southbound platform and says he seemed to be counting the CCTV cameras.'

'That's understandable behaviour,' remarked Owen. 'It's just so he can work out where he needs to disembark so he's least likely to be seen clearly, as I mentioned earlier. He's fine-tuning his plan, just as we are, exactly as predicted.'

Lexington took a hefty swig of the fruity red wine. 'We shall need to be much more careful. If he sees us then there's a small possibility that he'll back out of his plan, even at this late stage. He may already have noted the faces of Monica and Thomas from when Mehmet photographed him so it's best we travel in smaller groups from now on whenever we're working. The closer we get to the end, the more we need to take every precaution to ensure we get the usual result. I suspect this will not be as straightforward as the Cooper case or indeed Hunt, relatively speaking. Belinda, I wonder if Nikola could please ask his people to let us know, through him, the moment they spot Michael. We just need to avoid him until Tuesday.'

Belinda agreed that she would ask Nikola first thing in the morning. 'He's very much on side,' she added. 'I think he's actually rather excited to have a positive involvement in something like this. It's quite unusual for him. More often than not, he's having to bail people out of a night in the cells. He genuinely seems invested in the whole business, after our inauspicious start.'

'Owen, are you going to be okay without Graham for a while?' asked Monica.

Owen smiled, misty-eyed. 'Oh, yes, we'll be fine. We're not joined at the hip like we used to be. Besides, Catherine's going to stay with him for a few days to keep him company. He gets a bit grumpy if he's on his own for too long. That's what comes from being one of eight children, I suppose.'

Monica and Thomas shared a look. Thomas stifled a laugh and turned back to Owen. 'Have you and Graham been together long?' he asked, proud of himself for not mentioning Catherine too, just in case their arrangement wasn't common knowledge.

Owen paused for a moment and took a sip of wine as he calculated his answer. 'Let's see. It'll be about eighteen months, give or take. Graham joined The Twelve at the beginning of 2018, almost six years to the day after I did. We hit it off straight away, I suppose because we both lived fairly near each other and we were both in similar lines of work – police and homeland security – and we'd both lost our wives in car accidents. There was a lot of common ground. It didn't take long to get around to talking about bisexuality and that's when we started seeing each other as more than just friends and eventually becoming a couple. By the time you're as old as we are, you can start to sense when someone is going to be receptive, as it were. Obviously we were delighted when everything just fell into place. It's almost as if Lexington planned it.'

'I can quite assure you, Owen,' growled Lexington without malice, 'that the thought never truly entered my mind, although, as you know, I have always endeavoured to bring in new people who will ease effortlessly into our group rather than create unnecessary turmoil. I see little value in creating confrontation for confrontation's sake. We have enough on our plates without infighting and I'm delighted that this current group is the most harmonious that I can remember. It wasn't always this way, let me assure you.' He took a swig of wine and continued. 'The process of choosing new members isn't as haphazard as you might expect. Someone like Suzanne, for example, should assimilate seamlessly in a few years when the time comes, whereas someone like Dennis certainly would not.' He gazed proudly around the room with a look of satisfaction like a farmer surveying a recently ploughed field. 'The very fact that we now have a smattering of couples amongst us, official or otherwise, I consider something of a badge of honour, and although I never intend for such delights to happen, I like to imagine that somewhere in my decision-making process, there's an element of matchmaking semi-dormant just under the surface.'

'You're the Cilla Black of senior citizens,' said Chris, to much laughter. 'The Tinder of The Twelve.'

———

By Thursday, Chris was emitting a faint but perceptible odour. He had stopped washing two days previously in order to bring authenticity to his supporting role as the homeless target of a psychopathic murderer. 'I'm going method,' he'd explained. 'I'm Daniel Day Lewis. I expect you all to be giving me spare change by tomorrow so I can stay in the role. I'll give it back. Maybe. Michael won't be able to resist me.'

Other members of the team had spent the previous day filing the rough edges of the different elements of their plan – David and Terry had been tinkering in the outbuilding to ensure that everything was ready for the appropriate moment. Owen, with

Martin's help, had been hacking into the CCTV system, initially for only a few fleeting seconds at a time to avoid detection, but then on Wednesday evening for five minutes. This had resulted in a prickly text from Dennis to Lexington to inform him that "unusual activity" had been reported to senior management via an email from the IT systems supervisor, and that Lexington would be prudent to advise Owen to be a little less cavalier, certainly for the next day or so. 'It's okay,' responded Owen. 'It works now. I was just pushing the boundaries that last time. And that chap in the ticket office is enjoying a lot less buffering, by the way.'

Monica, Thomas and Chris had been shuttling up and down to Moor Park, ensuring they recognised every nuance of the journey, every bump of the camber, noting regular passengers and mentally registering where they got off so that it would be easier to identify which parts of the train might become emptier before others. It was also a good time to chat together as friends.

'When this is over,' said Chris, unsubtly sniffing his armpit for signs of progress, 'I think the three of us deserve a proper night out. My treat. I know a fabulous little place in Shoreditch if you can bear to venture that far east. Small plates, Italian with a bit of Spanish and North African thrown in. Incredible wines and a really friendly atmosphere. What do you say? You can't book but I know the owner so it's not a problem.'

'That sounds wonderful, thank you.' Monica smiled, touching his arm amicably as their train eased out of a station.

'How are you finding Martin to share a room with?' asked Thomas. 'Is he behaving?'

Chris laughed and rolled his shoulders to exercise them. 'Sorry, the single bed's a little uncomfortable so I keep having to stretch a bit to iron out the knots. Anyway, sorry – Martin. He's being a dream, if I'm honest. Snores a bit but I suspect I do too. And he likes a quick chat about theatre shows before bed but that's fine with me. It was *Cats* last night, which I haven't seen, but I feel like I don't need to now! He even sang a bit of it. Something about a Mr Mistopheles who seems to be magical in some obscure way.'

'Thomas doesn't snore,' said Monica, looking at her paramour with wide-eyed longing.

'That's because Thomas is the perfect man,' said Chris with no element of unkindness, and slapped Thomas warmly on the knee. 'Anyway, back to Martin, it's actually good to get to know him a bit more. Obviously, we've chatted a fair amount over the last five years or so since I joined, but we've been sharing more since becoming "roomies" as the young people would say. He's got some terrific stories from his time on the cabs. He claims he once drove Princess Diana home from one of her secret liaisons, you know. I've no idea if it's true or if he dreamed it but Martin seems convinced. Apparently she gave a large tip for him to keep quiet about it. He used the money to take his wife to the revival of *Company* by Stephen Sondheim.'

At that moment, all three phones collectively buzzed. The message from Belinda alerted them that Michael Burrows was travelling; one of Nikola's team had spotted him. 'We'd better move,' said Monica. 'Northwood is the next station, so we'll get off there and find a coffee shop for an hour until he's passed through both ways. We can't risk him seeing us together, particularly as we're due to all check out the golf buggies and the route to the outbuilding later. It's such a blessing we have Belinda and her connection with Nikola.'

The three of them found a chain coffee shop a short walk from the station and positioned themselves at a corner table away from other customers in case anyone caught a whiff of Chris. Somewhere in the distance, they could hear the sirens of a couple of emergency vehicles moving at speed. Monica texted Belinda to ask for an all-clear when Michael was no longer travelling. After two hours and three coffees, plus cake for Chris and toilet breaks for everyone, the friends began to feel a growing sense of anxiety. Monica decided to contact Belinda again for an update thinking it most unusual for their target to be spending so much time on the trains at this late stage. Belinda's response came not via text, but in a call, and in a voice breathless with worry.

'Sorry I've not been in touch. I've been on the phone almost constantly to Nikola. Michael Burrows has stabbed one of his people.'

28

'Where did this happen, Belinda? And how's the victim? How's Nikola feeling?' Monica's voice was calm although her mind was ablaze with questions. Thomas held her left hand as she spoke, stroking it reassuringly. Even Chris had stopped eating.

At the other end of the line, Belinda took in a long breath. 'Nikola's fine,' she paused, 'now. He was absolutely furious to start with and wanted to take immediate revenge, but I talked to him for about half an hour and he's calmer now; still not completely at ease but certainly no longer murderous. It happened at Pinner about an hour and a half ago. Michael was being monitored by a young lad named Dimo. I say "young", he's twenty-two.'

'You say "is" twenty-two,' said Monica, hopefully.

'Yes, sorry, Dimo's fine too. Well, he's going to be fine. He's in hospital but Nikola says it's not serious. Just lots of stitches and an overnight stay. No major damage to any organs or big arteries and nothing long-term. Apparently Dimo does martial arts and was able to deflect the blade, otherwise it could have been very different, but this of course creates new problems. It means that

Michael is armed and more dangerous, and there's also the possibility that he's aware that he's being watched.'

'Have you told Lexington?'

'Not yet. I was just about to when you called. I'll do it now. I haven't got much life left in this phone battery but there should be enough for a couple of minutes. Anyway, it's safe to travel. Michael disappeared into the park at Pinner and the area is crawling with police. I doubt he'll be travelling again today, not on the Tube at any rate.'

Monica relayed the information to her companions and Thomas clasped her hand tightly. 'This puts a rather different complexion on things,' he whispered, just loud enough for both friends to hear him. 'Maybe we accept Dennis's offer of help.' Monica recognised that the stabbing would intensify Thomas's concerns for her safety. She gently lifted his hand to her mouth and kissed it.

'We'll talk to Lexington later and see how he feels about the situation. Personally, I think it changes nothing, except that it means we need to be even more focused and on our guard. Chris, remind me how long it takes for the tranquilliser to kick in please.'

The former surgeon shifted slightly in his seat. 'I'll alter the dose so he'll be out in around ten to fifteen seconds from the injection. He'll start to come round after about an hour, possibly longer depending on his build. We'll know later whether that's enough time to get him to the outbuilding in practice, but Terry says it's plenty because the buggies are pretty speedy. He's done the journey in under ten minutes from the platform to the prison.'

'Okay,' said Monica with a steely expression. 'Thank you. Thomas, I know you're worried, but I promise I'll be fine. It's just another job. There will be three of us in close proximity and we've rehearsed it over and over. We can do this.'

She registered the anxiety on Thomas's face. 'Darling, listen to me. We all know about grief and how it works. It hides around corners, in cafes. It conceals itself in the touch of a hand, the colour of a shirt, a familiar sound. It lurks in the darkness and in the brightest sunlight. But we also know that, with time, the sharp edges of grief wear down and become smoother like a pebble, so that we can carry it around, always feeling its weight but equally always knowing it can be managed and that we can live with it.'

Monica traced her index finger softly down the creases on Thomas's cheek. 'Nothing is going to happen to any of us, but on the off chance that it does, we know we can get through it because we've all done it before. Plus, I'm not afraid of death. I haven't been afraid for many years. I was brought up to believe that death is simply rebirth so if I suddenly dropped dead at this table, yes it would be sad but I've had an extraordinarily full life and, if my lapsed Hindu faith is correct, then I have many more to look forward to. I just hope to find you sooner in our next life.' She looked at Chris for a moment and then back to Thomas. 'Anyway, I have a strong feeling we shall all be fine. Call it an old Indian lady's intuition.'

'You'll probably both be reincarnated as rabbits,' quipped Chris.

Back at the Harrow house later that evening, Lexington had gathered all eleven, as well as Suzanne, to briefly discuss the day's events before their evening excursion. The commissioner shared Thomas's concerns that their safety was at greater risk. 'The offer remains. If you'd like us to have officers on stand-by, you just have to say the word. You know that, Lexington.'

'Thank you, Suzanne, but I believe more than ever that we should do this in the usual way. Without weaponry. The day that

The Twelve resorts to crude methods then we have sacrificed our right to exist, in my view. Chris, Monica, Thomas, do you have any concerns? You'll be the frontline, as it were.'

Monica looked at Thomas. 'We don't,' she replied with conviction. 'We'll all take greater precautions than usual, of course, and we're well aware of the dangers. However, we're confident that everything will go to plan.' She glanced at a wall clock with a squirrel motif, which had been a housewarming gift from Mrs Mendoza. 'Should we be getting to Moor Park soon?'

Lexington agreed. Martin had arranged to take Terry and David up to the golf course in his cab so that they would arrive before the others and be ready with the buggies. Belinda, Graham, Anna and Catherine all joined too, in case they were required as backup for whatever reason; and most unusually, Lexington had decided that Suzanne should join them for this reconnaissance exercise so she travelled in the taxi too in order to avoid being noticed on the Tube – Martin confided later that night that he'd never stuck to the speed limit so assiduously in his life, 'even the bleedin' annoying 20mph bits with the bumps!'

It was 9.30pm by the time everyone had congregated on the now familiar platform, with the exception of Terry, who was guarding the golf buggies in a secluded side street not far from the station. Although it was a relatively mild evening for mid-March, a subtle shift in the direction of the breeze suggested a colder spell was approaching. 'The forecast for Tuesday is that it'll be just below freezing at this hour,' said Chris, 'so we'll need to prepare for that. On the plus side, though, that tends to mean fewer people travelling late. Your average commuter up this way is more inclined to want to get home early when there's a chill in the air.'

'How was your journey up here, Commissioner?' asked Monica, mischievously.

'Oh, Martin's an excellent driver,' said Suzanne. 'I'm sure all cabbies weren't like him when I used to take them a few years back. If he wasn't already busy, he could be my personal chauffeur anytime.' Martin blushed and remained uncharacteristically silent. 'And such music on the journey. *A Little Night Music*, wasn't it?'

'Original Broadway cast with Glynis Johns,' the cabbie whispered.

The twelve of them spent a few minutes doing final checks on the locations of the cameras. They also noted the scheduled times of the trains going in the opposite direction, knowing that Michael Burrows would have done the same to minimise the likelihood of witnesses, looking across from different platforms. That process completed, and ensuring the station was empty, they took the stairs down to ground level. 'These are quite steep stairs,' said Catherine with concern. 'Are you sure you can carry a dead weight safely to the bottom?' Owen explained that he and Martin, along with David standing in for Thomas, had already experimented with heavy objects on the stairs and had been successful each time.

'We filled a beanbag full of gravel for one of the tests,' said Martin, flexing his biceps. 'That would weigh more than Dennis, let alone Michael, and we managed it easily. All this bloody yoga does have its benefits after all.'

Owen also explained that once he'd restored CCTV footage on the platform, and when the main group was safely on the stairs, he would quickly pack up his laptop and overtake them to ensure that the larger 'luggage' ticket barrier was open, allowing them to move through quickly. 'I've got a master ticket that overrides the Oyster system and keeps gates open whenever needed.'

'Is that legal?' asked Suzanne, dubiously.

'Absolutely not,' said Owen, brightly. 'I invented it. Would you like one?' The commissioner replied that while she was grateful for the generous offer, she nonetheless felt it advisable to decline for now, at least until she herself retired in a few years.

Once outside, they walked the short distance to where the locksmith was waiting with the borrowed buggies in a quiet, darkened avenue with large detached houses on one side and a tree-crammed embankment sloping up towards the railway on the other. 'I've got three today,' Terry grinned, 'because there are so many of us. It'll just be the two on Tuesday. Today it's like *The Italian Job*, though. Without the coach and the gold, obviously. Luckily they're four-seaters.'

They climbed onto the three golf buggies, Monica, Anna and Belinda squeezing onto the back seat of the one driven by David as they were the smallest. The convoy set off for the outbuilding, first along tarmac until, after five minutes, turning off the road and onto the golf course and from there into dense woodland to the outbuilding, the plumber manoeuvring slowly between trees to avoid anyone falling out if they encountered a log or a root.

'Just a second,' said Terry as he expertly picked the lock. 'Voila! We've fitted low luminosity 10-watt bulbs so as not to attract attention from anyone looking this way from any distance. There's enough light to be able to see what we're doing, but not enough to really be noticed from afar. The nearest house is quite a way off anyway but we're not taking any chances. I've also added some electric heating so nobody's going to freeze to death, not even on Tuesday. Someone's electricity bill is going to be sky high, but that's not really my primary concern, if I'm honest.'

'I like what you two have done with the place; it's very homely,' smiled Monica, approvingly, running her hand over a deep red leather armchair, one of four in addition to a sturdy metal chair with handcuffs and ankle restraints. 'These are a particularly nice domestic touch.'

David took a bow, accepting the compliment. 'Gotta keep a

few creature comforts. We borrowed a van from one of Martin's mates. Have you noticed another new addition?' he asked, smugly. 'She's over there.' They turned to look towards a far corner of the room and, through the semi-lit gloom, their eyes settled upon a new, state-of-the-art barista-quality coffee machine. 'We reckoned good coffee might be needed if it's a late night. And it will be a late night. Does anyone fancy an espresso? The beans are finest Sumatran.'

'Impressive,' said Lexington, settling carefully into one of the chairs. 'I think we could all benefit, to be honest, although perhaps not an espresso on this occasion as I may not sleep. A latte will suffice, thank you. Decaf if you can stretch to it.'

For the next hour, and with the heating on, the thirteen of them discussed what would happen once Michael Burrows was captured. It was decided that they would call Suzanne first and then she would call Dennis to let him know that his stepson was safely interred. The chief constable was, according to Suzanne, still coming to terms with the overwhelming nature of everything that had happened over the last few weeks but was certainly edging closer towards acceptance of his stepson's fate, an inevitable prison sentence for life. Dennis had decided, wisely, to keep away from the immediate area on the day in question, instead opting to wait for any news.

'You're sure this chair will hold him?' asked Suzanne, rattling it noisily.

'We've based it on another one we have over in the City, Commissioner,' said Martin. 'We've tested it using either Terry, David or myself in the last few days and none of us can get out of it. We're all strong men, particularly David, so if *we* struggle then I can't see a problem, particularly as there will be at least five of us guarding Michael at any one time. Chris can always give him another sedative injection if he starts to get restless.'

By eleven, everyone was comfortable with the logistics of the plan, even those who were new to the finer points of it. 'We'll take you all back to the station,' said David, 'and then we'll get the buggies back to where they should be. They need to be ready for the morning to assist the businessmen of the home counties in their attempt to stave off obesity through the medium of golf. We'll see some of you back in Harrow. Commissioner, would you like Martin to take you home?'

'You're kind, but I think I've troubled Martin enough for one day. I'll arrange a Scotland Yard car from Harrow, thank you. I have to say,' she looked around at the lined, experienced faces, 'once again, that I'm continually astonished and impressed by everything that you do. The level of professionalism and detail is really quite extraordinary. I wish I had either the time or the resources to reach the same levels with my senior team. I'm actually envious!'

'I'll drive Lexington back to Harrow,' said Martin. 'He should have a bit of comfort as it's his last case.'

The older man smiled, gratefully. 'And I shall arrange hot water bottles for you all by the time you get back.'

Just before midnight, and after the return journey via buggy and Underground, the Harrow group was gathered in the living room, tired but energised by all they had seen. 'I'm going to see Dimo tomorrow,' said Chris. 'Belinda checked with Nikola that it was okay. I think we owe him a visit after what happened, so I'll be out from late morning.'

'Do you want company?' asked Thomas.

Chris reached out a hand and patted Thomas on the knee. 'Thank you, my friend, but I'd like to see him alone if it's all right with you. He's out of hospital now so he's convalescing at his flat in Preston Road. It's not far so I won't be long and I've warned him that I smell a bit strange. He understands the reason. Martin's going to drive me, so I don't inflict myself on the general public. We haven't got anything major on tomorrow, have we?'

'Just more fine-tuning,' said Monica. 'If you miss anything, we can fill you in.'

29

Chris returned from his four-hour visit to Dimo the following afternoon with a noticeable spring in his step. 'How is the patient?' asked Thomas, looking up from his book as the former surgeon took off his coat and joined his friend in the reception room. 'You were there a long time.'

'He's in excellent spirits,' said Chris, cheerfully, positioning himself on the arm of a chair at a safe distance from Thomas and Monica who had also been reading, 'considering he's been knifed by a murderer. He's still in a bit of discomfort but he's got medication from the hospital and I've given him something a little stronger, shall we say, from my personal collection to help him sleep better. He understands that he can't take both at the same time so he's going to try mine and see how he feels. I took a quick look at the wound and it's healing well. They did a good job at that hospital. The stitches are probably better than mine used to be. He'll be up and about in around three weeks as long as he eases off the martial arts for a bit longer.

'I had to apologise about my body odour and they were perfectly kind about it. Oh, I met his brother Ivo, too. Both of them were junior martial arts champions back home in Bulgaria.

They specialised in something called *Da Dao,* which personally I'd never heard of, but it looks like it saved his life on this occasion. Why they decided to come to the UK is a mystery to me but I suppose, like so many people in their position, there's this opaque promise of better opportunity in a foreign land. They didn't imagine in a million years that they'd be begging for pennies on a city transport system, but now that they're here, the two of them are trying to find regular jobs.'

'That must be a challenge,' said Thomas.

'It's really tough, particularly when they both have criminal records, albeit for minor offences. I might see if Suzanne can quietly do something about that when all this is over. Anyway, enough of me rattling on. Did I miss anything important?'

Monica explained that the only major thing he had missed was lunch: a tagine of lamb with a vegetarian option involving butternut squash, which Terry had prepared. 'I think there's some of the veggie one left in a pan on the hob if you ask Terry,' she added. 'Oh, and there's an impromptu yoga class later this afternoon and Anna's coming up, which will no doubt please you. She says it's more important than ever that we all keep our bits and pieces functioning. We're moving all the furniture to the walls to make space. It's at five so don't fill up on too much lunch if you want to take part.'

Chris managed to fill a small bowl with the remnants of Terry's vegetarian tagine and then spent a couple of hours in his room alone while the rest of the group gathered for their class. Martin peered in at one stage but Chris reassured him. 'I think it's best to give the official yoga a miss, old boy,' he had explained. 'I suspect my current aroma might affect everyone's concentration. I'll catch up with Anna separately.'

After yoga, Lexington announced that anyone who wished to go back to their own homes for the weekend was welcome to do so. He realised that although the Harrow house was comfortable, some members of the group may be missing creature comforts as well as their own space and, as they had made excellent progress in such a short space of time, there was no pressing need to incarcerate anyone so long as they all returned for dinner on Monday. As an incentive, he revealed that the meal would be a warming chicken and leek stew, which he would be making himself with a little help from Terry, who had agreed to perform the role of sous chef. 'I may even attempt a dumpling,' he added.

'That was utterly delicious, Lexington. Thank you. And Terry, of course.' Thomas was mopping the dregs of the stew with a piece of focaccia bread. 'How did you learn to cook so well?'

The locksmith raised his hands in a 'you're most welcome' gesture. 'It's all in the seasoning,' he began. 'Get your salt and pepper right and you're halfway there, and then add a tiny bit of very good vinegar at the end just to lift everything. White wine vinegar in this case because it's chicken. My wife taught me that, God rest her soul.' Terry looked momentarily wistful. 'She was a marvellous woman, but feisty and she never had any truck with that nonsense about a woman's place being at home, so we always shared the housework. Of course, it was a bit unusual in Stepney in the late seventies, as I'm sure you can appreciate, but I loved it. She taught me all about cooking and I taught her the basics of locks. She would have been a decent smith if she'd ever fancied a career change.'

'She was a teacher, wasn't she?' asked Monica, mopping the side of her mouth with a patterned napkin which Lexington had explained was named *Mottaga* for reasons unknown to all but the good folk at IKEA HQ.

Terry explained that his wife Irene had been an English teacher for thirty-five years until her early death. 'Cancer, I'm afraid. Started in her liver and by the time they caught it, the bloody thing was everywhere. It's a bastard of a disease as many of you know. But you move on; you have to.' He smiled feebly at the group. 'And when Lexington called me six years ago, she'd been gone for just over three years and I was in a much better place. I'd thrown myself into work, but I was also thinking about retiring and letting the younger guys have their turn. I didn't *want* to retire, though, not at all. I was worried that I'd just sit at home all day vegetating, and that's not good for a man of any age, let alone one in his autumn years. So this amazing opportunity that Lexington presented was right up my street.'

'We'd had our eye on you for a while, Terry,' said Lexington with a sympathetic smile. 'A couple of you long-serving members may remember a splendid old chap called Bennett who kept squirrels as pets. Anyway, he was getting on in years and he decided, much like I have lately, that the time had come to move on. He was a carpenter by trade but he'd spent time over the years on all manner of disciplines; he was vital to The Twelve and we knew he'd be tricky to replace. We looked around the carpentry world for a bit but the pickings were rather slim. There were a lot of decent carpenters, don't get me wrong, but none with quite the right temperament or circumstance. We managed to whittle down the list to a couple of possibilities but they were both a bit dour, as I recall. Plus, one of them had a massive and time-consuming family, which rarely works well in The Twelve if I'm honest. Too many demands; a wedding or a funeral every other weekend. Then another member of the group at the time, Miranda Andrews it was, said that she knew you, Terry. Do you remember?'

The locksmith nodded. 'I'd done a few odd jobs for her, nothing more. Nice woman. She started off needing a deadlock fixed and I ended up basically doing a bit of DIY all over the house. Massive house too, up in Hampstead with just her pootling around in it. I'm afraid she was going a bit doolally towards the end.'

Lexington frowned. 'Yes, dementia had begun to set in, sadly. She had to leave about six months before Bennett, but I suppose her priceless legacy was to introduce us to Terry. That and about twelve million in her will after we'd sold the house; I thought about keeping it as a Twelve house but there were too many small rooms and not really anything suitable for meetings. A delightful Ukrainian chap bought it for his daughter and her family. Obviously we're enormously thankful for both Terry and the money; more so for Terry, if I'm perfectly frank.' The locksmith's cheeks reddened.

'It may not be the time or the place, but have you given any thought to who might fill the gaping void once you're gone, Lexington?' asked Chris, who had taken on the role of sommelier that evening and was circling the table refilling glasses with a 2014 Chablis. The others had politely chosen to ignore his scent, which was by now rather pungent. Lexington had sent Martin out earlier in the day to purchase a scented candle as a distraction.

'In terms of replacing me at the helm, not quite yet.' Lexington took a sip of wine. 'Perfectly chilled, Chris. Thank you. I'm very nearly there but I thought it best to see how this Burrows business plays out first. However, in terms of making up the numbers after I've gone, as it were, do you all remember Veronica from my New Year party? I think she is ready and may be our best option. Belinda and Graham have been watching her for a few months now. She's highly intelligent, very well connected and largely at a loose end. I may put her forward for a psych test before too long. She'll enjoy the experience of meeting Mrs Mendoza. Of that I have no doubt.'

'Plus,' added Monica with a fiery look in her eye, 'the addition of Veronica would go some way to addressing the absurd gender imbalance that still exists within The Twelve, even in this day and age!'

Lexington explained that the final choice wouldn't be his entirely: that once they had moved beyond the Burrows case, the eleven of them could meet with Veronica either individually or in small groups, to assess whether or not she would slip seamlessly into the vacant position. 'Now, as it is most unusual for so many of us to be together on the evening before an operation, I should like to raise a toast. To a successful day tomorrow: to the safe return of everyone here involved, and,' he raised his glass, 'to new friendships in old age.'

The assembled members of The Twelve raised their glasses, each understanding in subtly different ways the meaning behind Lexington's words.

'Equally unusually for us,' Lexington continued, 'we have some dessert this evening. Earlier today, and despite the cold weather, a Mrs Archer from next door came round with a homemade apple crumble to welcome us to the neighbourhood; apparently she has a tree in her garden and she harvests the fruit in October and November to store over the winter. She also makes jam with them. They're cookers, not eaters, she reliably informs me. Terry let her in and, as only he and I were here at the time, I'm not at all certain what conclusions she may have drawn. Terry was carrying a feather duster as he was attending to some urgent cobweb unpleasantness in one of the bathrooms, but that didn't appear to cause any perturbation on Mrs Archer's part, and so an apple crumble is available to those who desire it.'

'With fresh custard which I've made,' added Terry. 'Or double cream from the local corner shop, which I haven't.'

The anniversary of the birth of Josef Mengele dawned with an appropriately vicious frost that adorned the outsides of the windows with a tissue of ice crystals. As predicted, the temperature wasn't expected to rise above three degrees Celsius for the entire day. Lexington had ensured that everyone had shoes with grip as 'the platforms can get slippery, despite best attempts at gritting by the relevant authorities.'

Chris, who hadn't washed for a week, had by now cultivated a musty and authentic odour, which everyone agreed was in keeping with his role as the evening's principal player. In order to accentuate the effect, Chris had been sleeping in the same clothes since the previous Wednesday and, as a result, Martin had moved his bed as far away from him as the internal structure of their room would allow.

Come the evening, the group had convened and gone over the final details of their plan, after which everyone retired to their rooms to nap. Monica and Thomas dozed fitfully, which was unusual for them, but Chris explained that their bodies were starting to create adrenalin in preparedness for the evening activities and so deep sleeping under the circumstances would be a challenge. 'It's like when you know you have to be up early for an important appointment and as a result you keep waking up every couple of hours for no reason.'

At eight, Belinda arrived with news that Nikola had called his working people off the Tubes for the evening and also that there had been no sightings of Michael at all that day, or indeed since the attack on Dimo, although Nikola had positioned his people inconspicuously at every station from Finchley Road to Pinner on lookout throughout the day and into the evening. 'I rather hope he's changed his mind about an attack this evening,' said Belinda.

'He won't,' replied Monica, firmly. 'He's the sort who has a plan and sticks to it, regardless of the consequences. Plus, if you're Michael then today is a date which demands celebration…

in his own macabre way.' She moved towards Chris and squeezed his hand, supportively. 'Are you ready?' The surgeon nodded that he was. He had with him three small, full syringes with plastic safety tips. He gave one each to Monica and Thomas, and kept one himself. Everyone would be wearing trousers with deep side pockets for the evening so that the syringes could be easily accessible.

'I shall be here until I receive news,' said Lexington, quietly. 'Belinda will stay with me and Suzanne will join later. I wish you all luck, particularly Thomas as it's his first one. I hope, as ever, and expect that you will have no need for it, but nonetheless…' He let the sentence evaporate into the air as the team donned their coats and set off for the business of the evening; David, Owen, Terry and Martin in the cab to Moor Park; Monica, Thomas and Chris on foot to the Underground.

Lexington and Belinda watched solemnly from the door of the Harrow house as the three of them waved brightly from the pavement before turning to walk down the hill, their condensing breath now visible against the charcoal sky. 'Au revoir!' said Monica, blowing a delicate kiss. A dog barked somewhere in the distance as the temperature dipped a degree further.

30

It was 9.20pm before a text came through from Belinda. Michael had boarded a northbound train at Wembley Park, wearing a long grey coat buttoned almost to the top and a baseball cap pulled down as far as it would go. According to Petar, the Bulgarian who'd spotted him, Michael was seated in the middle of the train, as expected, to avoid the CCTV cameras at Moor Park and also knowing that the middle would be the area with the quietest carriages by that point in its journey. Both of Michael's hands were reported to be deep inside the coat's pockets. 'A poisoned sandwich in one, of course,' said Thomas. 'And maybe a knife in the other, but we can't be certain.'

Monica breathed in deeply, her heart already beating hard. 'It's okay,' she exhaled, to herself more than anyone. 'I'm ready.' As they were at Pinner when the call came, the three friends decided to enter a small, cold platform waiting area until they could see Michael. Around seven minutes later, in an almost empty carriage, the baseball cap appeared, its owner's back to the platform, moving slowly right to left as the train eased to a stop. Chris scraped his fingers through the frozen earth of one of the station's empty flowerbeds as he moved quickly and purposefully toward the back of the platform to board.

The automatic doors opened. Thomas and Monica took seats in the compartments either side of Michael, each about twenty feet away from him. Monica had to walk past the poisoner to get to her position but he did not, she noted to her relief, look up at her. It took a fair amount of restraint for Monica not to grab and inject the poisoner there and then, but she forced herself to maintain composure and stick to the agreed plan. From their seated vantage points, they could both see Michael staring down at the carriage floor, slightly slumped, while all the time keeping both hands inside the pockets of the coat. Between Thomas and Michael were a couple of middle-aged women engaged in a lively conversation about one of their husbands, as well as an older gentleman, clearly returning from work, engrossed in his evening newspaper crossword, biro poised. On the other side of Michael, there were no passengers until Monica. She looked ahead towards the driver's cabin and noticed a handful of solo travellers dotted in various seats, the closest being an old man with a hat, dark glasses and a white stick with a curved handle who was in a window seat facing the platform.

Meanwhile, Chris had settled further down the train so that it would appear that he had been travelling for some time.

As they slowed for the next station, Northwood Hills, the two women rose from their seats to leave, still deep in conversation. Michael turned in their direction, towards Thomas but away from Monica, and smiled. To Thomas, it felt as though the poisoner was smiling directly at him, a thought he dismissed quickly as he reached into his own pocket and ran his thumb over the plastic casing of the syringe. He had practised with the syringe over a hundred times since the beginning of March and yet its contours suddenly felt alien to him.

The opening of the doors had brought a wave of icy air into

the carriage, which had the effect of heightening Thomas's anxiety. The high-pitched beep of the doors as they closed seemed to be louder than ever, a staccato electronic knell. 'I'm ready,' he repeated Monica's words slowly to himself under his breath. 'We're ready.' One more stop and then Moor Park. Thomas could feel his heart rate increase and suddenly became glad of the medical Chris had performed on him back in January – 'Your heart's very strong, old man. No major issues there for a while,' his friend had concluded, although at this precise moment it felt primed to burst.

The train set off again, picking up speed through the freezing suburban gloom before beginning its deceleration into Northwood, the stop before Moor Park.

Just as it was coming to a halt, Thomas's nose made him aware that Chris was beside him, holding out a quivering, dirt-encrusted hand. 'Spare any change, mate? It's a cold night to be hungry on the streets.' The surgeon and the sports trainer stared into each other's eyes. Chris's pupils were dilated in anticipation. Thomas had to force himself not to look in the direction of Monica and, of course, Michael.

'Um, no, I'm sorry,' he muttered, hoping he was loud enough to be heard by Monica. And Michael.

'Fucking tight old bastard,' grumbled Chris, adjusting his head slightly so that only Thomas could see and then winking quickly before moving down the train towards Michael. The commuter with the newspaper was getting off and almost bumped into Chris as he did so. Chris hesitated for a moment, pretending to fiddle with his underpants, but in reality giving the train time to set off before his scheduled encounter with Michael.

Finally, the doors closed and Chris shuffled towards the poisoner. Thomas was desperate to catch Monica's eye, but he knew that such a silly mistake might give them all away. The lights from bedrooms and living rooms outside the train had given way to darkness as the train moved further into the more rural suburbs, the black outlines of trees painted against the night's canvas.

'Got any change, mate?'

Chris was now standing over Michael, his left hand outstretched and expectant, his right slipping the safety cap off of the syringe in his pocket. A few feet away, Monica was doing the same.

The train began to slow.

Michael stood up, taller than Chris but not by much, his eyes on the floor.

'You've got really good teeth for a homeless fucker, haven't you? So I don't think you really need spare change, do you, old man,' he said calmly as he slowly drew the knife from his coat and looked up into the surgeon's eyes, now filled with fear. 'I think you need something else.'

31

From his vantage point a short distance away, Thomas watched in horror as Michael lunged at his friend. Chris quickly turned his body sideways in an attempt to deflect the blade, and then fell back on the opposite seats of the carriage, dropping his syringe in the process. Michael pulled the knife back and readied to stab again.

'Chris!' shouted Thomas without thinking.

Michael turned to face him, not five metres away, his face contorted in fury as the train slowed almost to a halt. 'Oh look,' he snarled, 'there's a pair of old fuckers, is there?'

Thomas pulled the syringe out of his pocket, knowing that against a knife he would need luck as well as agility as Michael moved purposefully towards him. Suddenly, the younger man straightened up, grimacing in pain, Monica's emptied syringe still sticking out of his left buttock. He swung around violently to see Monica already racing down the train, her heart pounding and her brain counting the seconds until she hoped the tranquilliser would kick in. 'Fucking bitch!' he spat furiously, and sped after her.

'Four, five, six…' in Monica's head, if she could reach fifteen before he caught her, then she would be safe, but after 'six' she heard a loud crash and turned to see Michael spread-eagled on the floor next to the elderly blind man she had noticed earlier.

'Fuck you!' breathed Michael weakly as his head lifted gingerly from the floor of the carriage and then dropped with a thud.

The blind man looked down at the poisoner, prostrate in front of him, and jabbed him hard in the side with his stick. 'I am sorry, young man,' he said with a strong Turkish accent, 'but my stick can get in the way sometimes. Such a nuisance. I always forget to tuck it in.'

'Mehmet?' Monica was gathering her thoughts as the doors opened at Moor Park station, permitting another blast of frozen air to invade the space, and just managed to pull the train's emergency lever before Owen entered the carriage. 'Mehmet, whatever are you doing here?'

The old Turk removed his sunglasses, tipped his hat and gave her a wink. 'I thought you might need some Ottoman help,' he smiled. 'As it turns out, I was right.'

'How did you know what time to be here?'

Mehmet ran a hand across the bottom half of his face as if to stretch it slightly. From his pocket, he pulled out a cheap pay-as-you-go mobile phone. 'You are not the only ones that Nikola likes to keep informed,' he said with a satisfied smile. 'Now, you had better go and check on Mr Chris.'

'Ladies and gentlemen,' the downbeat voice of the driver appeared unusually placid over the tannoy after the preceding thirty seconds of mayhem. 'Sorry for the delay to your service this evening. Someone has pulled the passenger alarm so I just need to check on that before we can continue. Hopefully we will be on the move again shortly. London Underground apologises for any inconvenience to your journey at this time.'

Thomas had already reached Chris, who was slumped in a seat, bleeding from a wound just below his shoulder. 'I need an ambulance, Thomas,' he gasped, obviously in some pain. 'I'm losing blood.'

Owen explained that he had already called for one the moment he'd seen what was happening from the platform. 'I'll stay with Chris,' said Monica. 'He'll need someone with him and it makes more sense that it's me. Can you two quickly get Michael off the train before the driver gets here? Take Chris's syringe. You might need it later. It's on the floor over there. You can use the safety cap from mine which, by the way, you'll need to remove from Michael's arse. I stuck it in quite far.' She pointed to where Chris had dropped the drug.

'Will you let us know how he is?' asked Thomas, scrambling to retrieve the syringe.

'Of course,' replied Monica, touching him tenderly on the arm. 'Stay safe. Please. One shock tonight is more than enough. I love you.'

By the time Owen and Thomas reached the stricken Michael, the train driver was only a carriage away, joined by the dishevelled station guard who had miraculously left the online distraction of his office to find out what was going on.

'Is this the emergency?' the driver asked, nonchalantly. 'Just looks like a drunk fallen asleep to me. A drunk in a baseball cap. In this weather!'

'No, mate. The emergency is further down,' said Owen, improvising quickly. 'Some old homeless fella with a medical problem. This is our friend's son. He's had a few too many. We'll take care of this. It's our stop anyway. You deal with the real emergency.' He pointed in the direction of Chris and Monica, noting with alarm that Chris had slipped further down the seat and that Monica was now cradling his head, which had drooped to one side.

The two of them reached under Michael's shoulders and lifted the dead weight off the train and onto the platform. 'Nice to see you,' waved Mehmet, rescuing the knife, which he had wrapped in a handkerchief and pocketed as soon as Michael had dropped it. 'You had better take this with you. Maybe Mr Lexington will need it as evidence.' He pulled a disposable carrier bag from his inside coat pocket and placed the knife in it before carefully handing it to Owen. Once off the train, Owen quickly secured the knife in a small bag along with his laptop as the half dozen passengers who had also left the train made their way hurriedly to the safety and warmth of their waiting rides.

Michael turned out to be even lighter than they had anticipated and, with the platform clear of passengers and the station guard already occupied, they were able to easily move him down the stairs and out of the station, his head lolling pathetically, to where David and Terry were waiting with the buggies.

'Everything all right?' asked the locksmith. 'Where are Chris and Monica?'

'I'll tell you on the way,' said Owen as the sound of distant sirens pierced the chill darkness. 'We'd better get out of here fast. In fact, is there a way to get off the road quicker? I just want to avoid bumping into any of these emergency vehicles.'

'Of course,' nodded Terry, who then shouted over to Martin in the other buggy. 'Scenic route, Martin. Put your foot down.'

Once inside the outbuilding, which, as Terry had put the heating on at eight, was a cosy relief after the biting cold of the buggy journey, David searched the comatose Michael's clothing. As expected, the other pocket did contain what looked like some sort of soft food like a bread roll wrapped in tin foil, which the plumber delicately removed as if it might explode, and placed on a table next to one of the armchairs. In addition, there was a roll of around a dozen twenty-pound notes, some small change, a one-month paper travelcard and some chewing gum. Unusually, there was no mobile phone and Terry also noted there were no keys – suggesting that wherever Michael was staying, it would most likely be somewhere with a code entry system. Either that, or there would need to be someone on the inside to let him in. Once they were satisfied that there were no hidden weapons, Terry and Owen secured the killer, still immobile, to the chair.

'And now, we wait,' said David, brightly. 'It should be around an hour before he comes round. I'll make the coffees.'

Owen telephoned Lexington to let him know the situation, although he was already aware about Chris, as Monica had called from the ambulance. 'Any news?' asked Thomas with growing concern when the call was finished.

'They've taken him to the general hospital in Watford, which is the closest to here with an A&E. Apparently it's a very good one. Monica will call with an update as soon as she knows anything.' Lexington had also kept Suzanne informed. 'She may arrive at some point over the next couple of hours, but it depends on her workload. There's a bit of a political kerfuffle she has to deal with, apparently. The Secretary of State for Education has been involved in some sort of sex scandal and she has to help to hush it up. I didn't tell you that.'

They sat drinking coffee, mostly in silence and more aware by the minute of the worrying lack of news from Monica. Just before midnight, Michael Burrows began to make a low groaning noise, his head cautiously moving from side to side like a newborn creature blinking into sunlight.

'Good morning, Mister Sleepyfuck,' said Martin casually, sitting in an armchair across from the prisoner with his legs stretched out and crossed at the ankles and his arms spread wide behind his head. 'Sweet dreams? I sincerely hope not.'

Michael tried to raise himself but quickly realised that his chair wasn't quite as built for comfort as those he could see before him, owing to its various cuffs and restraints, which he rattled angrily. 'Where the fuck am I?' he exploded with as much venom as his semi-awake state would allow. 'Who the fuck are you?' His eyes, wide and raging, darted around the room and settled on Thomas. 'Oh, *you*! I remember you. From the fucking train. Where's that bitch that stabbed me? I've got unfinished business with that one.'

Thomas had to dig his fingernails into his palms to assuage the fury that had been building up ever since he'd last seen Chris, weakened and bleeding, a couple of hours earlier.

'Never mind her,' said Martin, gesturing to the wrapped package. 'Would you mind telling us what's in the tinfoil?'

Michael clenched his fists and shook himself as hard as he could, hoping that there might be some small loosening of the ties. When it became clear that there wasn't, he flopped back in the chair, inhaled deeply and then spat violently at Martin, who shifted sharply to his left in order to avoid the gobbet of phlegm. 'See for yourself,' he hissed. 'Take a big bite. You'll like it. I made it myself using only the freshest ingredients for society's most discerning consumers.'

Owen, who was closest, took some disposable rubber gloves from his pocket and pulled them tightly over his fingers. He then picked up the foil package and carefully peeled back the layers to reveal what looked like an innocuous ham and salad roll, before lifting the top piece of bread and some lettuce. Sprinkled liberally throughout the roll was a crystalline white powder. Owen gave it a sniff. Nothing but the scent of cured ham. 'Potassium cyanide again? Or something else, maybe?' Thomas wished Monica or Anna were there to advise. 'Could be strychnine?' Owen proposed. Burrows' mouth curled slowly into an odious smile. 'Ah. I thought so. You mentioned it in the chat room about a week ago. And enough to kill within a couple of hours by the look of it.

Unless it's been mixed with something else. So, what was the knife for?'

'Why the fuck should I tell you?' shouted Michael at the top of his voice. *'Help!'*

'I wonder why they always do that,' mused Martin to no one in particular, as Michael continued his desperate cries. 'As if we'd deliberately incarcerate someone within earshot of the public. Let us know when you're finished, Michael. We have time.' Martin sat back in his chair and started ostentatiously nibbling a fingernail.

'I'll ask again,' said Owen when the noise had subsided. 'What was the knife for?'

Michael was silent for a moment, struggling to decide whether cooperating and trying to befriend these strange old gentlemen might somehow be his best chance of escape. 'Security,' he said finally. 'That's all. It felt like someone was following me the last few weeks and when that fucking stupid beggar kid got involved, I knew it. Is he dead, by the way? Not that I give a fuck who lives or dies in this shithole world.'

'Why do this in the first place?' continued Owen, ignoring the question. 'What have any of these people done to hurt you?'

Michael shrugged as best the handcuffs would allow. 'Why the fuck not?' he growled. 'These people are vermin. Smelly fucking scroungers. If they don't fuck off, then they deserve what's coming to them.' There was a pause while everyone took in what Michael was saying. Thomas was willing the phone to ring and for Monica to tell him that Chris was okay, but no call came.

'Why the Underground?'

'Oh, I think you know. You old people are clearly quite smart. You know who I am and where I've come from.' The snarl in Michael's voice had returned with thoughts of his stepfather. 'So, what happens next? Do you torture me or something? Hit me with incontinence pants until I give in?' The poisoner grinned as if the thought of torture was quite appealing.

'Sadly not,' said Martin. 'Tempting though it is. Not on this occasion anyway. Thanks to your stepfather, we'll hand you over to the police and you'll go to prison for life, possibly to some sort of secure hospital if you're lucky. You'll stay here with us until the commissioner arrives and she can decide what to do with you. Incidentally, just out of personal curiosity, why go from the District Line to the Jubilee Line back in January when the pattern suggested you were working in a clockwise direction? That confused us for a while.'

Michael adopted a calmer tone, more resigned. 'I don't really know, mate. If I'm honest, I don't really like going south of the river,' he explained. Everyone looked at the cabbie, who was now grinning triumphantly.

'Don't!' said David, raising an admonishing finger at Martin before turning his attention back to their captive. 'You're quite chatty for a psychopath. I'll give you that.'

Michael did his best to sit back, almost relaxing into the restrictive position on his chair like a demented prince on a throne. 'Well, you know, there isn't really a manual for this sort of thing. It's not like there's a one-size-fits-all character profile. I can be silent and uncooperative if you prefer.'

There was a knock on the side of the building rather than the door, a coded signal. 'That'll be the commissioner now,' said Martin, getting up to greet the visitor. He unbolted the heavy wood and swung it wide open, then stood in the doorway shocked, as Michael Burrows looked past him at the outbuilding's newest visitors.

'Oh hello, Dad,' he beamed sarcastically, emphasising the nominative. 'It's really been far too long. Have you enjoyed watching what you made me do?'

32

Dennis Burrows was standing slightly ahead of the commissioner in the pale light of the doorway, his face expressionless. Suzanne held out a hand to usher him into the outbuilding and they both edged forward tentatively, cautiously, climbing into a cage with an unpredictable wild animal.

'This is somewhat unexpected,' ventured Owen, giving Suzanne a look which asked, 'Are you absolutely sure about this?'.

The commissioner closed the door behind her, keeping her eyes firmly on the young man pinioned to the chair in the centre of the gloomy space. 'Dennis and I had a long chat earlier this evening, in between all of this ongoing nonsense with the government minister. All things considered, I believe it's for the best. I've also spoken with Fiona, Dennis's wife. I've given it as much thought as I could in the time available and I also sought the advice of Lexington, who agreed that the implications of not having Dennis here were on balance, potentially more challenging than having him here. Ergo, here we are. How are you feeling, Dennis?' She turned to the chief constable, who was staring blankly at his stepson as if in a daze.

'I'm all right,' he said mechanically, not turning from the young man secured to the chair in front of him. 'Michael,' he nodded, 'good to see you again. After so long.'

Michael sat up straight in the chair and flexed his wrists under the handcuffs, digging his fingernails into his palms. 'Have you come to tell me what a naughty boy I've been?' he sing-songed. 'Or have you come to hit me again? And is Mum coming? Because that would really make it a family party to remember.' He spat out the last four words as if they were gristle.

Dennis looked up at the ceiling of the outbuilding and inhaled deeply. 'Your mother isn't coming,' then he paused before adding, 'but she wants you to know that despite everything, she loves you and she wants what's best for you.'

A sense of regret flashed fleetingly across Michael's face before the feral scowl returned and he reverted back to his default sarcasm. 'Oh, that's so nice. But the feeling isn't mutual. I hate that woman and I hate you.' The ankle cuffs rattled as he tried again to make some progress, however improbable, towards freedom.

Thomas's phone vibrated. A message from Monica made him catch his breath. 'Chris is in the operating theatre having emergency surgery,' he shared while typing a quick reply. 'He's lost a lot of blood. She says it could be a while before there's more news. The surgeons say it's too early to tell whether he'll pull through.'

'That's a pity,' said Michael without emotion, 'I really hoped I'd killed that interfering old fucker there and then. A second stab would've finished him.'

In a heartbeat, Martin hurled himself towards the captive and grabbed him round the neck. 'How fucking dare you, you little shit!' he screamed. 'You're not fit to breathe the same air as that brave man.' Thomas and Terry simultaneously lunged at Martin and dragged him off, but not before the cabbie had landed a right jab to Michael's head.

'Martin!' shouted Terry, aware that they had witnesses to this unusual outburst. 'For God's sake, man. We all feel the same way but you've got to keep it together. You know the way we do things. Anger doesn't help.'

Martin muttered a muffled apology, directed more towards Dennis than to Michael, and went to sit down. 'I watched *West Side Story* earlier,' he explained. 'That always puts me in an emotional frame of mind.'

'I think,' said Suzanne, calmly, 'that under the exceptional circumstances, Martin's feelings can be understood. Although you're right, Terry. We all need to keep our heads.'

David decided to defuse the situation by offering the new arrivals a coffee, which they both accepted. Over the whirr and hiss of the coffee machine, Owen shared what little information they had so far gleaned from Michael. 'I've known for some time,' stated Suzanne, 'that you've been using cash for everything: the travelcards, minicabs and the rest of it. But where are you getting the cash from? There's no record of you having a bank account for around eighteen months, Michael. It's as if you've been using cash and only cash for the last year at least, in order to be virtually impossible to trace. So, someone must have been supplying you with unlimited cash. Who is it, Michael? If you tell me, then I can help you if and when this gets to court.'

Michael smiled. 'Come closer, copper, and I'll give you a little clue.'

The commissioner looked around the room for a supportive face. 'I wouldn't,' warned Owen. 'He spits.' As if taking this as a cue, Michael launched a blob of sputum in the direction of Suzanne, missing her by inches. 'Warned you. Charming, isn't he? Quite the catch.'

'Blame my upbringing,' growled Michael with a glance to his stepfather who remained impassive.

The commissioner thought for a moment, struggling to decide the best course of action, before telling the group that she was going outside to speak with Lexington. The six men – a stepfather, a stepson and four pensioners – sat or stood in silence listening to the gentle winter wind tickling the budding trees until, after five minutes, Suzanne returned and offered her phone to Thomas. 'He wants to speak with you,' she said, pensively.

Somewhat surprised to be singled out, Thomas took the phone and listened intently to what Lexington had to say. For a moment, he considered disagreeing but on reflection, and with images of Chris in surgery filling his head, as well as horrific thoughts of what might have happened to Monica if the circumstances had been different, he decided that the wisdom of years was, on this occasion, to be respected, regardless of his own personal feelings.

He returned the phone to Suzanne and looked round at the other members of the group. 'We should give Dennis some time alone with his son,' he said calmly.

'Are you sure?' asked Owen, anxiously.

'Oh, please no!' whined Michael, weakly. 'You promised you wouldn't torture me.'

'Quite sure,' confirmed Thomas, suppressing his own misgivings. 'He's not exactly going to help Michael escape, is he? We're the only ones with the keys to the cuffs. Ten minutes. That's all. Before we all start to catch a chill. It's minus two outside. Is that okay, Dennis?'

'Yes,' said the chief constable flatly, almost robotically. 'Thank you, gentlemen. Commissioner.'

Owen refilled everyone's coffee mugs and all bar the two Burrows stepped out into the cold where most of the men, after placing their drinks carefully on the ground by the wall of the outbuilding, disappeared in the direction of various trees – 'that's what three cups of coffee in quick succession does,' as Terry pointed out – leaving the police chief alone with Thomas.

Sensing his thoughts were elsewhere, Suzanne drew him into an uneasy hug. 'I know what you're thinking,' she said, her breath condensing in the night air, 'but try not to worry. From what I know, the people at that hospital are excellent and they certainly won't want anything bad to happen to one of their own. I'm sure Monica will be in touch with good news as soon as she can.' Thomas relaxed into the hug as it became a little less awkward. A year ago he would have recoiled from this sort of contact, but life with Monica had made him more tactile, or at least less likely to shy from situations such as this one. He briefly allowed himself to focus his attention back on their current situation but, once again, the commissioner was ahead of him. 'You know what we're going to find when we go back in, don't you? Lexington has explained it to you?'

Thomas moved a couple of feet away from her. His head dropped slightly as he ran his left hand through his thinning hair. 'I do,' he said at last. 'And I think I believe it's for the best although I can't help worrying about Dennis and particularly his wife. And I'm not sure why Lexington chose to tell me of all people.'

The commissioner smiled and took a sip of coffee as the steam from her cup condensed around her face. 'He told you because he believes in you. And he also knows that the first case can often be a challenge. And there's no need to worry about the Burrows. They'll be looked after. I'll make sure of it.' They stood in silence for a moment, listening to the strengthening breeze tickling the buds of ashes and oaks, and trying to block out the distant sounds of urination coming from different directions. 'Do you... need to... go?' asked Suzanne, waving a hand in the direction of the trees. Thomas shook his head. Somehow the events of the previous three hours had distracted his bladder as well as his brain.

Owen was the first to return, followed by Martin, David and finally Terry with an upbeat, 'Ah, that's much better, if a little chilly on the old you-know-what.' A couple of minutes later, the door opened and Dennis, subdued, ushered everyone back in.

To the casual observer, nothing had noticeably changed in the critical minutes that stepfather and stepson had been alone, apart from an obviously more docile Michael, and yet both Suzanne and Thomas knew that everything had changed.

The tinfoil package had been reopened and its contents were gone.

33

'Do you want to leave now?' Suzanne asked, looking at Dennis with sympathetic eyes. 'Before the next stage.' He was sitting, slumped in one of the chairs facing Michael. 'You should probably get home to Fiona. She'll be worried about you. My driver can take us both and I'll drop you off. There's little need for us to stay now. What's done is done.'

Dennis raised his eyes to meet hers and it was obvious that he had been crying. 'I just need a moment,' he said. 'This isn't easy.'

Eventually, the chief constable rose from his chair. Without looking at Michael, he stumbled towards the door, stopping only briefly to address Thomas. 'I hope Chris will be okay,' he muttered. 'And I'm sorry.' Dennis turned to Suzanne, wiping the remaining moisture from his cheek. 'I'm ready to leave now,' he whispered.

'I'll send some people over in the morning to tidy up,' said the commissioner. 'Thomas, can you relay what needs to be said to the others, please? Just so it isn't too much of a shock.' Thomas explained that he would.

'Fill us in then,' said Martin, as the door closed and the sound of footsteps faded into the night. Just then, Michael raised his head, looked at Thomas and then at Martin. His eyes were full of defiance but there was something else: a resigned sadness.

'I'll tell them,' he murmured, his voice already fragmented. 'While I still can. Take a seat, gentlemen. This won't take long.' Michael rattled the cuffs again, but with less ferocity this time as his muscles began to weaken. He explained how stepfather and stepson had finally found some common ground, the older man regarding his action as a form of paternal kindness, the younger man considering it more a work of symbolic martyrdom. 'Ideally, I would have wanted this to happen in April for the Fuhrer's birthday. That was my intention all along. I wanted to get tonight out of the way and do another quick one on Saturday and then focus on my grand finale on the twentieth. I had a spectacular plan for that over at Heathrow. Lots of blood, there would have been, and then, just like him, I'd take the cyanide myself at the last possible moment as the coppers closed in. It would be quicker than this filthy hybrid substance that's in me now. It's really only suitable for the scum, but, you know, best laid plans and all that. At least this place looks a bit like a bunker. I appreciate your efforts to at least make me go with style.'

Within minutes, Michael was struggling to breathe, the sheer quantity of poison swamping his system and causing his lungs to fail. Forty minutes later, he had slumped forward, groaning in agony, and shortly after that he was motionless. David checked for a pulse but there was none. 'We could really do with a medical type to be absolutely sure,' he said, thinking of Chris, 'but I'm pretty certain he's dead.'

Thomas called Lexington to let him know the news, and then tried Monica, but her phone diverted to voicemail. He was comforted by the sound of her voice. Then the five of them stood in silence for a few minutes, taking in all that had happened since leaving the Harrow house many hours earlier, the only sound the wind fizzing sporadically through the sparse branches.

'One of our more eventful evenings,' said Martin, softly. 'It's not always like this, Thomas. Don't panic. What next?'

'I'll stay with him,' said Thomas quietly, wishing with all his heart that Chris was there. 'You can all get back if you like. Get some sleep.'

'If it's all right with you,' said Owen, 'I'd like to stay with you.' Thomas, secretly grateful for the companionship, nodded, and the two men embraced spontaneously, out of relief more than anything.

'Come on, then.' Martin smiled. 'Group hug. Before some of us get some shut-eye.'

'Don't forget to turn the heating off when you leave,' said Terry as they separated. 'I'll be back with David and Martin in the morning to clear everything out and have a wipe down, as it were. I trust someone will text when there's any news from the hospital?'

Thomas promised to keep everyone informed, and he and Owen settled into an armchair each as the sound of the two buggies receded into the distance. 'You have a snooze,' said Owen. 'I'm too full of caffeine to drop off any time soon.' Thomas closed his eyes and thought of Monica as he drifted in and out of shallow sleep for the next couple of hours.

Monica's text arrived at 5.27am. He was distracting himself by scrolling through a news website as Owen dozed when the news from the hospital arrived.

Chris was out of theatre where the surgeons had to stitched up a small artery just below his shoulder; he was now in intensive care and was stable. Two of Chris's daughters were with him and Monica had had to explain, with some improvisational skill she thought, why he was dressed as a tramp and why he smelled so strange. Quite how Chris was going to keep up the pretence of being part of a senior citizens' acting troupe would have to ultimately be his problem, especially as the younger daughter appeared unconvinced.

Monica's text explained she would stay at the hospital until he woke up and that Thomas was welcome to join her as soon as the police had picked up Michael Burrows' body.

Just before 8am, Owen heard an engine approaching and ventured outside to greet two non-uniformed officers who had arrived through the trees in an unmarked Jeep, the registration and identification details of which Suzanne had texted an hour earlier. 'You gentlemen need a lift anywhere?' the younger detective had asked, chirpily, once Michael had been zipped into a body bag and loaded into the back of their vehicle. Thomas and Owen had both declined, feeling that an early morning walk through the woodland dew and across the golf course would shake off the cobwebs of the night before and the minimal sleep they had each managed.

'Where are you taking him?' asked Owen, nonchalantly. 'Just out of interest.'

The detective stared into the far distance to where suburbia was breakfasting peacefully. 'We'll check with the commissioner, but I think the idea is untraceable disposal,' he said, quietly.

'We've got an acid bath if you need it,' offered Owen, wiping his nose where the cold had begun to make it drip.

The young detective smiled, opening the passenger door. 'I'm sure you have Mr Pook,' he said. 'But we can manage.'

Owen and Thomas watched the Jeep drive away and returned to the outbuilding. Thomas washed up all the coffee mugs as

Owen dismantled Michael's chair in advance of the arrival of Terry and the main clear-up team which, according to a text, was planned for just before ten. Once they were happy that the place was in an acceptable state of tidiness, the two men turned off the heater, left the outbuilding and locked the door behind them.

They reached Moor Park station at around 9.30am and travelled back to the Harrow house where Lexington was waiting with fresh croissants and tea and a congratulatory handshake. After showering and changing, Thomas took a cab up to the hospital where, after navigating various lifts and corridors, he found Monica sitting alone on a yellow plastic chair in a corner of a small room near to Chris's ward. When she saw Thomas, she ran and clung onto him so tightly that he felt – he hoped – she was never going to let go.

'They say he might come round in the next few hours,' she whispered, tearily. 'And then we can see him. His daughters are in with him now.' Monica's eyes began to slowly overflow. 'Oh, Thomas, I was so scared. What if we'd lost him? What then? I've spent the night thinking of that and about us and about whether I'd even want the top job if Lexington offered it and… Oh God, my brain just wouldn't switch off!' Thomas saw that her eyes were red with tiredness. 'All that talk beforehand about one of us getting hurt or worse. I was so dismissive and then it happened to Chris, for God's sake.'

'Let's just sit,' he said, gently cupping her face. 'We can talk later. It's best that you rest.' Monica lay her head on his lap and Thomas stroked her hair until, a couple of minutes later, he registered the familiar change in her breathing and he could tell that she was fast asleep. He leaned back on the rear of the plastic chair and felt his shoulders and the back of his head gently meet the wall. Thomas closed his eyes and soon, he too was dozing peacefully.

It was just getting dark when a doctor came to let them know Chris was awake and could receive visitors. His daughters had gone home to freshen up. 'He's a lucky man, Doctor Tinker. The blade made a mess of a small artery, but it was fairly easy to fix in surgery. A couple of inches lower and to the side and that knife would have pierced a major artery or even his lung. He's on morphine, so he may be a little drowsy, but you can see him if you like. He's been asking for you.'

Chris was in a private room, his shoulder and left side bandaged, but his bed was propped at such an angle that he could raise his head slightly to be better able to see Monica and Thomas as they entered.

'Greetings, welcome visitors,' he whispered, his eyelids heavy.

'At least you smell better, old man,' said Thomas, holding back tears.

'Bed bath. About an hour ago. Apparently Monica had to explain when I arrived that I wasn't a real tramp so at least that bit was convincing. Apart from the teeth, apparently. Schoolboy error. I'll know for next time.'

Monica explained that he was lucky to be alive and relayed what the doctor had said. Chris smiled knowingly. 'Do you remember when I went to see Dimo and his brother Ivo? The martial arts experts? They taught me the move that saved Dimo's life. The best one to use when confronted with a knife. Looks like it also saved mine. You just twist your body and… ow!' Chris had automatically twisted. 'Probably shouldn't do that for a while,' he grimaced.

Thomas told them what had happened after the events at Moor Park station, at the outbuilding, with the surprise arrival of Dennis – and what became of Michael.

'I suppose it's disappointing in some ways that he won't be tried,' said Monica, 'but equally, it somehow feels like the right conclusion in a weird way. What do you think is going to happen to Dennis?' Thomas replied that he didn't know and explained about the detectives who'd collected the body. He turned to Chris for his educated opinion, but the ex-surgeon had already closed his eyes and was snoring gently.

34

The apple blossom in St John's Wood had carpeted its tree-lined avenues with May confetti as Monica and Thomas, hand in hand, made their way slowly to a Twelve house just a few doors up from the London Planetarium, which Lexington had chosen as the location for his grand announcement, the last of his impressive tenure. Unusually, Monica had never visited this particular house before and was intrigued by it; a series of texts had revealed that, apart from Lexington, only Owen and Martin had known about this place before today, increasing the sense of anticipation and mystery.

This particular Tuesday was a warm one, the second day of an unseasonable but welcome spell, which seemed to have helped to bring the city to life after a damp and breezy April. Thomas and Monica had decided to leave themselves enough time to amble through the side streets to the outskirts of the park before finally arriving at the intriguing location.

Monica knocked on the blue door of the Georgian terraced house and was delighted when, after a series of unlocking clicks, Chris opened it. 'A gentle hug is fine,' he said, gesturing to his left shoulder and wincing momentarily, 'but just be careful on this side for a few more weeks, okay? No lifting me up, for example – and for goodness' sake no bumps on my seventieth birthday next month.'

The hallway of the house, Thomas noticed, was decorated with sketched portraits which, as so often, looked oddly familiar in style. While Monica and Chris eased ahead, already chatting away, he paused and looked at one closely, trying to make out the signature. 'Van Gogh, Thomas,' said Lexington's lowered voice behind him. 'Originals. Only drawings, mere scribbles in pencil and chalk of course, but still worth millions. It's one of the reasons why we don't generally come here as a group. It was late 2012 that we were here last. Martin had just joined and he nearly caused chaos when he accidentally knocked one off the wall.' The older man winked conspiratorially. 'The insurance is a nightmare. I've considered selling them time and time again, purely to avoid all the paperwork. To whom to sell them, though; that is the question. Delightfully, it will no longer be my decision after today.'

'How on earth,' began Thomas, 'did The Twelve acquire these?'

Lexington stepped back and regarded the drawings carefully. 'According to the diaries,' he explained, 'one of The Twelve lived next to the unfortunate Vincent in Brixton in the 1870s and they were a gift, apparently in return for some half decent wine and a loaf of bread. Valueless at the time, of course. The member of The Twelve, whose name was Shillingford as I recall, moved to this house in 1880 and they've been here ever since. They moved the sketches into the cellar during the last war, of course.'

Thomas felt the old man's hand on his shoulder. He smiled and closed his eyes, reminded fleetingly of a time long ago when his father, in a rare moment of pride, had done the same. Gathering himself, Thomas asked how Lexington was feeling about retirement. The former diplomat reflected that as anticipated, there was a colourful mixture of emotions involved, although the primary one was of grateful relief. He had spent a few weeks deciding how he wanted to spend his late autumn years. Lexington being Lexington, he had managed to assemble a daunting list of tasks and objectives which would take at least twenty years to complete, even at a decent canter. 'A couple of the more strenuous ones may have to remain on the back burner, but you never know. Especially if I keep up the yoga. Anna has kindly offered weekly private sessions.'

The two men moved towards the back room which, in keeping with the other properties, had been long ago adapted to comfortably accommodate a group of between twelve and fifteen people with armchairs, side tables, sofas and, naturally, an extensive drinks cabinet. Thomas checked the wall art in this new room to see if there was anything notable, but it looked to be merely good quality landscapes, the sort you might pick up in a car boot sale. 'I don't bother to insure these,' whispered Lexington, sensing his friend's curiosity. 'None of them are worth more than about fifty quid.'

In addition to the twelve members of the group, Suzanne was in attendance as well as Veronica Madison who had been slowly introduced to everyone since the beginning of April and who was now, it was widely accepted, a de facto member pending Lexington's retirement and the formal creation of a vacancy. A series of one-to-one meetings, particularly with Catherine Daniels and also with Monica, had confirmed Lexington's original opinion that the ex-newsreader would be beneficial to the group as well as a perfect fit, character-wise. A night out watching greyhound racing with Terry, Martin and Belinda had similarly strengthened her case.

Once everyone was seated and duly refreshed with tea and coffee, Lexington began the meeting by enquiring after Dennis. Suzanne explained that he had taken early retirement, as expected, but was being looked after by the police force both financially and in terms of his mental health. His wife was also taking advantage of professional counselling. The commissioner had spoken to them both at the weekend and reported that they seemed to be making good progress. 'Naturally, Dennis hasn't told her what exactly happened that night, but it's something *he's* going to have to live with. In other news, they're thinking of moving to the Canaries,' she said. 'And of course, if that's their decision then we shall ensure that they have everything they require in order to make that experience a positive one. He's been replaced in the role by Charlotte Pearson, as you'll know, from Scotland Yard. She's an old friend as well as a former colleague of mine so it's worked out rather well. We should have a bit more joined up thinking going forward.'

'Did you ever find out where Michael was getting the cash?' asked Chris. He was being fussed over by Anna who continually made sure that the cushion in his armchair was allowing him to rest his arm to avoid unnecessary pain.

The commissioner sipped her tea. 'We did a bit of digging and tracing after he died and managed to find a young woman with whom he had spent some time. Not exactly a girlfriend but someone he would occasionally visit; I suppose even psychopaths need a friend from time to time. She wasn't terribly communicative to be honest, but she did let slip that he would always have loads of cash and once told her that he had "rich benefactors" who he "helped with their long-term aims". She also said that he could be quite frightening at times, which is why she never introduced him to any of her friends and she would never know when he was going to turn up because he didn't have a phone, which she admitted was unusual. We are aware of several well-funded groups of extreme right-wing fanatics and conspiracy theorists in London so I would expect he was in the pay of one of those. An apparently lone wolf is rarely that. Michael was a bright yet troubled young man of no fixed abode who could do someone's dirty work for them and would be hard to track. He would have been a highly attractive prospect to a certain type of organisation.'

'And just out of interest,' asked Owen, 'what did happen to the body after it was driven away?'

The commissioner paused for a moment, trying to construct a politic answer. 'Owen, I would happily tell you but today is Lexington's day and I would rather not tarnish it with unpleasant details. Let it suffice for me to say simply that you are not the only ones who are able to make things mysteriously vanish as required. As I'm sure you in particular would appreciate, the State has its methods, rarely used though they may be.' The commissioner's demure smile left no one in any doubt that the matter was firmly closed.

Lexington then formally welcomed Chris back, delighted and relieved that he had made an almost full and relatively speedy recovery. 'Furthermore,' he added, 'I'm sure you'll all be interested to know what happened to that delightful house in Harrow, which was a welcome home from home to some of us for a few short days in March. As you'll recall, I fully intended to sell it at a meagre profit, but after the events on the train I had second thoughts. Frankly, we don't really need the money and you never know when you might need somewhere out in the suburbs again. I also felt that Mehmet – who probably saved Monica's life, let's not forget – could do with a change of scene. I've let the house to him, free of charge, naturally. This has allowed him to sell his previous home so that he can live out his remaining years without financial worry, even if he requires live-in care. Mind you, I hear that he has already taken a shine to our friend and apple connoisseur Mrs Archer next door, so who knows what the future will hold for both of them.'

Monica smiled at Thomas and clasped his hand tightly. 'Young love may be blossoming yet again.'

Lexington nodded towards the couple. 'He's also letting Dimo and his brother stay in a couple of the rooms in the house, so that they now have a permanent address, which will help them to get the full time jobs which they so desperately desire. Nikola is apparently fine with this arrangement and is even thinking about changing career himself, although I suspect he's in no particular rush. Besides, Nikola's immediate concern is the visit of his father next month, a man who has never before boarded an aircraft or indeed spent any time in anything larger than a small town. Needless to say, Nikola's feelings of intense joy are merged with filial concern, but hopefully the visit will pass without incident.'

Martin raised a hand politely. 'If the old fella needs a lift anywhere, he just has to ask,' offered the cabbie. 'And I mean Mehmet as well as Nikola's old man while he's on holiday.'

'That's very kind of you, Martin,' said Lexington. 'I'll be sure to pass that on. Anyway, now I'd like to formally induct our newest member to the group. As I will be standing down at this meeting, the vacancy will be filled, I'm very pleased to say, by Veronica whom you all know by now and who, I am sure, will be a most wonderful asset and friend going forward. I appreciate that you have already bonded, by and large, so this announcement is merely a t-crossing and i-dotting exercise on my part.' At this, there was a round of applause as a blushing Veronica stood up and took a sedate bow as Lexington asked Terry if he might open a couple of bottles of the Dom Perignon 1988 which had been patiently chilling in wine buckets.

'You've all been enormously welcoming,' the former television presenter began, 'although Terry does still owe me a tenner from the dogs.' She smiled as laughter filled the room. 'I shall do my best to earn your belief and trust in me and I cannot wait to get started on the next case.' The laughter was quickly drowned out by applause as Veronica took her seat.

'My final duty,' continued Lexington as the locksmith deftly teased the corks out with dampened but audible pops, 'is to announce my replacement at the head of this wonderful organisation.' He paused for a moment, amplifying the significance of the moment with a breath. 'It will, I'm sure, come as no surprise to many of you when I tell you that I am handing over the reins to Monica who, for over eight years now, has been the most dedicated, humble and determined of companions to us, as well as a woman who demonstrates great intelligence, compassion and bravery in equal measure. These qualities, along with her keen sense of moral duty and assassin's eye for detail, make her the perfect option.' Monica smiled broadly, kissed Thomas on the lips and was then embraced by Catherine and Anna while being warmly applauded by everyone else. 'I have spent the last few weeks gradually and, may I say rather subtly, briefing her on what's what. I shall spend the next fortnight going through the very fine detail, particularly with a view to the rather tedious paperwork involved with some of the low-level admin. I'm sure you will all give her your full support over the coming years and all that remains is to allow Terry to furnish you with a glass of extremely fine fizz and raise a toast to Monica. Commissioner, I know you're on duty, but perhaps a small glass on this occasion?'

Suzanne gratefully accepted and joined in the toast. 'Will you say a few words, Monica?' she nudged, excitedly.

Monica bent her head forward, taking in the enormity of the moment. 'Thank you, Suzanne.' She paused again, regaining some composure and feeling her way carefully through the series of words tumbling around her head. 'I think I can speak for all of us when I say that this extraordinary group is unlike any other, being as it is composed of people who are individually brilliant at what they do, but who, collectively, are a force to be reckoned with. At its foundations are people who care, both about society as a whole and about justice for those who often can't get justice. As we've seen all too clearly in recent months, the most vulnerable in society are often those most at risk. Although they don't realise it, indeed they cannot know it for obvious reasons, we will always be there for them. But our group is more than that. Much more. It allows us all a distinct purpose just at that point in life where we could too easily wind down and take up bingo or canasta or–'

'Nothing wrong with a spot of bingo from time to time,' muttered Martin, which inspired another loud ripple of laughter throughout the room.

'Agreed, Martin.' Monica smiled before continuing. 'It's a group which has also forged many deep, wonderful and strong friendships late in life and,' she gently reached back and took Thomas's hand, caressing his fingers softly, 'in some cases more than that. I'm enormously honoured and humbled to be taking over from Lexington. I'll do my very best to make him proud, to make all of you proud. And I'll do everything I can to continue to earn your support, your friendship and your love.'

If the walls of the house had not been surprisingly thick, and had the neighbours on either side not been absent, the applause, accompanied by more hugs and champagne, would have led the occupants to believe that some virtuoso musical performance had just concluded.

'I have no concerns about your aptitude for this role, Monica,' said Lexington later, on his third glass of fizz and leaning on the arm of a chair for support. They were in a huddle with Thomas, Catherine and Suzanne. 'You're extremely well qualified; probably more qualified than anyone has ever been.'

'Even more delightful,' added the commissioner, raising an empty glass, 'your appointment means that there are now three women in charge of Scotland Yard, this group and the British Transport Police for the first time in history. Something else to be celebrated.'

Lexington explained that he would need to spend some additional time with Monica just to get her up to speed with everything but – and he was looking at Thomas at this point – that he had no intention of eating into evenings or weekends and that he anticipated it would take no longer than ten days to finalise matters. 'And naturally, you may call on me anytime if there is anything that doesn't make sense. Now, if I may, I just have to borrow Monica for five short minutes, but I shall return her to you imminently.' The outgoing and incoming senior partners joined hands and one led the other along a corridor to a short set of stairs heading downwards to another closed room. Monica took a quick glance over her shoulder and winked at Thomas as Lexington took a key from his pocket, unlocked the door, ushered her inside and secured the door behind them. After a few minutes, the two of them returned, but this time Monica had the key with which to lock the door.

'Shall we walk home?' asked Monica, brightly. 'It's such a lovely day and I could do with shaking off some of that fizz with some fresh air.'

Thomas gave her a cuddle. 'We could even take a detour while we're in the park,' he said, 'as we're in no hurry. Sit in the shade for a bit.' They walked lazy and carefree, hand in hand through back streets to Regents Park, where they found an empty bench next to the pond. 'I don't suppose you're allowed to tell me what was in that room,' he mused. 'Was it a magic mirror that shows the future, by chance?'

Monica laughed. 'I'm afraid not, darling, although if there

were such a mirror, I hope I would see you in it.' She kissed him three times on the lips. 'But no, I can't tell you. Not yet. But one day, I hope. It's nothing to worry about but right now, it would be a burden to you if I'm honest, and I'd rather not weigh you down with anything… especially after what happened with Chris.'

Thomas understood. After a challenging first case, he was rather hoping he could take it a bit easier on the next one, although his suspicions were that it may be unlikely. The mystery room, however, wasn't the only matter weighing on his mind. 'Monica,' he started, in a tone that she recognised meant a statement of great importance might be circling to land. Monica turned her head towards him, her big eyes twinkling. 'I was wondering whether you might like to meet Emily and the twins at the weekend. I've told them all about you and you could say they're very excited. I could cook Sunday lunch at my place if you like. If you're not quite ready yet then that's fine; I understand.'

Monica grasped his face, pulled him towards her and planted a kiss on his mouth. 'That sounds perfect, you sweet man,' she said, beaming and ruffling his hair. 'Right now, I can truly think of nothing I'd rather do more.'

35

'Simon. It's Dad. Are you well?'

'Dad. Is anything wrong?'

'No, not at all. Quite the opposite. I was just aware that we hadn't actually spoken this year and it's nearly June. Look, I've been thinking. You're my son. We should talk more. In fact, do you fancy coming over for lunch one weekend?'

'Sure. That would be great. Can I bring a friend? There's someone I'd like you to meet.'

'Of course. In fact, now you mention it, I have someone to introduce to you too…'

THE END

ACKNOWLEDGEMENTS

It takes a village to raise a book, so thanks firstly to my family, Debi, Caitlin and Ella for all the tea and encouragement. When I was little, I dreamed of a family like you, and I love you.

Thank you to everyone who read terrible early drafts of this book and yet somehow offered advice and support. These extraordinarily kind and brave folk include Owen Bywater, Simon Ponsford, Simon Collins, Chris Rowland, Matthew Christmas, Justin Somper (Go Pirate Academy!), PJ Norman, Ben Edwards, Ian Bamford, Dave Crowder, Jonathan Bailey, Dave Brabham and Andy Sutcliffe. Sonia Patel, without your magical talents, there would simply be no words.

Enormous gratitude to Betsy Reavley at Bloodhound Books for taking the leap of faith and also to the brilliant Shirley Khan, the fabulous Tara Lyons, and everyone else at Bloodhound for the general greatness. Thanks must also go to Justine Solomons at Byte The Book, along with Andy Macleod and Nicole Johnston for their timely advice and crucially, to Dominic Wakeford at Reedsy for reaffirming my faith when it was wavering.

Thank you to Marian Keyes whose online fora at the beginning of 2021 brought such joy and reignited the flame to scribble words. Chantelle Sturt, for ten years you have inspired me to be better. Thank you. You are truly amazing.

Finally, a big thank you to my first English teacher Patrick Carpmael who, in 1978, instilled in me a love of words and stories which eventually led to this place.

A NOTE FROM THE PUBLISHER

Thank you for reading this book. If you enjoyed it please do consider leaving a review on Amazon to help others find it too.

We hate typos. All of our books have been rigorously edited and proofread, but sometimes mistakes do slip through. If you have spotted a typo, please do let us know and we can get it amended within hours.

info@bloodhoundbooks.com

Printed in Great Britain
by Amazon

57328597R00169